BOOM TOWN

GARRISON KEILLOR

also by Garrison Keillor

That Time of Year: A Minnesota Life, 2020

The Lake Wobegon Virus, 2020

Living with Limericks, 2019

The Keillor Reader, 2014

O, What a Luxury, 2013

Guy Noir and the Straight Skinny, 2012

A Christmas Blizzard, 2009

Pilgrims, 2009

Life Among the Lutherans, 2009

77 Love Sonnets, 2009

Liberty, 2008

Pontoon, 2007

Daddy's Girl, 2005

Homegrown Democrat, 2004

Love Me, 2003

In Search of Lake Wobegon, 2001

Lake Wobegon Summer 1956, 2001

ME, 1999

Wobegon Boy, 1997

The Old Man Who Loved Cheese, 1996

The Sandy Bottom Orchestra, 1996

Cat You Better Come Home, 1995

The Book of Guys, 1993

WLT, 1991

We Are Still Married, 1989

Leaving Home, 1988

Lake Wobegon Days, 1985

Happy to Be Here, 1981

BOOM TOWN

A **LAKE WOBEGON** NOVEL

GARRISON KEILLOR

PRAIRIE HOME PRODUCTIONS

ISBN: 978-1-7330745-5-1
Library of Congress Control Number: 2021920782

Visit our website at garrisonkeillor.com

First Edition

This is a work of fiction. Names, places, characters, and incidents are either the products of the author's imagination or are used fictitiously. "Lake Wobegon" is a registered trademark of Garrison Keillor.

Cover and book interior design by David Provolo
Cover illustration by Rodica Prato

1

A NEW WORLD

I flew back home to Minnesota for my best friend's funeral last spring over the objections of my wife who was leery of COVID, which was raging in Minnesota thanks to anti-vaxxers, many of them devout Christians like my cousins who put up "Prepare to meet thy God" signs along the road and who believed the virus meant a quicker trip to glory but Norm went down from cardiac arrest in his driveway, an easy death. He wanted to go in his sleep, but anyway it was quick. He was a big person in my life and so was his sister Arlene and to skip the funeral out of fear of infection seemed to me unworthy and a denial of reality even worse than the evangelicals' resistance to medical science so I boarded Delta at Terminal D at LaGuardia and returned to my origins. He died on May Day and it was a shock but not a surprise: Norm always said, when asked how he was, "Never better," but in March he switched to "Okay" and a few weeks later to "Not bad," a rather steep decline.

I rented a car at the Minneapolis-St. Paul airport and drove north to Lake Wobegon and noticed, nearing town, that the "Prepare to meet thy God" sign was gone. I stopped and got out of the car. It lay in tall weeds by a barbed-wire fence. Someone had shot it with a shotgun and the *Pre* was gone and the stake was busted. I left it lying there but the phrase "Pare to meet thy God" stuck with me. Cut back on excess, trim the nonessential. A good motto for a man nearing 80. Set aside ego and the craving for widespread approval, ditch your bag of stupid regrets, abandon pleasures no longer pleasurable, love your neighbor, and you will find yourself in God's presence. My cousin Rose, who was named not for the flower but for the Resurrection, sends me a birthday card every year: *God is moving the waters. He is bringing this dispensation to a close. We may not be here tomorrow. I pray you are waiting on Him.* It's sweet. To think of someone waiting decades for Rapturization. I do appreciate her interest in me.

I called Giselle in New York and left a message that I love her and drove into town and noticed the ruins of the EZFreeze. Not much happened in the town of my youth and when something did, my dad would say, "It was the biggest thing since they got the bug zapper at the EZFreeze." The zapper was a big neon ring under the eave that electrocuted mosquitos. Now it's gone, the symbol of progress.

So is the Lake Wobegon Maternity Hospital, the big white house where I was born in the summer of 1942, which caused no stir at the time nor does the fact that I'm still living. I am here as a result of good luck. As a kid, I stood on the front seat of the car, no seat belt, as Dad drove 80 mph on a two-lane road to get to Bible camp in the Badlands of South Dakota, driving at top speed so we wouldn't need to stop at a motel. I survived it and also the preaching, which was all about imminent death, ships sinking, car crashes, furnaces blowing up, storms with lightning. We fundamentalists were grim, like people living in a coal mine, but if I looked grim, my cheerful mother would say, "What's the matter? Did the dog pee on your cinnamon toast?" and that made me smile, and it still does, imagining a dog going to the trouble of getting up on the table to do that. Wobegonians were cheerful stoics and if you asked "How are you?" they said "Fine" unless they were lying on the ground and there was external bleeding. Lighten up. Life is good. It could be worse. Don't feel sorry for yourself. Winter is not a personal experience: everybody else is just as cold as you are. Take it one day at a time. Make something of yourself. Don't be a ten-dollar haircut on a 59-cent head. Find out what you're good at and do it. That was our way.

Growing up in the coal mine, your people warn you against ascending

6

to the surface, but eventually you do and WOW you see trees, the sky, you feel rain and wind, you get to know Catholics, Jews, Buddhists, you go to movies. I left when I was 18 to make my way in the world and I married a girl from New York who was not a coal miner and we moved there to make her happy and now I go back home mainly for funerals, which these days are for people my age, which gets my attention, an obituary with my number in it. Old rocknrollers, ballplayers, movie stars, cousins, classmates, I pay attention, I read the story closely and guess at the omissions.

So I came back to pay my respects to my old pal Norm who'd stayed a good friend though I was a writer and he took over his dad's trash route, and we confided in each other, he was the only one I told about my cruelty and disloyalty, my vanity, my miserable sins, dumb things I did, dumber than you'd think a grown man capable of, dumber than a boxful of hammers, and I walked into Lundberg's Mortuary and there he was, freshly laundered lying in a box with floral arrangements around him, and I felt a sort of relief. The man knew all my sins, which would now go to the grave with him. I hated to think it but it felt like I'd been given a fresh start in life.

A woman spoke to me and I jumped. She was looking over my shoulder at the corpse. "They got the wrong tie on him," she said. It was Pastor Liz from the Lutheran church. "Nancy gave them a blue tie. Norm never wore a red tie in his life. Lundberg is such a fuckup." She laughed: "Did I just say 'fuckup'?"

As it happened, I was wearing a blue tie so I took it off and got Norm's red tie off and looped mine around his neck, which was rather wooden, and stood up at the head of the casket so I could figure out how to tie it, and it came out pretty good.

"It's good of you to come all this way," she said. "Hnnhh," I said.

I've come back for the funerals of teachers, Mr. Faust, Mr. Bradley, Miss Story, LaVona Person. I meant to come back in 2020 for the funeral of Julie Christensen who was a year older than I, a seventh-grader, who watched me walk by her yard on my way to shoot baskets and she said, "Do you want to wrestle?" and I stopped. She was a long-legged girl in green shorts and a white T-shirt. I walked over to talk to her and she grabbed me and threw me down on the grass and sat on me, her hot mint-scented breath in my face, her legs scissored around me. She said, "Try to get up" but I didn't want to. She was strong. She said, "Have you ever been kissed?" and then she kissed me and stuck her tongue in my mouth. I'd never seen that done before, never imagined it. She said, "I'll bet you want to see my tits, don't you." I shook my head no, and she lifted her shirt, and I closed my eyes. It was a big moment. I shook my head because a Brethren boy should, but I did want to see, and I didn't close my eyes, I squinted, and it was very interesting. She said, "If you tell anybody, I'll beat the crap out of you. I mean it." When she died at 79 from myeloma, the funeral was on a Saturday and I had to do a show in New York, but I grieved for her, my liberator. So was Norm's sister Arlene but that's a whole other story.

Norm and I each grew up in homes where pennies were pinched, our mothers darned socks and mended clothes until they wore out and then cut them into strips and wove them into rag rugs. We were brought up to use bars of soap until they were thin slivers in our hands and then wash with the slivers. We each experienced shame early: his dad was a terrible speller and liked to write letters to the editor, which the printers at the paper, both of them drunks, never corrected and so his dad was often in print with hideous errors that our fellow third-graders were highly amused by such as "hangkerchiff" and "judgmint" and "without acception." In addition to my Brethrenness, I was the first boy in the class to get glasses, which made me a lousy ballplayer in grade school and got me the nickname "Perfessor." So Norm knew where I came from and I confessed most of my sins to him except the sin of feeling superior to him, which anyway faded out after 65. There is not much superiority in old age, just good luck. He and I grew old together and became relics, the last in our circle of pals to have driven a Model T Ford, the very last to have participated in the prank of privy tipping, which we did at the age of twelve, along with older boys, all of them dead now, at the lake cabin of Harold Starr the publisher of the town paper, sitting in his outhouse one evening, on the throne with his trousers around his ankles, as we crept through the underbrush and heaved the privy over onto its door as the gentleman cursed us, trapped within, left with only one exit.

We were the last ones to have used the Sons of Knute's Big Boy fiberglass duck decoys, eighteen feet long: the hunter lay on his back inside the duck and pedaled the driveshaft that turned the propeller as he looked out through a periscope in the duck's neck, scanning the skies for incoming ducks. The Knutes had six of them and they were too tippy and four decoys sank and Norm and I found the two survivors and paddled them around, with concrete blocks for ballast. Nobody else remembers this.

In recent years, I'm sure, we looked at each other and wondered which of us would be standing and looking down at the other one in the box. So it's me, and I miss him. There is nobody left for me to talk about Julie Christensen with or our teachers LaVona Person or Helen Story or reminisce about the county fair back when it had a dirt racetrack and the older brothers of boys we knew went tearing around it in souped-up cars and dared death in order to impress girls. And now here was Norm waiting for the right moment to spring up from the coffin and say, "It was only a joke!" but death has disabled him, there's no spring left in him, he's become ornamental. The line has gone dead.

He stayed in Lake Wobegon and I went out into the world and had a career, and he remained my trusty friend and faithful informant. He told me a few years ago, "It's a whole different town. You wouldn't recognize it. The guys you and I grew up with are old coots sitting in the corner and grousing. We used to play hockey on rinks we flooded ourselves and we built goals out of packing crates and we used magazines for shin guards, now they drive the kids into Willmar to an indoor rink. Now they close the schools if more than two inches of snow is forecast because falling snow can trigger anxiety for some kids who may need counseling or medication." (Back in our day, school was never canceled unless the building was no longer visible. There was no windchill index or misery index, we didn't think in those terms. In a blizzard, your dad tied a clothesline to your belt so he could reel you in if he had to and the clothesline was a hundred feet long, the distance from the house out to the county road, and when the line went taut you knew you were there and you waited for the headlights to appear in the whiteness and if it was windy, you might have to dig a cave in the snow and if the bus didn't come for a couple hours, you reeled yourself back home. Snow was not a mental health issue.)

It troubled Norm that the Christmas program at the high school was now called the Happy Holiday program, and the word "Savior" was changed to "Teacher" and Vacation Bible School was now called Spiritual Awareness and was about showing respect for others and not about the rough stuff, Noah and the Flood, Cain and Abel, Abraham and Isaac. And the old songbooks have been banned with old faves like "Frankie and Johnny" ("The first time she shot him, he staggered. The second time she shot him he fell. The third time there was a southwest wind from the northeast corner of hell.") and "The E-ri-e was a-rising and the gin was getting low and I scarcely think we'll get a drink till we come to Buffalo."—songs that we sang in the third grade, they've been replaced by songs about brotherhood, meanwhile, thanks to the internet, words considered obscene by truckers are being used freely by small children.

"Me and you were the end of an era, mister," he said. "The last of the free and the brave. Our neighbor lady has three kids and has an app so she can track them around town by their cellphones. Turn on the computer and there's a blue and a red and a yellow dot to show where Mason, Logan, and Salem are. Surveillance of children. It wouldn't surprise me if she taps their phones too.

"You and me were lucky to live when we did. It wasn't all Zoom and Facebook. People got together in person to chew the fat. The men sat in the living room and watched football and talked about crops and hunting and the women in the kitchen talked about births and surgeries and now they just post pictures on Instagram and no secrets are told for fear of who might be reading. It's a damn shame."

Liz left to go looking for Norm's wife, Nancy, and the moment she left, Lundberg came in, not George Lundberg, whom I knew, but his son George Jr., who took over the business when the old man developed dementia from inhaling preservatives and one day he dumped Mrs.

Soderberg's ashes into the toilet. She had wanted them to be scattered on the river and the old man figured flushing them amounted to the same thing, so he had to go to the loony bin and the son, who wanted to be a painter, not an undertaker, stepped in, a sour man with a woofy voice who never developed the warm avuncular unctuosity of a funeral director. He glared at me and said, "Huh. So you came after all. They said you were coming but I figured a big shot like you's got better things to do with his time. Guess I was wrong. Anyways, two more of your classmates died over the weekend, Ronnie Hansen from a car crash and Peter Flanagan from what he thought was cancer but it was COVID. So I guess your timing is perfect. How're you doing? I don't suppose you'll have your funeral back here. Have it in some big cathedral in New York City so all your famous pals can attend. Right? Well, good luck with that. The problem with being famous is that when you die they can't wait to say bad things about you. Any scandal, no matter how small, it goes into the second paragraph of your obituary. All your so-called admirers, they love to dish out the gossip. But I'm sure you know that."

I didn't bother correcting him. What I love about New York isn't famous friends but Giselle, eating lunch with her down on Grove Street in the Village, oysters on the half shell, meatballs, an iceberg wedge, driving up to our summerhouse on the Connecticut River, and Giselle has my permission to put my ashes in her flower bed by the garage where they likely won't bother whatever man takes my place in her life, and meanwhile I'm glad to return home in honor of my ghosts.

I got out of Lundberg's and headed down the street and there, fifty feet away where there used to be a driveway next to Ralph's Pretty Good Grocery, was a little sidewalk café called Laura's Lunch and there, sitting around a table under an umbrella, were my old classmates Clint and Dave and Billy and Daryl, and Clint looked at me and said, "Well, look what the wind blew in," which was exactly the sort of thing I'd expect to hear and Dave pulled in an extra chair and said, "Good of you to get out of the fast lane and come join us common folks" and I sat down and suddenly it wasn't 2021 anymore, it was a moment of timelessness.

Billy: "You look a little lost. Can we help you find something?"

Dave: "You look a lot like someone I used to know. The class oddball."

Daryl: "Sit down and take a load off. We just ordered lunch."

And I sat down and I was back home.

Clint: "So do we call you Garrison or can we call you Gary?"

I said that my name is Gary and that Garrison was only to make it sound like I went to an Ivy League school instead of a land-grant university.

Clint: My wife went to New York last year.

Me: Is that right?

Clint: I don't know if it was right but she did it anyway. Said she had a wonderful time.

Me: What did she do?

Clint: I don't know and I don't want to know.

They were all dressed like retired guys, which they are, and I was in a suit and tie, but it didn't matter. A kid came out with a menu and Daryl said, "The egg salad sandwich is really good," so I ordered that.

Daryl: "Good of you to come all this way but I knew you would. The class of 1960 is fading away fast. Pretty soon there won't be any of us left."

Dave: "So you finally figured that out, huh?"

Daryl: "What?"

Dave: "Death. It's a definite trend. I read today that more than a billion people who lived on this planet are now dead. Including our parents, all gone."

Daryl: "Well, when it's your time, it's your time. Makes no difference. My brother's brother-in-law was a marathoner, cross-country skier, lifted weights, worked out, one morning he had a stroke, died the next day. My uncle Danny had two shots of bourbon for breakfast and maintained his alcohol level all day and lived to be ninety-five and was killed by somebody throwing a sofa out of a sixth-floor window. You just can't tell."

Billy: "Marilyn just texted me that Bob Anderson died."

Clint looked at me and said, "You and I need to find us some younger friends so we don't sit around on a beautiful day and talk about death." Darlene passed by and he said, "Who do I have to sleep with to get my coffee warmed up?" She said, "Coffee is supposed to keep you from sleeping."

Daryl said, "He's Norwegian, sweetheart. They only think about sex when they're too drunk to go fishing. A Norwegian likes to go to bed with two women so when he falls asleep right away they can keep each other company. If he wants sex, he goes downtown with a pocketful of cash and goes looking for a warehouse. They're not only lousy lovers, they're bad spellers."

I was the only one who laughed at these old jokes; the others just smiled.

The front of Ralph's was now a yoga studio and the back half where Ralph did his butchering and baking was the Laura's Lunch kitchen. On the table was a brochure advertising a solar plunger that fits over your solar plexus, creating harmonic vibrations in the pelvic enclosure that cause the body's own meridian powers to drive invasive toxins from the lymph system to create positive energy and expectations. I thought about asking, "Whose is this?" but didn't. If it belonged to one of my pals, I didn't want to know.

Next to the outdoor café, in what had been Halvorson Hardware, was a grocery, The Common Good. Up the street I could see the signs of the Sidetrack Tap and the Chatterbox Café but across the street where Bunsen Motors, the Ford dealership, had been was a carved wooden sign, *AuntMildred's.com*. There was Clint Bunsen sitting next to me and I wanted to ask, "Why?" but it's as obvious as the nose on your face. He's 78, almost 79, just like me, and his brother Clarence is 81. You get to be 78, maybe you don't feel like sticking your head under the hood and working on the carburetor. And maybe the carburetor isn't a carburetor anymore but an app and the old mechanic has to reprogram himself to deal with it.

Dave was talking about Ronnie Hansen. "Died in a car crash chasing ass down in Florida. And Pete Flanagan had colon cancer he was treating with Clorox."

Billy: "I heard it was Lysol."

Dave: "Six of one, half a dozen of the other. Either way, death by stupidity. Doesn't speak well for our class, I must say."

Lunch arrived and my egg salad sandwich. Which, according to the menu, was made from eggs laid by local free-range chickens raised on wholesome grains, no GMO or GOP or SUV. Anyway, it was a perfectly good sandwich.

Norm had told me about the start-up companies that had taken over the town, like Universal Fire, which made artisanal twenty-year-old white oak and ash firewood, non-GMC, upper-altitude, seasoned with sea salt. It was getting into the field of artisanal ice as well, made from Lake Superior water, and was bottling virgin oxygen from the northern wilderness. The founder, Rob McCarter, had an MFA in creative writing and the artisanal firewood business was right up his alley. He was the one who wrote the fan mail from customers: "Our petty troubles disappear in the twilight when we light Universal in our fireplace. And now your bottled Boundary Waters air has cleansed our spirits."

A woman named Willow owned a dozen horses and started a manure works to make an organic sun-dried ethical/sustainable manure, Wholly Shit, $15/lb., nicely wrapped (*Each creature is full of beauty. Spread it around.*), a crisp well-balanced manure with a warm nose, smooth texture, and a complex structure. She said, "It's all about continuity, waste is a nutrient, the end is the beginning. Manure is universal, it's part of who we are."

Norm said, "I've come across crappy products but I never knew you could sell absolute shit. Not at that price." The old men groused about it but the stock kept going up, up, up.

A company, Tomorrow Tomato, made an inclusive tomato sauce from diverse varieties raised on family farms in a variety of eco-societies. Norm and Nancy's granddaughter Normandy invented a very soft facial tissue with 8 percent lamb's wool and 5 percent spiderweb woven into the paper. Her husband, Max, created a nameless ginger ale aged in oak barrels: very successful. People asked him, "Why no name? You need a name." And he said, "Whatever," and so that became the name and he put out a Whatever mug, an earthy clay mug that became a Thing and went viral for a while, like Totality Tote Bags, which became wildly popular after the price was doubled. "These kids understand the New Economy," said Norm. "Plenty of people have way too much money and that's your market. Don't bother selling stuff to paupers." Normandy married Max when they were eighteen. He had hair down to his shoulders and it was an alternative ceremony, with an epic Walt Whitman poem (*"O comrade and aficionado, come, take my hand, you are comely and possessed of secret longings, come travel the open road under a banner of affection, shameless, glistening with wordless desires."*) and the soloist sang "Purple Rain," which is odd for a wedding—"I never wanted to be your lover, I only wanted to be your friend" and Nancy's mouth was bleeding from biting her tongue. Norm said, "We thought it'd last six months but it's been a year and a half." He admired their enterprise. Normandy was 20 and drove a green Jaguar and had Zoom meetings with executives at Chanel and Dior and Pankake. Elon Musk called her once. She knew Sandy Frazier. She was hot stuff.

Lake Wobegon had been a farm town of two thousand, an exporter of its young people, and now it was booming. Two brothers, Jake and John, created Woke alarm clocks that sound like crickets and a woman says, "Rise and shine, renew your spirit, resume the struggle, resist the system" and a carillon plays "We Are Strong Together" and you hear marching feet, a bass drum, and a gong. They were made in a factory in Mumbai for $1.75 apiece and retailed for $68. Jake's girlfriend Ashley came up with a dance video that teaches math, *Let's All Go Rithm.* Nobody learned from it but the concept was fantastic. Her business partner, Hailey, created a detoxifying spread made from honey and locusts and then developed an app called Constant Companion that traces your daily routine and if you forget why you've walked into the kitchen, a voice in your earpiece says, "You probably came to warm up your coffee." Then it lists other options.

Clearly, this was no longer the town I told stories about on my award-nominated radio show, *A Prairie Home Companion.* Nothing like that town. I walked around and saw notices on bulletin boards for personal trainers, dog walkers, yoga instructors, a veterinary aromatherapist, jobs that never existed here before. The Central Building, now renamed Main Street Lofts, has two social media consultants, an accountability coach, two content writers, an ergonomicist, a data analyst, a fitness advisor, and three massage therapists, shiatsu, hydroponic, and audiovibratory. Snazzy new cars are parked up and down Main Street. A woman named Nona Loso runs a lucrative business leading grief seminars and an annual grief cruise to Greece. She does a podcast for pet-loss grief, "Puff & Spot Are Gone," and a monthlong summer camp—Norm called it a "death camp"—at which people divide up into grief pods and are assigned hugging partners. He said, "Promise me you won't let Nancy organize a grief pod for me," and I promised and she didn't, probably because she wasn't all that grief-stricken.

Norm lived in Lake Wobegon his whole life. He was in the trash-hauling business but was very spruce and well-informed and instead of a trashman, he might've been taken for an envelope salesman or an economist. He was astonished when Death caught up with him. He'd been to a doctor only twice, once for a bum hip that he managed to hobble along with and once for random appendicitis but it went away. He got too old to lift trash barrels so he sold the business to a young guy, Tom Paradise, who turned it into Paradise Recycling, which, thanks to the righteous name, he built into a multimillion-dollar business. Norm hated retirement. I was busy doing my show and offered him a job driving the tour bus, and he said he couldn't leave Nancy alone for weeks at a time, she being a major worrier, and also (he added) he wasn't that fond of the show personally, being more of a jazz guy, not so interested in people playing dulcimers and singing about the death of small children. We were close so he could be honest with me.

The last time I talked to him was in February. He called me, ecstatic that he'd tried to kill himself and had failed to. A month before, he said, he was in a bad way, had a pain in his side, couldn't stand up straight, saw double, felt dizzy and nauseated, hung onto walls as he walked through the house. The doctor said it might be cancer and wanted to send Norm down to the Cities for tests. "They might need to poke a hole in your side and put in a tube," the doctor said. It sounded to Norm like a bad idea and he kept putting it off because if it was bad he preferred not to postpone death with radiation or chemo because he was already deeply depressed about losing his girlfriend Elaine.

"Elaine who was married to Steve?" I said. He said, "After Steve died, she and I jumped into the sack—we got together twice a month out at my cabin. Every other Friday. She was a teacher, she liked having a schedule. You remember that cabin. You spent a summer there after high school. Nancy knew about me and Elaine, and she wasn't thrilled about it, but she'd lost interest in sex years ago so it was no skin off her nose. Nancy's life was all about gardening, grandkids, *Jeopardy*, and jigsaw puzzles. For her, mutual nakedness was as alien as pole vaulting. I had two years with Elaine and it was a happy two years and then one day she called and said she couldn't see me anymore. She said, 'I don't want to be the object of gossip and walk into the hair salon and see people stop talking and I know they were talking about me.' I pleaded with her and remembered the great times we'd had, but she had made up her mind and that was that. Well, if she was embarrassed to be my lover, shacking up with the trashman, it depressed the hell out of me. I went in the hospital for an X-ray or MRI or something and I was in pain from an umbilical hernia, my belly button was the size of a golf ball, and Nan was down in the Cities and the ER was full of COVID people and the dying and demented, people wailing and weeping, screaming, 'Somebody come and help me! Please!' and I freaked out and left the ER and came back to town and drove out to the lake cabin and decided to pull the plug. I'm an old fart who gets in everybody's way, no use to anybody and I didn't want to put Nan through all the trouble, and I've lived long enough. So I downed half a pint of bourbon and took a couple tranquilizers and sat in the car with the motor off and waited to freeze to death. It was twenty below. An easy exit. No sickness, no long decline hobbling around the Good Shepherd Home looking spooky and cadaverous and dribbling coffee down myself, peeing my pants, rocking back and forth like a caged animal in the zoo, my mind turned to sawdust, one hip shooting with pain at every step. To hell with that.

A person has only so much time and that's all the time there is. A quick exit, like Elvis after a concert. *Norm Gunderson has left the building.* I had made a list of several jerks I didn't want invited to my funeral and some instructions to Nan: No eulogies, nothing, just the 23rd Psalm and one hymn, 'Abide with me, fast falls the eventide,' And I cut my son out of the will, the little prick, because he refused to say hello to Elaine at a Whippets game. I wrote a note to Nan saying thank you and I sat there thinking about Elaine and the good times we'd had committing adultery and then I remembered the picture of Elaine naked in her bathtub, her phone in hand, and it was in the drawer of the bedside table, and I don't want Nan to have to see that picture. Jesus. I could see the story in the paper: he died of hypothermia outside the cabin where he canoodled with his tootsie. Well, I had no feeling in my arms or legs but I managed to open the car door and fall out into the snow and my legs were like two wooden logs but I crawled fifty feet to the cabin and somehow I got inside and I crawled into bed and woke up on the morning, and looked in the drawer and there was no naked picture of Elaine and I remembered, I had burned it a week before at her request. Memory loss saved my life. I tell you, when you almost die and then you don't, life is incredibly beautiful. Just dazzling. I looked and I felt like a new man. I cried, I was so happy. I have never been so happy as that day of my death and resurrection. I felt like the luckiest man on God's green earth. I went ice fishing a day later and caught a two-pound walleye and roasted him on an open fire: best meal I ever ate. There's nothing like almost dying and then coming back to the world. Take my word for it."

Nancy asked me to say a few words at the service, and it was hard to think of what to say about a man who died happy, but I wrote a poem on the plane and stood up to read it. I'd never written a love poem about another man. I wrote a formal sonnet, as a way to avoid gush, and it was okay.

Time passing and the old man with the scythe
Is mowing. He hasn't been merciful, has he.
My best friend, a good and generous guy,

Is gone, leaving the world less jazzy,
He awoke one fine day, felt ill,
Lay down for a nap and never arose
And now we carry him up the hill
Seventy-nine years old, in his Sunday clothes.
But Norm wouldn't want us to be sorry a
Long time. Weep, say your prayers and your
Eulogies and then resume the beautiful aria
Of life in all its generous grandeur.
Each day is borrowed but let us own it
And find beauty in our coffee and doughnut
    And love this world before we have flown it
    And find what we would've wished for, had we only known it.

Nancy smiled and whispered, "Thank you," and Norm's grand-daughter Normandy came to the piano, wiping away tears, and sat down and played a few rolling chords and sang:

May you have eternal happiness
In the land you're going to,
May everyone be loving
And always kind to you.
May you play a round of golf each day
And have a perfect score
May you live forevermore.
May you have a double cheeseburger
Along with double fries
May you play Bingo every night
And always win the prize
And be reunited with your dog
And walk the golden shore.

There was more. I looked at Pastor Liz who managed to keep a solemn face though I could see twitches at the corners of her mouth.

Her funeral homily was based on the passage in 2nd Corinthians, about we mortals being jars of clay containing the light of God. *We are hard-pressed on every side, but not crushed, perplexed but not in despair, persecuted but not forsaken, cast down but not destroyed.* Norm was no more perplexed than most and certainly not persecuted. He survived his suicide attempt and the colon cancer turned out to be a Grade A case of constipation and a nurse gave him a nuclear enema that cleaned him out and he got five bonus months of life. He told me he never felt so happy as the day he went home twenty pounds lighter and told Nancy he loved her and meant it. He was able to enter the Sons of Knute Guess The Ice Melt contest and guess the Pontiac would go through the ice on March 8th (the 14th was the winner) and he got to witness the first week of April, which was springlike and buds emerged and a week later came a snowfall of elegant crystalline grandeur, every twig of every bush and tree glazed with frost, every photographer in town out snapping pictures, and the next day it melted, and then there was fall in the air and the next day a high of 72, four seasons in one month, and he put out tomato plants and sweet corn and he sat with Nancy in the backyard and drank half a bottle of Pinot Noir I had sent him two years before, which he postponed drinking because he didn't think he knew enough about wine to appreciate it, but he loved it, Nancy said, and he sang her a song, "Till There Was You," which she'd never heard him sing, and the very next day he died.

The heart attack struck on May 1 at two in the afternoon at home and he took a couple Alka-Seltzers, while Nancy called 911 over his objections and the EMTs loaded him, protesting, on the cart and headed out the door and he died in his own driveway. The shock of being rescued was probably what killed him, the man had never asked for help in his entire life, being carried bodily on a gurney to a van with flashing red lights made him think, "I'm dying," so he died. The EMTs got out the paddles but he was gone, no struggle, he simply ceased to exist.

Clarence Bunsen gave a eulogy, Norm being his brother-in-law, and it was about Norm being such a good listener and a friend to all, from the working stiff to the well-to-do, and he glanced at me and for a moment

I was stricken with the thought that my secrets were about to spill, and when he sat down I noticed Arlene in a wheelchair beside him. I'd heard from Clint that she was ill and that Clarence had shut down Bunsen Motors on account of it but the wheelchair was hard to look at. I looked away as Norm's neighbor Bud gave a talk about Norm encouraging him (Bud) to pursue his hobby of painting and how this changed Bud's life and then the Four Norskmen stood up and sang:

Life is not land we own.
O no, it is only lent.
In the end we are left alone
When the last light is spent.
So live that you may say,
Lord, I have no regret.
Thank you for these sunny days
And for the last sunset.

As they sang, Bud set out several of his paintings—for sale, the proceeds to go to a Norm Gunderson scholarship fund—and what this showed all too clearly was (1) abstract painting is not easy but requires talent and technique, and (2) tastelessness has arrived in my hometown and people are helpless to ward it off.

Arlene slipped up behind me, wheeled by her niece Normandy who'd sung the awful song, and said, "Hey, stranger," and I turned as she stood up. "Hello, stranger. I hope you don't mind if I give you a hug." And she put her arms around me from behind. I know you don't come from hugging people," she said. "I hope I'm not embarrassing you." She turned to her niece: "Am I making a scene here? Actually, I don't mind if I do. The world could do with more scenes."

"I heard you were in the hospital," I said.

"Ehhh. Pffft. In and out. It was a lot of nothing."

"So what's the wheelchair about?"

She let go of me. "Laziness. Got tired of walking. And it's a great way of getting attention. You get in a wheelchair and suddenly people are twice as nice as they ever used to be. But you're looking pretty good for a guy almost my age. She turned to her niece: "Believe it or not, I used to go skinny-dipping with this guy. Don't tell my husband. We were teenagers. Children. Stripped naked and jumped in the lake."

Normandy was impressed. Very. "She was your girlfriend? Really? What happened?"

Arlene said, "Go ahead, tell her. She's twenty, she's been around, she knows what's what."

"Norm was my best friend and she was his sister. We were like family," I said.

"So it was incest then?" Arlene said, a little too loudly. People around us stopped talking. Heads turned. I heard whispers: *What'd she say? Incest?*

Arlene was delighted. "Look! I made his face turn red. A big-shot writer from New York and I've made him blush. Wow. This is the high point of my week. I've embarrassed a New Yorker."

Normandy said, "Did you go all the way?"

Arlene laughed. "Honey, we went around the block and came back and went around again. But don't take my word for it, ask him."

I was walking away to look at the paintings, which seemed like the polite thing to do and I managed to avoid eye contact with Bud and then smelled geraniums and a woman threw her arms around me; it was Ronnie Hansen's wife, Shirlee. "Oh my god," she said. "That was the most beautiful poem and you read it so perfectly. Oh my god, I can't believe you're here. We loved your radio show so much. I suppose you heard"—and she wept—"we lost Ronnie. Friday. In Florida." She seemed to be about to collapse and I put an arm around her—she said, "Could you read a poem for my husband? It would mean so much. Or say a few words. You were so important to him. He was so proud of your friendship. It'd mean so much."

And I heard myself say, "Of course." I may have said, "It's my pleasure," I'm not sure. And she was so grateful, it was hard to remove myself from her grasp. "Oh, thank you, thank you, thank you. You're the greatest. I love everything you've written. Oh my god."

So I agreed to eulogize a shithead. The problem was distraction.

During the service I had discovered a small hard protuberance on the roof of my mouth that I couldn't remember having felt there before. I felt it with my finger and my tongue, and though it didn't hurt, it bothered me, what with death on my mind and Norm in the box and people around me who might well attend my funeral, given the opportunity. God has a plan and maybe it's that, after the trashman's demise, his friend the radio show host will be struck by mouth cancer, the mellifluous baritone silenced, the democracy of death demonstrated for all to see. And then, walking to the cemetery, I heard a shout and a bicycle whizzed past, inches away, I smelled pizza, he yelled *Sorry!* And I realized I was in a bike lane. We never had bike lanes in Lake Wobegon back in the day or pizza delivery but here it was. The obituary would say, "He was struck by a pizza deliveryman only two blocks from the house where he was born. Police said he died instantly. According to onlookers, it was a sausage pizza, extra large, which may have obstructed the deliveryman's view." It won't mention my classy memoir, my radio monologues, no link to a video of me singing "I'll Be Your Baby Tonight" with Heather Masse. In people's minds, I will be forever linked to sausage pizza.

I got to the cemetery and phoned Giselle in New York and mentioned the protuberance to her and she told me to send a picture. I hid behind a tree while they got Norm set up among the Gundersons and I opened my mouth as wide as I could and took some cellphone pictures and texted them to Giselle and she said, "Oh my god, that is horrible, you have to see a doctor. Today." She grew up in Greenwich Village and her dad was a doctor who took care of E.E. Cummings, Dylan Thomas, William Burroughs, Jack Kerouac, and a lot of dedicated carousers and scapegraces, so she knows a thing or two about human foolishness and I obey her in all medical matters.

I walked around the cemetery, over by my parents' graves and they looked up and said, "What is he doing here and what's wrong with his mouth?" The protuberance felt larger. Life is all about brevity and how easily the world can get along without us: nobody fills our shoes, they're simply thrown into the old shoe bin and all the books we wrote are made into roadbed, you drive the interstate, you're driving on literature, I read that somewhere. People were busy conversing and I didn't see anyone of a doctoral demeanor present. I saw the former Diane Magendanz, now Mrs. Dan Durand, whom ages ago I danced with at the SnoBall and experienced carnal desire as the band played "Vaya con Dios" and pulled her close to me as we bumped around trying to cha-cha-cha and my hand was on the zipper of her dress and she sneezed directly into my face and apologized and I drove her home. I remember it clearly, lust followed by nasal precipitation. I felt no desire for her now. None. My mind was on death.

Then I saw Elaine, standing alone at the back of the crowd, Norm's great love. She taught health in high school, and I figured, "Why not ask?" So I walked over while Liz was sprinkling holy water and consecrating the grave, and I whispered hello to Elaine. She was weeping. I said, "I'm sorry for your loss, I know he loved you a great deal." She said, "It's not that. It's my son Bailey, the one who lives with me. He's forty-two and ever since he had that traffic accident he's been obsessed with sweet corn and craves it, but he's also allergic to it, except for white corn, which is okay, but he prefers yellow even though when he eats it, he hears voices that tell him to jump off the roof or run naked around the yard, and I do what I can for him, I got him a therapist who got him on an anti-obsession medication but it also dulls his taste buds so he loses his appetite and now he's down to a hundred and forty pounds, he's a scarecrow, and it's all I can do to help keep him halfway sane and not in a loony bin, so I have no time for myself, I haven't read a book in ten or twelve years, and now I got a call from a neighbor saying that my son is knocking on their door, he's naked, and he's singing 'Unchained Melody' and I'm sorry to throw this all on you and babble on about my problems when I'm sure you've got plenty of your own, but honestly I don't know what to do."

I tried to think of something encouraging to say, and then she said, "How are you?" so I opened my mouth wide and pointed to the protuberance and said, "Do you know what that is?"

She said, "I can't understand you with your finger in your mouth." I asked again. She looked. "I have no idea," she said. She asked if Giselle and I still live in New York. I said, "Yes, we do." The gravedigger was lowering Norm into the ground. Then, walking away from the grave, I saw Dorothy who owns the Chatterbox Café and I asked her if there is a doctor in town and she said, "No, Dr. DeHaven died, and all we have now is a holistic healer and an aromatherapist. What's wrong?" I said, "It's some sort of swelling on the roof of my mouth."

She said, "Open wide." We were walking back to the church for the coffee hour, we were on Main Street, across from Mark's Meats and what used to be Dr. Nordquist's office, the dentist who hated to give novocaine, feeling that suffering would motivate better dental hygiene, which now was the This N That Shop run by a lady in a green suit and big golden specs that made her look like an angry grasshopper, across the street from Krebsbach Chev, which was gone, disappeared. "It's a long story," she said, "open your mouth." I did. "Wider," she said. She stuck her finger in and felt the protuberance. She said, "It's nothing, I have one of those too. It's called a torus palatinus. It's just part of your hard palate. Nothing to worry about." I noticed a young woman in what used to be Bunsen Motors, now AuntMildred's.com, staring at us as if she'd never seen a palate exam in public before. I smiled and waved. She ducked down.

After coffee hour, I called Giselle and lied and told her I'd seen an otolaryngologist and he'd said it was an ordinary torus palatinus and nothing to worry about. She said, "I still think you should have someone look at it when you're back in New York." As if a Minnesota otolaryngologist might only have a two-year degree from a vo-tech and not be fully aware of bony growths. "I'm fine," I said. I told her that I'd decided to stick around town for a few days and help Nancy get rid of stuff and also talk to people and fill in some gaps in my past, and she said okay. "There's so much I still want to know and there aren't many people left to ask," I said. "Fine," she said, "you do that. Just don't put yourself in the path of old girlfriends."

"My old girlfriends have other things on their minds. They're not interested in me," I said.

"I was joking," she explained. "I know," I said.

"I'll miss you," she said. She and her cousins Russ and Kerry had been talking about hiking a stretch of the Appalachian Trail in Vermont, she said. She'd bought a great pair of hiking boots. "You'd be welcome to come, but I know you'd hate it, being with hikers. You're a stroller," she said. "So I'll see you when I see you."

So there it was: I was sort of hoping she'd rush out to Minnesota to see to me after my protuberance experience but she is an independent New York woman and makes her own plans and she loves to hike, not sit and reminisce.

Twenty-five years we've been married—no, twenty-six—and I adore Giselle but we're quite different people. She grew up in the narrow streets of the Village among brilliant screwed-up people who keep walking into lampposts, and urban canyons make her restless and she needs brisk walks and broad vistas of mountains and seashore. A day of hiking clears her head of confusion. I'm from the prairie, where, if it's not the end of the world, you can see it from there, and I love narrowness, it comforts me, which is the appeal of narrative prose so I am a writer and parodist, not a big thinker, I don't want to stand on the summit, I need to wend my way into the arroyos of subordinate clauses, through groves of metaphor, following the streambed of anecdote toward the river of genre that leads to the ocean of literature, but I don't expect to get to literature, I'm content to be an imitator. She accepts our differences. She plays a variation of Scrabble in which sounds are permissible like *feh* and *ta* and *pssst* so we argue over *meow* and *miaow, argh* or *arrgh,* and she is crazy about Broadway shows so long as they have a big dance number with arms in the air and high kicks. Like the Act One finale of *Gravy Boat!* with the chorus singing *You've got stature/You're on the dais/ With Margaret Thatcher/And General Petraeus./You're an apple pie with a satisfying belch./You're David Bowie, Gabby Pahinui, you're Gillian Welch.* And she stood up and sang with them: *You're Neil Young and I love you heartily/As an aria sung by Cecilia Bartoli./I'm a fraud, a fake, a big mistake, a creep./I'm over a barrel and you are Meryl Streep.* She's seen the show ten times, she knows it by heart. She loves Italian opera and she doesn't eat lamb nor can she tolerate the misuse of pronouns (*Her and me went to France last year* is enough to make her lie down with an ice pack on her forehead). She can only drink fresh-ground, dark-roast coffee, one of three brands ground in New York, and she is very fond of Portuguese olive oil but not Spanish and she is intolerant of wool. She is extremely fussy about her pillow. She has hours of BBC talk shows on her phone, men talking about cod fishing and wickets and Ibsen and Finnish fiction, which she needs to put herself to sleep at night. I adore her and I have never doubted her love for me though I've taken her on a dozen or so disastrous vacations, which she can recite in a very funny monologue. The New Year's flight to Norway to see the aurora and instead we got the flu. My seizure in London and the rainy week in Florida and the time in Paris when I sat in the hotel and worked. She has stories about me and that's why I wrote a memoir, to get my version out first.

I told her I loved her with all my heart and went to the Chatterbox to talk to Dorothy who was behind the counter, the only familiar face in the place, all the others were new to me, younger faces, some with hairstyles that didn't exist back in my day, some with hair colors not found in nature. Stylish dressers who looked like they'd never weeded a strawberry bed in their life and wouldn't know which end of the hoe to hold. Very strange. I looked at the menu and noticed that tuna casserole was gone, a classic. "What gives?" I said. She said tuna casserole is offered at the Lutheran church's Saturday lunch for seniors: nobody comes to the café for it.

"What about the Commercial Hot Beef Sandwich?" Missing. I loved the Commercial. Two slices white bread with big dollops of mashed potato and three slabs of pot roast in a gravy lake. She said, "Three of the regulars had heart attacks, one had quadruple bypass, two died, all of them good eaters, and it put the fear of cholesterol in their pals and they switched to vegetable pad thai. Men who'd avoided vegetables for fifty years but death changed their minds. Have some. It's okay." I ordered a cup of coffee, black. The waitress looked familiar and her name tag said "Darlene" and I thought I knew her but wasn't sure because her hair was a dramatic crimson, so I asked Dorothy, "Is that Darlene?" She said, "Of course. She got tired of being a brunette and she had a jowlectomy." Darlene is my cousin Alex's daughter, married to the son of my classmate Carol. I said hi to her and she said, "I figured you were just being aloof."

I couldn't believe it. Me, being aloof? I have less aloofness in me than your average graduate student. I was brought up humble and I've been going downhill ever since. Give me a break.

She said, "My brother-in-law in Waco, Texas, send me your book *Lake Wobegon Days* for Christmas. His name was written on the title page. He'd tried to erase it but I could see the indentation. Anyway I started to read it and I got about twenty pages in and I was waiting for something to happen, somebody to leave town and go to California, something, anything, and I put it down and I haven't picked it up again. It's been a busy winter."

Meanwhile Dorothy was saying it's hard to attract a physician when so many of the new people believe in alternative medicine and think that regular exercise and hydration are the answers to everything. "Alice, our mayor, and the town council are offering to finance a new clinic, because they're all over sixty, but one of these days the newcomers, who pay most of the taxes, will vote them out of office, and we'll get a Chinese acupuncturist. Which is okay by me. Dr. DeHaven was the worst doctor ever, right out of the nineteenth century. No matter what the problem, he always said, 'Let's wait and see what develops,' which isn't medicine, it's malpractice, but we lived with it because we were brought up not to complain. People came to see him who were suffering from stage four colon cancer and went home to take a couple aspirin."

"As long as I've got you here, Mister Big Shot—" She poked me in the chest with a sharp fingernail. "While you've been busy weaving your little tales about sleepy Lake Wobegon, Mister Big Shot Writer Man, the town has boomed, and you can make fun of it to your heart's content but it's a boom that we desperately needed. Everyone was moving away, tax revenue was down to a trickle, the birth rate was about what you'd expect when the median age is fifty-five, so we were about to board up the schools and consolidate with Millet's and have our kids go to class with those dummies. What a horrible thought. No Milletite has finished college in years. Nobody there has Wi-Fi. The newest encyclopedia in their town library is a 1978 Collier's. So LifeCycle and Universal Fire were a goddam godsend. Now our kids graduate from Lake Wobegon High, they don't have to move to Minneapolis to find a job putting price stickers on cans of creamed corn, there are jobs here, good jobs, and they can look around and see entrepreneurs a few years older than they who are prospering mightily. You've got teenagers talking about starting companies and turning into tycoons.

"Like Jordan who bought fifty acres of Daryl Tollerud's farm and planted sassafras trees and sarsaparilla vines and he makes the first genuine organic root beer in America, *American Roots*, which sells for $10 a bottle, it's a gold mine. He's twenty-one. He sent his parents to Europe on the Queen Mary 2 in an Executive Suite. His wife, Jamie, and her sister Kaylee raise cockapoo dogs that are trained to provide child care, including bottle-feeding and diaper changing. Some of the dogs can even push a stroller. The root beer grossed three million last year, its first year, and the cockapoo caregivers are going to be in an article in *Vogue*." Kaylee, she said, had won the National Gift-Wrapping Tournament once, wrapping a motorcycle, unboxed, with only two tiny rips, and she worked as a gift-wrap consultant to catalog companies. But training caregiver cockapoos was her true calling and seemed to be the cockapoos' too.

Dorothy said, "I love you like a brother but frankly you're a little past your expiration date. You ought to meet Pastor Liz's sister Alyssa. She was in Silicon Valley for three years, got stressed out working for Google, cashed in her stock options, and came to live on her great-aunt Mildred's farm two miles west of town, the farm with the goats and gardenias. Did you ever meet Mildred? She's a widow, eighty-five, suffering from dementia, but it's good dementia. She was a lifelong Lutheran, rather tightly wired, but dementia loosened her up and made her funny. She can't tell you what she ate for breakfast, but she remembers a dozen Cole Porter songs and she's led the Women's Bible Study down some interesting paths and now at eighty-five she loves to dance and twirl around and tell scandalous stories about men taking liberties and she adores Alyssa and Alyssa's girlfriend, Prairie, and treats them like sisters.

"They were two nerds, humanities dropouts, who couldn't so much as boil an egg and she taught them the basics of cooking and in her kitchen they formed AuntMildred's.com and created Aunt Mildred's Gourmet Meatloaf and Mashed Potato frozen dinners, using ground sirloin and lamb to make the only gourmet meatloaf on the market. The top frozen meatloaf dinner, Hillcrest, was produced for penal institutions and retailed for $2.29. Aunt Mildred's retailed for $18 and was worth every penny."

I held up a hand to ask a question but Dorothy was on a roll.

"It was the first American meatloaf to win the coveted Grand Prix du Carne Baguette in the Entrée Exotique category of the Académie Délicatesse Culinaire Française and Oprah mentioned it on her show and sales went through the roof. And then came Aunt Mildred's Hometown Brownies with lavender honey, brown eggs, dark caramel, unbleached artisan flour, and Costa Rican chocolate. And Pumpkin Bread with Nicaraguan Nutmeg. And Fifteen-Minute Pomme de Terre Tot Hotdish with Mushroom Cream Sauce. It was Grandma cuisine but made for well-to-do connoisseurs of historic cookery, and it all happened here in Lake Wobegon and now the dishes come out of a factory in Kansas City and six months ago Consolidated Foods offered them fifty-five million for AuntMildred's.com and they turned it down."

She poked me again. "Fifty-five million dollars. Anybody offer you fifty-five million for something? How about five million? I don't think so. Sweetheart—" She pinched my cheek. "It's a new world. It's a whole new town. There is overachievement in the air. Multimillionaires riding their bicycles around town, and our kids trying to emulate them. And real estate is booming. Old people are getting three times what they expected to get for their little crackerbox houses. What's not to like about that? I realize it doesn't make as good a novel as bachelor farmers and the Sons of Knute and an overturned pontoon boat, but we are happy campers up here, so watch your step. If you came here to write another novel about us, show some respect."

And then Dorothy looked up and waved to someone. "I want you to meet her," she said. A tall woman with black wiry finger-in-the-outlet hair approached and Dorothy stood up and they hugged. I stood, unhugged, my hand unshaken. "This is Alyssa," said Dorothy. She said, "Garrison's a writer. He writes books. Or used to." The woman said, "What sort of books? Mysteries? Thrillers?" Her gaze went over my right shoulder, watching for the next person to come through the door, a friend perhaps, maybe a celebrity. "Not mysterious to me," I said. Dorothy said I had done a radio show and Alyssa asked if it was a podcast. "No," I said. I enjoyed the fact that there was a little bit of creamy soup on her upper lip and she seemed not to know about this. Dorothy said, "He's written some books about this town."

"You come from here?" said Alyssa. I nodded. "Hnnhh," she said. Dorothy said that I lived in New York with my wife, Giselle. "I lived in Brooklyn for six months," Alyssa said, "and paid two thousand a month for a fifth-floor walk-up and everywhere I looked, I saw highly intelligent people working full-time to impress each other who had no idea of the world except that New York was the center of it and they slaved at lousy jobs in tiny cubicles out of fear that leaving New York meant sudden death, and one day I got on a bus to San Francisco and took charge of my own life." She looked over my shoulder again and still didn't see whoever she was hoping for. She told Dorothy, "I've got to scoot" and said, "Nice meeting you" to me and was gone. I was perfectly okay with her lack of interest in me. I'm a Minnesotan, from the Gopher State, our state bird the loon, so I don't expect strangers to be impressed by me. My wife the hiker loves me dearly, and I have friends—five or six, maybe more, and that's good enough. Adulation would only go to my head and lead to expensive spas and a winter home and Percocet addiction. Who needs it?

Dorothy was right. The new people were no dummies. While old coots like me are mourning the passing of the hour of splendor in the grass and glory in the flower, Alyssa and Prairie started a beauty line, NutriSoft nontoxic face cream and beeswax eyebrow balm. The nontoxicity was writ large right on the label and for emphasis, below it, the line

"Guaranteed to contain no sulfates, phthalates, nor anything from form-aldehyde. Not ever tested on cats or dogs." Maybe ordinary lotions don't contain toxic phthalates either, but if so, why don't they say so on the bottle? NutriSoft does. And it contains oatmeal and lavender, a big step up from formaldehyde. The nontoxic guarantee propelled NutriSoft to No. 5 on the Top Twenty lotion list, two slots ahead of a lotion from the same factory in Akron that makes NutriSoft. The lavender and oatmeal are blended in at a bottling plant in Pittsburgh. Nontoxic lotion and gourmet meatloaf—I thought, "The quicker they get rid of us geezers, the jazzier the world will be." An unspeakable thought but there it is, I thought it. *They can't be stopped, once we've dropped. When we're dead, they'll get ahead, their profits increase when we decease.*

2

LAKE CABIN

Lake Wobegon was booming, meanwhile classmates of mine were dying, Norm and Bob Anderson and Ronnie Hansen, and then Peter Flanagan, four boys who appear at age twelve in a 1954 class photograph, all wearing plaid shirts, their hair with comb marks, hands folded on the desks, so hopeful, anxious to please, and now they had all at once gone over the cliff. Bob left town and hitchhiked to New York to become a dancer and changed his name to Lindsay Longet and started a dance company of six dancers that worked with electronic music of a random sort, dancing in half darkness with plenty of writhing around in a pile of flesh on the floor and occasional strobe lights, which mostly played in smaller towns in the South. He died crossing Columbus Avenue in New York, crossing against the light, a lifelong habit but the cab that killed him was driven by a man from Indiana where stoplights are respected. His body was not returned to Lake Wobegon, his family having moved to Florida years before, and his funeral took place in Tampa. His brother called Arlene and said they'd like the school hymn played at the service, and she wasn't feeling well so I FaceTimed her and we sang a duet and her daughter recorded it and we got a thank-you note a week later, saying it was very well received.

Hail to thee, our Alma Mater,
Would that we might dwell
Longer in thy hallowed hallways,
But we bid farewell.
Through life's dangerous lonely passages
'Long the coasts of grief and fear,
In our hearts we'll e'er remember
How you loved and taught us here.

Bob certainly knew about dangerous and lonely passages. I thought Arlene and I sounded rather good in duet, her with the melody, me singing alto, I thought it was very tender. It sounded like a love song. I think the average listener could hear that there was an emotional tie between these two people and if someone asked me who that woman was, I might've told them: she was the first girl I loved. She took me into the lake and we made love, she baptized me into grown-up life.

I wasn't sure how Nancy felt about me, Norm's buddy, who'd gotten an earful about her idiosyncrasies over the years, but she was calm and friendly and invited me to come and have coffee. She sat on her front porch in her dark blue polka-dotted dress with her granddaughter Normandy who was weeping. Nancy said, "He wanted to go exactly the way he went, in a flash, no waiting. I got in the ambulance with him and he blew me a kiss and then he was gone. I didn't say anything, I didn't want them to be pounding on his chest or using electric paddles and making his legs flop around. I just let him go. It meant so much to him that time you met him for a beer in St. Cloud. He was afraid you'd lose track of him, you being a big success and all." She put a hand on my knee. "Which brings me to the hard part. Norm wanted you to have his lake cabin. He said you and he used to spend summers out there. I imagine he talked to you about it." I nodded; he had. "I know you're probably on your way back to New York but I just can't bear to go into the place. It was his hideout, his secret life. I don't want to see it. The place is falling apart. If you could just spend a few days out there, that'd be good enough, and then, I don't know, we can burn the place

34

down or something." She handed me the key. And then she broke down and cried. "He was so happy this spring. He had a wonderful couple of months. He drove me nuts sometimes but I miss him."

The cabin is a 20x30 one-room wood frame house, white siding, screened front porch facing the lake, outhouse behind, at the end of a dirt road serving a string of similar cabins all from the 1920s. Norm's grandparents built it. I hadn't set foot in it since the summer after high school graduation but that summer is so vivid to me still that when I parked on the grass and walked up to the back door, I could feel the music of the past, as if the movie was about to start, and Norm's older sister Arlene would come out and take my hand, wearing her dad's unbuttoned white shirt over her green bikini. She was nineteen that summer and her boyfriend Lance had dumped her. Norm had enlisted in the Army to avoid a jail term for vandalism and his mother missed him and so I became a substitute son and Arlene's retribution boyfriend. I sat with the elder Gundersons listening to them reminisce about life in the Thirties, the dust storms, dust blowing into the house, dust in the breakfast cereal, the drunken father weeping in the barn, the insane aunt upstairs yelling at the dead, the broken-down Model T—funny stories about hard times. Harold was small for his age, having been a premature baby, not expected to survive. His mother swabbed him with Wesson Oil and laid him in a cigar box on the open door of the oven at low heat and he survived. He was a gentle soul, thanks to his slightness. He fended off bullies by his good manners. He and Marjie met at a dance in Chaffee, North Dakota. She wore a nice dress of her mother's and the zipper broke and he tried to help her and it came off the rails and he put an arm around her to protect her modesty and found safety pins and they danced, she and her protector. She was a good dancer, very lively. They had no money and were engaged for four years and finally could wait no longer and she got pregnant and they were married by a judge in the town park on an August day and the sky turned dark, a hailstorm, hail the size of ping-pong balls, and they dashed to the car and Harold's uncle got him a job delivering mail and they settled in Lake Wobegon and had Arlene and he went into ceramic tile and life was good. He loved to talk about his good fortune and I listened to him, listening was the rent I paid. Brethren men didn't tell stories, they looked forward to the Rapture, not backward at their own lives.

I enjoyed Harold and Marj's patronage, their cheerful outlook, Marj's pot roast and sweet corn, and the lazy evenings, the sting of gin and the burn of smoke. I slept in an upper bunk, Arlene in the lower, a canvas curtain between us and her parents' bed. I read Ferlinghetti to them on the screened porch and we drank gin and tonics and I practiced smoking Pall Malls, exhaling stylishly. I couldn't have done these things in my Brethren home. I was on the road to sophistication and a life as a writer, whatever that might mean. Arlene had felt lost in her freshman year at St. Olaf, she thought she might go to the U, she said, "We could be roommates." That was a thrilling thought. A bedroom with her in it, waiting for me at night.

She knew I was a virgin; I was quite aware of it myself. She told me I was sexier than her ex-boyfriend, that he wanted to get into her pants but had no idea what to do if he got there. I had a few vague ideas I'd gotten from an old marriage manual, *Light on Dark Corners*. You kiss and touch and get excited and Point A goes into Slot B. Meanwhile, the Gundersons treated me like a son and Arlene said she was attracted to me and I let my parents believe that I might join Norm in the Army, which was the last thing on my mind. It was an idyllic summer, more than idyllic, dreamy, glorious, heavenly. I read Liebling and Cheever and Thoreau and imagined being a writer and meanwhile a girl was in love with me and sat next to me on the porch when nobody was looking, her hand on my bare knee, sometimes moving up to my bare thigh. Once she said, "Kiss me, you fool" and I did and then she did it again and again. "What else would you like?" she said. I didn't know how to say it: *everything*. I was a good boy but I wanted to see beyond goodness. A writer needs to go to the end of the road so he can write about it.

Marj and Harold skipped going to church those summer Sundays. Sunday was a day of relaxation. It wasn't like the Brethren life at all, a life that ran on the steel rails of doctrine. There was no hugging among

36

Brethren, men didn't even show affection to their wives in public, but the Gundersons were patters, embracers, smoochers. Marj liked to put her hand on the back of my neck, maybe slip an arm around me. She was a secret Democrat, she told me she was going to vote for John F. Kennedy. She wanted Arlene to go to college because she, Marj, hadn't had that opportunity. "It never even crossed our minds back in the Depression," she said. She admired me for wanting to be a writer. "You are so creative! Where do you come up with these ideas?" She said she hoped she'd live long enough to read the books I'd write and I promised to hurry up and write some. She said, "You seem so serious sometimes but I think you're very funny." She liked the limerick I wrote for her:

A woman from Chaffee named Marj
Believes in living life large.
The spirit will chafe
In a life that's too safe,
So climb on your horse and cry, "Charge!"

She posted it on the refrigerator. She said, "Sign it, you'll be famous someday." Marrying Arlene would give me Marj for a mother-in-law, a big bonus.

Harold was a classic dad. After it rained, he always said, "We needed that rain." If he ran into a friend in a restaurant, he said, "Guess they let anyone in here." When the waitress brought the check, he said, "What's the damage?" If you left to go to town but came back because you forgot something, he said, "Back already? How was it?" We sat on the porch, a gin and tonic in one hand, a Pall Mall in the ashtray, my hand on Arlene's bare leg, reading Thoreau to her—*If one advances confidently in the direction of his dreams, and endeavors to live the life which he has imagined, he will meet with a success unexpected in common hours.* She asked, "What do you dream of?" I said I wanted to be a writer but really what I wanted was for her to touch my leg, which she was always doing. Thoreau said to build castles in the air and then put foundations under them. He said he would rather sit alone on a pumpkin than sit crowded with others on a velvet cushion. I sat next to Arlene on a swinging couch, her head on my shoulder, her hand on my thigh, admiring the texture of my green swim trunks. She said, "Do you know you have a beautiful body?" I did not. Nobody had ever said anything of the sort to me before. She said, "I don't know why we should be ashamed of our bodies. I think we should enjoy them." I agreed. Whatever she meant, I was in favor.

I was intoxicated by *Walden* that summer and fascinated by Arlene's interest in me—no other girl had seen erotic potential in me except Julie Christensen and that was only for the purpose of domination, and one night, sitting on the porch after her parents had retired for the night, Arlene mentioned swimming in the moonlight, and I got up to go get into my swim trunks and she said, "You don't need those, it's dark out" and we proceeded out down a dark path to the dock where I took my clothes off and she did too and we stood in the water up to our shoulders, embracing, a delicious historic moment when you trust yourself to another, skin to skin, and I kissed her and her tongue was in my mouth and then the porch light came on and Marj stepped out the door and she could see what was what, I'm sure, but she said, in a soft voice, "Don't go in too deep, kids," and disappeared back into the house, and Arlene grabbed hold of me, asked if I was excited, and it was beyond excitement, more like transfiguration. This was the significance of the old Gunderson cabin, the place where, under the influence of Thoreau, I dreamed of touching a girl in secret places and met with success. Arlene took hold of me and said, "Oh my" and she hoisted herself up on the dock and opened her legs and eased me inside her and thus my ordinary Brethrenly life was touched by magic. You could put up a brass plaque: *My adult life began on this very spot.*

Sixty years later, I unlocked the back door and walked in, and seeing the green linoleum of my youth, the old wicker furniture, the yellow kitchen table, the woodstove, the bunkbeds with the canvas curtain between them, it was thrilling—even with the mounds of junk every-where, it was as if the historical society had preserved the place and a docent named Meredith would give a talk about Fifties conformity and what was expected of "nice" girls and the fieriness of fundamentalists' condemnation of carnal desire and also how the lack of birth control heightened the drama of premarital sex and she would lead the tour group down to the dock and read from my diary. *I stood naked in the water, not sure what to do, but she knew and then we were united in a way entirely new to me and I was afraid someone would come, my parents, a preacher, my uncles, the county sheriff, but nobody came and I held her close and it felt good and then it was amazing.* And Meredith talked about the romanticism of the small-town adolescent misfit intellectual and how the intoxication of my loss of virginity had sprung me loose from the burden of my puritanical roots and maybe diverted me from dangerous drugs and booze. And the surrogate parenthood of Marj and Harold had eased me out of judgmentalness and into normal habits of amiable sociability. Of course I'd have to write a couple of great works of literature in order to justify the historical society going to the trouble and Meredith becoming an authority on my upbringing, a Smith College *summa* grad who's read twice everything Edith Wharton ever wrote but needed a summer job and this was all she could get. But traffic is light, five or six visitors a day, and she has time to work on her own novel, *Guilford Girl.*

Three days a week I worked as a dishwasher in Jack's Café, which eventually became the Chatterbox, and I lived with the Gundersons, and Arlene went around in that white shirt, and sometimes she lay in bed and pushed at my mattress above her and dared me to come down to her bunk for a visit. One night, with the Gundersons in town at a church council meeting, we made love in her bed, which was rapture and exaltation, skin to skin, our lips, tongues, rocking, rocking—"Not too fast," she said—and then I shuddered and she laughed, and headlights lit up the room, and I climbed up and lay naked in my bed, breathing hard, as her parents came around the cabin and into the porch and sat talking about church things.

"Are you okay?" Arlene said. I said I was. "That was fantastic," she said. It was also the end. I went to Minneapolis to take an entrance exam at the U and she went back to St. Olaf and she wrote to me and said that Clarence Bunsen had asked her to a dance and would I be offended if she went with him and she signed the letter *Love* and I wrote back rather casually that of course I didn't mind if she went with him, not grasping her unspoken message, which was *Are you still interested in me?* and six months later she married him, and I felt hurt, rejected, and avoided her for years, but the shine of that long-ago summer still shone brightly, Arlene and me with our hands all over each other. For an evangelical kid raised by Brethren, it was the gates of the Garden of Eden flung open wide. The folks in the tour group ask if I ever wrote about that summer love affair and Meredith says no, that I am guarded about sexual anecdotes due to my background in radio, which I guess is true, but the beauty of our love stays with me, our nakedness, feeling the heat of her desire for me, something no woman had ever demonstrated. I left in September. Harold drove me to town to buy my 1956 Ford and he saw some horses in a pasture and he said, "Look, horses." I drove to Minneapolis, a new man, and set out to be a writer. And now I look in the kitchen cupboard of the Gunderson cabin and there are all my books, twenty-four of them, they look well-read. Norm had bought them used, some for as little as fifty cents. He was my good pal but he was frugal.

He was a hoarder and the cabin was the warehouse for his treasures, stacks of *Popular Mechanics* and *Saturday Evening Post* and boxes of stuff he'd rescued from the trash, shoeboxes full of old eyeglasses, pennants, plastic statuettes, antique keys and doorknobs, used postcards, campaign buttons, convention badges, several dozen streetcar conductor caps, boxes of autographed baseballs, including a Mickey Mantle and a Tony Oliva and a Billy Martin, a leather satchel once owned by Harold Stassen, a bunkbed from the Pullman car of the North Coast Limited, and all manner of doohickeys and thingamajigs, gewgaws, rummage. A hubcap for an ashtray and a New York skyline picture puzzle, half assembled. A picture of a wolf on a snowbank on a moonlit night. He was addicted to estate sales and couldn't resist Minnesota novelty items such as a Harmon Killebrew Casserole Dish and a Golden Gopher Savings Bank and framed menus from Murray's and Charlie's Café Exceptionale and Dayton's Sky Room, hundreds of interesting useless items. And there, not in a drawer but folded and tucked into his old 1960 *Wobegonian* yearbook, was the photo of Elaine, a naked old lady, taking her picture with a cellphone. A man freezing to death had remembered this picture and the thought of his wife seeing it and being offended had saved his life and clearly he hadn't burned it, it was still here, but if Nancy had seen it, I doubt she'd be in a jealous rage. Elaine was not attractive, naked. But the picture saved his life and he survived suicide and got to see spring blossoms and hear the meadowlark.

There was a CD player on the table and I pressed ON and heard Dylan sing:

Judas tears flowed past my ears
Despite my warm earflaps
And doused the fire of financiers
As Sears guitars played Taps.

Half-deserted towns back east
Were screaming in despair,
The lilacs of the late deceased
Were showing at the Fair.
Unconscious of the cattle pen
I saw the sacred cow
I thought I knew what those lines meant,
I find them crazy now.

I had no idea Norm was a Dylan fan. It was like finding the *Book of Mormon* at his bedside, with underlined passages. I rolled up the picture of Elaine and stuck it in an empty bourbon bottle, capped it, and threw it into the lake and it floated off to the west. Let some old fisherman find it and put it in his tackle box and forget it and then, six months from now, have to explain it to his wife.

His dirty laundry I doused with kerosene and burned it out back. I wet-mopped the place, dusted, set out termite traps. The bedding smelled lived-in and I buried it in the yard. I went to town and bought new bedding and insecticide. I rented a U-Haul trailer and backed it up to the back door and shoveled the accumulations in, all except a blue *LW Lutheran* cap. Norm was captain of the Lutheran Men's Softball Team back in 1970 and he put me at third base for a game against Jack's Auto Repair. I had two good plays, a hard grounder on the baseline, one bounce, that I backhanded and planted my right foot and threw the batter out at first. And I hit a triple, which should've been a single but went through the right fielder's legs and was bobbled and thrown wildly to the first baseman as I rounded second and the catcher threw it to third base and nobody was there, and I slid in safe, the only triple of my entire life on Earth, a great memory even if it has an asterisk beside it (*opposing team was drunk*). Now I had a souvenir of my last ball game. I hauled the rest to the dump. I sat on the porch and called Giselle and read some Thoreau to her and said I wanted to sit on a pumpkin with her and front the essential facts of life and follow the drummer of our dreams and she laughed and said she'd see me whenever I was ready to come home. She said, "Don't brood too much about the past the way you tend to do. Get out and walk. Two miles a day. It's good for the brain." She thought I was in mourning for my lost youth, but I wasn't at all, I was overwhelmed by gratitude for that fortuitous summer, the adult talk, the snap of the gin fizzed with tonic, the expressiveness of exhaled smoke, Arlene's thigh, a natural wonder in my hand, the steam of the scullery by day and the intensity of a girl at night, and Thoreau telling me to proceed confidently in the direction of my dreams. It's all well and good to make millions off a gourmet meatloaf and I take nothing away from a manure tycoon or firewood artisan, but in this very cabin I hit my stride years ago and against the odds I made a good life. I don't need to persuade anyone else, I just need to know it myself. My people were self-denigrating and fled from praise as if it were rat poison. I am now done denigrating myself. I have standing in this world. It's a new world and I maintain the right to observe and render judgment. I spread some poison behind the beds and took a broom and cleared cobwebs out of the outhouse and peed. I made a third final load of trash. I stripped the place down to its historic 1960 details, as you'd do with any important site, the Emily Dickinson house in Amherst, the Clemens house in Hannibal, Valley Forge. It took me two whole days but I did an excellent restoration. Norm had made no improvements so it was not hard.

I saw Carl Krebsbach's truck at the dump and I wanted to talk to him about having a look at the cabin to see what repairs are necessary. I didn't need to improve it but I didn't want it to fall down on my head. But he was on his phone and it sounded like he wasn't having a good day so I brought back another load of accumulations and then he was gone. I called him and got his wife, Margie, who told me he had a month's backlog of work but she'd pass on the message.

I said, "What happened to Bunsen Motors and Krebsbach Chev?" She was frying up walleye for supper but she told me the whole story. One April morning a couple weeks before I got to town, Arlene Bunsen awoke with sharp stabbing stomach pains and Clarence drove her straight to the Mayo Clinic in Rochester where, several hours later, the oncologist said, "It's pancreatic cancer and like most of them, it's being discovered a little too late. Your wife has about a 20 percent chance of living more than a few months. We can talk about chemo and of course we'll do as she wishes but my advice is to go home and make the most of what's left. Chemo would only extend the suffering." Clarence called Clint and said, "We're done. It's over. Arlene has cancer. Time to close up shop. I should've done it years ago, my mistake. Anyway, we're done. Hang up a Closed sign and lock the cash register and I'll bring in the accountant next week." Clint agreed. A guy from Universal Fire was looking at the used cars and Clint told him, "We're closing." The guy said, "I'll come back tomorrow." Clint said, "We're closed tomorrow too." It was done in fifteen minutes.

They had thought of selling the business two years before and listed it with an agent in St. Cloud and the offers they got were ridiculously low, insulting. "It's about customer loyalty," the agent said. "A new owner can't count on that loyalty transferring to him. Your best bet is to have your son or a nephew take over." Clarence's son Duane is a video game expert in Houston, Texas. He sits in a dark room looking at three screens for twelve hours a day, assessing level of difficulty though every game is rather simple for him, and Clarence hasn't heard him speak more than four words in a row except the time he dropped an oak table on his foot and then all the words were the same. He could no more sell cars than he could translate French. Clint's son Walter went to Philadelphia and married into a family of nonstop talkers and so he's gradually lost half his English and is mostly reduced to expressing approval or indifference. None of their daughters care to return to live in town and besides the men they married are not the brightest bulbs in the chandelier. So closure was the only option. Ninety years of history from the Model T to the SUV and it ended with one brief phone call, one brother to the other.

Clarence was too shaky to drive home. He got a hotel room in Rochester and sat looking at the wall. He ordered supper and didn't touch it. He went to the hospital. Arlene, semiconscious, said, "Don't tell the kids. I don't want them to worry." She took Clarence's hand: "I love you so much, and I assumed you knew that, otherwise I would've told you," she said. "My mother thought I could've done better but she gradually came around to liking you. I liked you from the start, the time you asked me to dance. You thought I was my sister Irene who wasn't a good dancer and you were sort of alarmed when I did the Twist but you accommodated yourself. You've always been an accommodator." He stepped out in the hall and wept and called his daughter Barbara Ann who was giving a talk about community outreach at Walker Art Center in fifteen minutes and she said she'd come home that night. He called Duane in Houston and left a message: "Your mother's at Mayo. It's serious. Call me when you get this." Duane is easily distracted: he's someone you can send to town for a box of nails and he'll come back with a crucifix and a model train. He didn't respond for a week and a half. Dorothy of the Chatterbox came down to Rochester on the bus the next day and drove the two of them home. She is that sort of friend: if you need her, she's there, on the spot, ready to take orders or take charge, whichever is needed.

Meanwhile, Clint moved fast, afraid Clarence might change his mind. He hung a big "Closed" sign on the Bunsen Motors showroom door, and by the time Clarence and Arlene got back from Mayo, he'd made a deal with a Ford dealership in Minneapolis to buy out the fourteen used cars on the lot and the SUV and Mustang in the showroom and he'd sold the lift and two truckloads of tools to a garage in St. Cloud. Alyssa and her partner, Prairie, offered Clarence $300,000 for the Bunsen Motors showroom, garage, shed, and two-point-six acres, and he accepted it. Meanwhile, Kenny Krebsbach, who two years ago twisted his back playing golf in Florida and got on painkillers that made him stupid and led to him chasing around after Claudia as she worked her rural mail route until she explained to him that it is a federal crime punishable by up to five years in prison—he decided to close up Krebsbach Chev at the age of 72. He never liked the car business and only took over the agency to please his old man who lived to be 98 and was Kenny's constant critic. Old Man Krebsbach never went south in the winter but visited the shop daily to complain that Kenny was selling the cars too cheap, the parts department was screwed up, the mechanics were rude, and the kids who pump the gas need to do a better job of cleaning windshields, meanwhile, a dozen Krebsbachs were demanding hereditary discounts. It drove Kenny nuts, and 72 is old enough to choose sanity for yourself. The old man was dead and Kenny wrote *Going Out Of Business* on the window let his relatives come in and take what they wanted. He sold the building to a company called Mellow Marsh that makes natural vanilla-bean marshmallows enriched with CBD, whatever that may be, which seems to appeal to the college crowd.

And then Kenny abandoned his wife of fifty years, Beverly, and took off with his niece's kids' second-grade teacher Samantha. He was on Percodan or Tryptophan or something with a barbiturate additive and he had bought himself a Mercury Marauder. He wouldn't have taken up with Samantha in a Chevy. But Beverly went to court and the judge awarded her the $200K that Mellow Marsh paid and also title to their house, another hundred grand, and Samantha left him and split for San Diego and Kenny wound up in Iowa City pumping gas and living alone in a camper. He told his brother Florian that Samantha was great in bed but, as Florian said, $300,000 is an awful lot to pay for sex.

45

What could a woman do for an old man that'd be worth that kind of money? It became a topic of detailed conversation at the Sidetrack Tap. Poor Kenny. For years you're an upstanding businessman and stalwart Republican and then the local barflies are discussing your sexual proclivities. If you mentioned Kenny to Carl Krebsbach, he held up his hand and said, "I know nothing about it. Nothing." Carl and Margie have been together 43 years and are happier than ever, after a couple rocky stretches that were kept strictly private. The town gossips have their theories but no solid evidence. He is still the town carpenter/contractor and his pattern of hammering a nail into a two-by-four—five strokes, *whack whack whack whack whack* with perhaps an extra tap for good luck—is familiar to just about everyone in town.

The death of the car dealerships was an earthquake event. The demise of Bunsen and Krebsbach felt like the fall of the Pantheon or the Washington Monument. Every Lutheran in town had sat at Clarence's rolltop desk and signed the contract to buy a Ford. Driving a Chev would mean you worshipped the pope in Rome and contributed money to buy pagan babies for baptism, so you didn't. A few rebels bought Buddhist or Shinto cars but the Lutheran/Catholic binary order was the prevailing one. I myself once sat at his desk and bought that 1956 Ford to drive away to the U in. I was eighteen, had tasted gin and made love to a girl, and pulling out of the lot in that 1956 Ford, I was a man and I have been one ever since.

A major historic event but we are a minimizing people. I ran into Clint one afternoon at the bank where I'd gone to see the new ATM. There'd never been one in town before, the bank held out against the idea of easy money, and now here it was. Even a stranger could get American cash, no questions asked. Daryl Tollerud was there, depositing a check from American Roots who'd raised sassafras on fifty acres of his land and here was $220,000 for rent and share of profits. He showed me the check. Clint walked up. "How you been?" said Clint.

"Not so bad," I said. Daryl held the check folded in two, not wanting Clint to see it.

"How's the writing business?"

"Petering out. I'm an aging white male. Nobody's interested in me or my ilk. But I keep going for my own amusement."

"Well, you had a good run," said Clint. "Same with us. No sense in waiting too long."

I said, "It's odd to see Bunsen Motors gone. It's been there forever."

"Ninety-eight years. One of the oldest Ford dealerships in the country. Grandpa Bunsen bought the first Model T in Mist County. Drove it home, forgot it was a car, pulled back on the wheel and yelled, 'Whoa,' and crashed into the ditch. Opened the business a year later. Clarence hated the idea of putting on a centennial party and serving cake and lemonade and hiring a band and having a hundred people congratulate him. He hates festivity. And then Arlene got sick and that gave him a perfect reason to close up shop."

"What's going to happen to the building?"

"This woman Alyssa bought it for her meatloaf company."

"Lots of new businesses starting up," I said.

"Yeah."

I said, "I'm going to miss Bunsen Motors. That was an institution here."

"Well, I'm glad I didn't wind up in an institution," he said. He turned to Daryl: "If you need a lug wrench, I got a bunch of extras." And he did. In a gunny sack he was holding.

"Don't mind if I do." Daryl selected lug wrench. Clint looked at me. I said, "I'm a lug who doesn't know a wrench from a rent check."

"Well, good talking to you," he said.

"Good talking to you."

I was like that when I retired from radio. People came up and said, "I miss your show," and I said, "I miss some of them. Not many." What's the problem? I'm old. What else is new?

It was almost time for Ronnie Hansen's funeral and what to say for a eulogy? He was well past the car-crash age, but his dad, Jerry, was the town drunk and also our school bus driver, who drove with his knees because he had a cigarette in one hand and a bottle in the other. So there was some precedent. Ronnie was good at math and had a crush on Arlene who bore a resemblance to Natalie Wood and who resisted his entreaties and one evening, walking with her, he took a stick and whacked a tree full of June bugs, which fell on her and he unbuttoned her blouse so he could get at the bugs that fell down her bosom and she had to outrun him, she was very fast, but not in the way he was hoping.

Ronnie was quite successful right up to the day he died. He owned a big house on Cedar Lake in Minneapolis, collected paintings, his wife was beautiful, he retired from airline piloting and used his free miles to fly around visiting his girlfriends while his wife did volunteer work in Minneapolis. Arlene told me, "He flew to Florida with only four hours before his return flight and he was in a big hurry to get naked and he drove over a hill going eighty miles an hour and suddenly the road was all yellow from a load of bananas that fell off a truck with a busted tailgate and Ronnie hit the brakes, which is the wrong thing to do when you're driving on bananas, and the car skidded three hundred feet and into a eucalyptus tree and so he died with the smell of cough drops in his nose. A true story and no surprise to anyone who knew Ronnie, but the story got quashed and the family asked me to do the eulogy, since I'd done such a good one for Norm, so I did. Arlene was surprised. She said, "But you didn't like him. Nobody did."

"I didn't know what to tell them when they asked me."

"How about, Hell, no?"

I met Pastor Liz in the mortuary office before the funeral and she said right out, "I hope you're not going to make this guy into a hero of our time, I hope. He was a jerk, you know."

I said no, I was just going to read a poem the family suggested I read, no reference to the deceased or to virtues of any kind.

"Good," she said. She reached under her surplice and pulled out a tiny bottle of gin. "If you're nervous, this helps," she said. I shook my head.

"A shot or two of gin really steadies a person before a funeral," she said. "In seminary, if you were a Christer, someone who takes it all too seriously, which I did, they made you stand up after supper and sing—" and she sang, softly:

Everything goes faster for the deacon or the pastor if there's gin.
An itsy-bitsy teeny-weeny little gin martini ain't a sin.
Bourbon is southern and it tastes like death,
Scotch is Presbyterian and gives you bad breath.
Beer's for squares and vodka for the dim,
Jesus drank wine but I'm not him.
Gin is a blessing so dive right in.
But choose a liquor store that's far away
And be prepared to pay the full amount
And don't ask for the clerical discount. (They do not have one.)
And do remove your collar and your little Jesus pin.

"Ronnie," she said, "never set foot in church even to use the lavatory. Speaking of which, I recommend you do. It's like we say: *Empty your bladder, don't be a culprit. Remember there is no pissing in the pulpit.*"

So I did and she was right. I had a half-gallon in me.

I didn't tell her that I had written a long eulogy with a made-up letter from a dying priest, Father Antonio, thanking Ronnie for his good work flying sick children to doctors in New York and I said he was on his way to visit Antonio and that was why Ronnie was speeding and when he saw three little crippled kids from the treatment center crossing the road he did not hesitate but steered the car into the tree, an act of self-sacrifice. I even gave him dying words. I had a cop peel Ronnie off the eucalyptus tree and he said, "Dígales a los niños que Dios los ama," which, according to Google, is Spanish for "Tell the little ones God loves them." It was a good eulogy about three pages' worth, and it turned the jerk into a candidate for sainthood. But it was way too much, a wretched excess of false piety, and I ditched it and read the poem instead, one by Alfred Lord Tennyson's nephew Artie, "Crossing The Yard."

Sunset and evening star,
And headlights of a car
And may I feel no tremors of alarm
When I head for the barn.

49

My family asleep upstairs,
The house nice and warm
May nothing need repairs
As I head for the barn.
I leave the keys in the pickup truck
As I depart,
The pigs asleep, some chickens cluck,
As I cross the yard.
I notice that the lawn needs mowing,
And there's a loose board
On the shed but I must be going
To my reward.

One last backward glance
At those I'll see no more
Then I'll buckle up my pants
And open the barn door.
Farewell to Time, Farewell to Place
Like other mortal men
I soon shall see my shepherd's face
As he leads me to my pen.
There I'll lie and know that I
At last have bought the farm.

Arlene told me, on the way to the cemetery, "Nice poem but Ronnie never set foot on a farm. He was terrified of dogs. The poor bastard was helpless when it came to lust. The honest thing would've been to tell the men in the audience that if you're going to commit adultery, you better do it close to home where you're familiar with the roads." I told her I didn't see it that way, I saw it as doing good to those who persecute you. "I saw him at our last class reunion. A kind of miserable reunion where all the people you wanted to see aren't there, and most of the people are the ones you avoided in high school, like Ronnie. He and I were standing at the urinal in the men's room and he looked down at me and said,

'That looks just like a penis except it's a lot smaller.' And I turned toward him and said, 'That's rather immature' and I accidentally pissed all over his leg."

"I wish I'd been there," she said. "But frankly I wouldn't have pissed on Ronnie Hansen if he was on fire."

"It was his brand-new seersucker pants. He jumped back and slipped on the wet floor and he broke his wrist but he didn't realize it until he got up and took a swing at me and there was a loud crack and he fell down again, he was in terrible pain. He sat in a puddle of piss and he cursed me and you realize at a time like that how very few good curse words there are in English and how they don't fill the need sometimes."

"The man was a well-known creep. Back in high school, he and I were walking home and he told me my bra strap was tangled up and before I knew it he had unzipped my blouse and unsnapped the bra and he stuck his hand up under my blouse and I had to kick him in the shins. The man was out for ass his whole life. He died in his rush to get some nookie."

"I never heard you say 'nookie' before," I said.

"I used to be a Girl Scout leader. So I'm making up for lost time. We're fading away, sweetheart. I hit my peak at the age of nineteen. That night you and I took our clothes off. Then I wasted two years at St. Olaf College and came home and got engaged and I became a moron. So tell me, why did the little moron carry a transparent lunchbox?—So he could tell if he was going to work or on his way home. Do you remember that night? I hope you do.

"Of course I do."

She stopped wheeling her chair and looked up at me. " I think you got scared and you left town because you were terrified you'd have to marry me and it turned out to be the smartest thing you did."

"I don't know."

"You were a very nice boy and it was 1960 and you figured a one-night stand meant we'd have to go to a justice of the peace and you'd have to find a job at the post office so you ran away and became a big-shot writer. So I get some credit for your career. Does Giselle love you?"

I said, "Are you asking if I get enough nookie?"

"Nookie, poontang, pussy, canoodling, copulation, whatever you call it out there."

"We call it consummation. And yes, I'm a very happy man married to a lovely woman."

"So on your third at-bat you finally got on base."

She smiled, the first girl I loved, the first girl who loved me enough to want to be naked with me, and she had tears in her eyes remembering that night naked in the lake.

"Don't you love Clarence?" I said.

"Of course. He's a good man. We made a good life. But I'm still in love with you."

And when she said that, she could say no more—I could tell, she was weeping. "I'm sorry," she said, and she turned and wheeled back the way we'd come.

I went on to the cemetery. Clint and Billy and Dave and I looked at the crowd around the tombstones and weeping angels as the pallbearers brought Ronnie's coffin through the gate and Clint said, "God, those pallbearers look awful." They were Ronnie's teammates on the football team and three of them had been badly concussed and looked like dead men walking so the procession moved slowly over uneven ground and stopped as one pallbearer switched hands to get a better grip and the front right corner of the coffin dropped a couple feet and the undertaker had to grab hold and then the rear left bearer tripped on a stone and the back of the box dropped and the lid sprang open and a pale dead hand flopped out and they had to set the thing down and put the hand back in and tuck in the blanket and close the lid and by this time the pallbearing team looked like they'd borne as much as they could bear. Clint said, "Those guys are so far gone they can't even carry him into the end zone." He grabbed my arm and the two of us stepped forward and took hold of the rails and so did three of Ronnie's grandsons and we took him to the grave and set him down. The benediction was brief and a soprano stepped forward and sang:

I come to the garden alone,
When the dew is still on the roses,
While the birds all flock round the path I walk
And I feel creation knows us.
And the bright sunshine warms this heart of mine
And it tells me here I belong,
And the fragrant air dispels despair
And it makes my faith more strong.

She was about to sing more when a distant bugler, missing his cue, blew Taps and did it almost perfectly. "I need a drink," said Clint. "It's not often you see a dead man trying to escape."

I kept him company in the Sidetrack. He had a whiskey and soda and I had a glass of mineral water and then Dave joined us and Daryl. It was two in the afternoon and Daryl ordered a gin and tonic and Dave a vodka martini and I looked at their drinks and didn't say what I was thinking so Dave said it for me. He said, "I've come to the age when you don't postpone pleasure. The big heart attack can hit you at any time so if I feel like jerking off in the morning, I do it, I don't wait until after dark." We sat and tried not to think about Dave masturbating and Daryl said he had put off martinis for years, thinking of it as a Republican drink, and now he was enjoying two a day, with a good nap in between.

Clint said, "I don't think about death much but I got to say, I almost bought the farm back in February. Went for a walk out around the lake with my dog Benny because the doc said I needed to walk a mile a day and I saw a money clip out on the ice about seventy feet from shore, and I tiptoed out there to get it.

"It'd been warm for a week, and I knew it was crazy, but I walked out on the ice. I had Benny on a leash and he didn't want to go. I had to half-drag him out there. The dog was smarter than I was. So I got out there and it was a money clip with a five and two ones in it. I could feel how thin the ice was and so could the dog. He looked up at me with grief in his eyes. And I thought to myself, 'Of the stupid things you've done in your life, this takes the prize.' The ice was mushy, and I figured the lake was probably about twenty feet deep right there, so I had just decided to give up my life for seven bucks. And the dog is looking up at me and trembling and I'm wearing a heavy down jacket and if I go through the ice, I'd never get the jacket off and I'd die for seven dollars. And I got angry at Irene who, when she saw me put the jacket on that morning, she said, 'You don't need that, it's warm out' and she said it in such a dismissive tone that I felt obligated to wear the damn jacket as a matter of self-respect, so I stood there and I could feel my feet sink into the ice, and I let go of the dog's leash and he dashed for shore and I imagined my death.

"Irene'd be grief-stricken for a while but she'd get over it. She'd sell the house, give away my stuff, and she's a forward-thinking person, she'd start a new life in Florida. Irene always said she hated Minnesota's four seasons: Almost Winter, Winter, End of Winter, and Summer. So maybe she'd live with her cousin Donna in Boca Raton, and she'd take up golf and I could imagine her meeting a guy who'd help her with her game. A guy like Donna's neighbor Bradley who took a shine to Irene when we visited down there last year. A dreary clueless sonofabitch, a Trumper, an anti-vaxxer. The SOB invited her to come to his health club and work out with him. The guy wanted to see my wife bending down in a little tank top and maybe put a hand on her abdominals to check her breathing. And now, with me dead and out of the way, he'd stand behind her with his arms around her showing her how to hold the 5-iron. It made me furious to think of her infidelity, and I dashed to shore and ten feet from shore, I broke through the ice but the water was only a couple feet deep and I walked home and I tell you, it was quite the near-death experience."

"Well apparently you didn't die, so what's the point?" said Dave.

Clint: "Who is telling this story? You or me? Shut up."

Daryl: "Let the man tell his story."

Clint said, "The point is: it was jealousy that saved my life, imagining Bradley with his arms around my wife. I could see him clear as day and I ran so fast my feet hardly touched the ice. I got home, my pants wet, I was shivering so hard my teeth were clicking, and she threw her arms around me and was horrified I'd gone out on the ice. She put my pants in the dryer, she brought a blanket, she hugged me, she wept at the thought of my narrow escape, and I realized how wrong I was to be jealous even though it was the thing that saved my life. If I'd stood out there and forgiven her, I'd be dead. I think that's what they call a logical contradiction. Anyway she put my pants in the dryer and I got out of my wet underwear and looked for a clean pair and she said, 'What's your hurry? You going someplace? Let's go to bed,' so we got in bed and made love and I tell you she was like a new woman, she was all over me, it was unbelievable. Fifty-six years of marriage, and it was honeymoon night at the Sunrise Motel. And it was jealousy that saved my life. The thought of her infidelity."

Dave: "So what does this have to do with anything? You're just bragging about having sex."

Clint: "It's not bragging when you tell the truth. When we were done and we lay there exhausted, she said, 'That was the best sex I ever had.' And I said, 'Compared to who?' And she said, 'There is no who, there's only you. You're my everything.'"

Daryl: "So what happened to the seven bucks?"

Clint: "I put it in her purse and I suppose she spent it."

I was hoping he wouldn't make me promise to keep the story confidential and he did not. Often people do if they talk about their sexual experiences: they say, "You better not put this in a book." He did not say that.

3

SEEING ARLENE

Out at the Gunderson lake cabin, I crawled into Arlene's former bunk and slept the sleep of the righteous and dipped myself in the chilly lake and soaped and rinsed and went to the Chatterbox for breakfast. Steak and eggs over easy. I'd taken one sip of coffee and one bite of steak and opened up the *Times* on my cellphone when Dorothy plopped down and was all over me about the cabin. "You're in town one day and already you've done a stupid thing, taking over that wreck of the old Gunderson cabin," she said. "It's an eyesore and it ought to be torn down before it falls down and Mike over there"—she pointed to a big, bearded guy sitting at the counter—"can do it for you. It's infested with mice and bats and cockroaches and Norm used it to rendezvous with a girlfriend and smoke dope and drink himself into a stupor. I hate to speak ill of the dead but he lost his mind after he retired and he sold his business to Paradise for a nickel and a song. What do you need a lake cabin for? You've got an apartment in New York. That's got to be worth a pretty penny. What do you need a shack for? You planning to shack up with someone? You??" She chortled.

It made me feel good that I knew something she didn't, that Norm survived his suicide and it changed his life—and that I had lived there for a summer when I was eighteen and Arlene and I did stuff together and the Gundersons treated me like family and thanks to that I drove to

Minneapolis when I was eighteen bursting with self-esteem and so I can enjoy her amiable abuse. Arlene and I crouched in the dark by the dock, both of us naked, and her mother knew it and chose not to humiliate us, and from small acts of kindness come the anticipation of good luck. When I exploded and Arlene cried out in pleasure just as the headlights lit up the room, that was perfect, and I'm not sorry she went off to other things—perfection is not sustainable. I've forgotten most of whatever happened to me in college but I remember the night at the cabin and the simultaneous ecstasy and illumination. One is a searchlight and one is a flashlight but in the dark each is remarkable.

Dorothy brought Mike over and he sat down at the table. He owns the hardware store across the street from Ralph's Pretty Good Grocery, which is still in business thanks to their excellent sausage and bakery, and the hardware is in what used to be the Bon Marché Beauty Salon where Luanne sprayed lacquer on women's hair to make structural bouffants that made them four inches taller and protected them from injury if someone dropped a rock on their head.

Mike married a Pfleiderscheidt except by that time they had dropped the "scheidt" because it sounded like "shit." Mike's name was Smith. He said, "We don't have a whole lot to do with her family." He was very chatty, I think he was angling to get my business. "We weren't Smiths originally," he said. "We were Kruegers."

"Like Wally, who owns the Sidetrack?" I said.

"Exactly. Same great-grandfather. Alphonse. Came over from Stuttgart in 1910 soon after the Wright Brothers' flight hoping to get rich off the silk parachute he had invented. He fell in love with a girl in town, Monica, who happened to be the daughter of one of his parachute investors, and he climbed up on the windmill to demonstrate how the parachute worked. She was very eager to see this and he had her hold a long strip of gauze so he could gauge wind direction, which of course was only to make her feel like a participant, and he climbed the tower and then they heard a distant engine and she looked away to the west and saw a biplane descending. She had never seen a plane before. She put

58

the gauze in her pocket and powdered her face. The plane landed in the meadow, piloted by a handsome young man in a brown leather helmet and a white silk scarf. For some reason, he carried a pistol in his belt. If it had gone off, it would've blown his nuts off. Anyway, he climbed out of the cockpit and conversed with Monica. Alphonse had to fold up his parachute before he could climb back down and as he did, he heard the pilot offer to take Monica up for a ride. The pilot had a French accent and Monica spoke to him in French. Alphonse had no idea she spoke French but she did. She said, 'Oui, monsieur.' Said it with great enthusiasm, and he helped her into the cockpit and squeezed himself in behind her and reached around her for the control stick, which was between her legs. It was obscene. He revved up the engine and the plane turned into the wind and took off and rose in the sky and then made a tight loop and Alphonse heard her scream with delight. He climbed down, disheartened, and walked two miles to town and went into the tavern and broke his promise to his mother and had a double shot of whiskey and it was the cure for the loss of Monica. He bought a couple rounds and soon he was surrounded by friends. A man picked up an accordion and there was dancing and hands of cribbage and there was a buffet of cheese and sausage, egg salad and meatballs and doughnut holes, and right then and there he gave up on romance and decided that he preferred friendship. He married Gertrude who was a friend of his sister's and when Prohibition struck, he became a manufacturer of brandy and gin."

"What about Monica?"

"She became engaged to the pilot and they intended to fly to New York but a few weeks later in Wisconsin his plane flew into a dense cloud and hit a flock of geese and he lost control, geese honking around him, and crashed into a tree and the plane caught fire and burned with him hanging in it. A parachute might've saved his life. Monica went to New York, hoping to be a Broadway dancer, but after a few auditions it was painfully clear to her that hundreds of New York girls could dance circles around her and soon she married a streetcar conductor. Alphonse grieved over her but he and Gertrude had eleven kids so I guess there was some interest there. They became Smiths in 1918 because they didn't want to be associated with the Kaiser anymore."

He gave me his business card and said he could get me a good price on demolition of the cabin. He said, "Probably one good shove and it'd fall over." I told him I'd think about it. What I thought was that I wanted to live in it for a few weeks and remember everything that happened that summer, no matter how trivial, remember Marj saying that Kennedy made her feel happy every time she read about him, remember Arlene stubbing her toe on a chair leg and crying out in pain and her dad examining the toe and saying, "Well, I guess we'll have to amputate." Remember Norm's gloomy letters from boot camp about the sadistic sergeant who enjoyed ordering trainees to get down and give him fifty. Marj serving us hamburgers and potato salad and reading the story I wrote and saying, "But it's so sad!" and how kind she was to me afterward. Arlene's white shirt flapping, the delicate breasts in their green hammocks.

Thoughts of that beautiful summer: I walked into the Chatterbox kitchen and back to the scullery where I'd washed dishes that summer of 1960 and the same old dishwasher was there, a conveyor, you racked up the dirty plates and they were conveyed through the washer and out the other side. A skinny kid with green hair was running it. I said, "I ran this dishwasher when I was your age" and then saw he had headphones on, listening to loud banging and shrieking. I let him be.

Walking back through the kitchen I heard a voice I've known most of my life, Myrtle Krebsbach with her husband, Florian, eating their eggs and sausage, and Myrtle on the phone with her son Sheldon in Minneapolis, her voice loud and shrill due to deafness. She said, "I don't suppose you saw the story in the *Star* about the woman from Mankato. She was depressed and her kids sent her on a Caribbean cruise and she went on board and realized they'd gotten her the cheapest cabin, no window, no balcony, and one night she went out on deck and put all the shuffleboard discs into a duffel bag and hung it around her neck and climbed over the rail and was about to throw herself overboard and be eaten by sharks and a sailor grabbed her by one ankle as she was about to go over." Myrtle wept and Florian looked away and pretended not to hear. "I know exactly how that woman felt," she said. "That woman was living my life." Evidently Sheldon had been in the midst of taking a shower—she said, "I don't care if you are standing there wet and naked—I saw you wet and naked once. I remember it well. After nineteen hours of excruciating labor that I wouldn't wish on a Nazi war criminal. I remember it vividly, the blood, the doctor in a panic thumbing through the obstetrics textbook, my husband passed out on the floor, the nuns saying rosaries. Your head was so big, it was like trying to push a football through a garden hose. Nineteen hours of sheer agony and the nurse messed up the epidural and you practically tore me in half, Sheldon, and when they handed you to me, I handed you back. They told me I could never have another baby because if I got pregnant and so much as hiccupped the fetus would fall out on the floor and that's why you're an only child and you'll inherit all the money when we die. Speaking of which, I'm not kidding about the cruise ship. Or maybe I'll sit in the car in the garage with the door shut and run the engine with a potato stuck in the tailpipe. Or maybe I'll take a pill or something—or take a whole handful. In fact, here's a bottle of Enderol. I could end it all right now."

And then there was loud talk at the other end—Sheldon trying to explain something to somebody—and Myrtle looked up and saw me and said, "My son the great intellectual just locked himself out of his house naked and the neighbors called the police and he's trying to prove to them that it's actually his house. My son who is forty-seven years old and has not yet found a woman who meets his standards. Well, all I can say is, if he had a wife he could just knock on the door and she'd let him in. Beggars can't be choosers." Then she yelled into the phone, "I do not want to talk to the officer, Sheldon. You have a master's degree in psychology. Use it."

Myrtle is a dramatic tragedian in a colony of the meek so wherever she goes she has an audience. Ask her how she is and she'll give you a monologue for as long as you stand and listen. I was glad to see her. I walked over and introduced myself. "I know who you are," she said.

"What do you take me for, a fool? You're the guy who missed the two free throws in the game against St. Margaret's that cost us a trip to the State Tournament." Those free throws were missed in 1959: the woman hasn't lost a stride. "Two easy shots and one hit the rim and the other rolled off it. I know people in this town who never recovered from that embarrassment. It didn't mean diddly to me but there were cheerleaders who contemplated suicide after. God only knows if eventually they went through with it. They moved away. We'll never know."

Then Dorothy had me by the elbow. "I know you saw Arlene, but they're very secretive about her cancer and frankly I don't think she has long to live. Barbara Ann moved back. We got Arlene set up in the dining room so she doesn't have to climb stairs, and Clarence rented a hospital bed, and the bathroom is a few steps away. Thank God, Barbara came back, and her husband, Bill. They're renting Kenny Krebsbach's old place temporarily. You wouldn't know Barbara, she's got very short red hair now and round black glasses. She gave them so much trouble back in her day—my God, what a pain in the ass. Do you remember? I do. She was wild. Arlene and Clarence held their breath for years, fearing she'd either (1) announce she was pregnant or (2) she was lesbian, but she got scholarshipped to Athena College in Vermont, which had open dorms—you want to keep a llama for a pet or cook on an open fire or practice witchcraft or take in some homeless people, fine. They eliminated the study of literature from countries that exploited other peoples and eliminated rectangular writing paper in favor of oblong and every May first the student body ran nude through the campus with streamers to entwine around the Maypole. She enjoyed the goofiness for a while and then got interested in math and that calmed her down.

"She was a feminist terrorist and now she's a caregiver. Amazing. Anyway, we managed to keep Duane from coming. No need for aimless bewilderment when you've already got pain and suffering. His wife, Monique, is from Florida, you know. She feels vulnerable if the temperature drops into the fifties. Fifty years old and she decided not to be brunette anymore and now she's blonde and a facelift so tight she can't say her t's or d's and she goes around in a bikini with less cotton than

62

you'd find in an aspirin bottle, but anyway we're fine. And I'm available when necessary. I've been caring for the dying since I was a teenager and took care of my grandpa when he had his stroke, and was he an easy patient? Is the pope Unitarian? He took his time dying. He lingered for almost a year, unable to speak but deeply pissed off. After him, the aunts were pretty easy. I got myself a black bag with a stethoscope to look official and a stash of drugs, painkillers, I could probably be arrested and locked up for practicing without a license but what in hell are you going to do? No doctor in town and anyway Dr. DeHaven was useless. 'Doctor Wait-and-See.' So I made myself a bed on their porch for whenever I'm needed, and meanwhile Barbara Ann is doing fine."

I got to know Dorothy when she helped look after my dad at the end of his life. She got him to tell the story about the double team of horses pulling the manure wagon who bolted and ran in panic and how he held on and tried to control them until they crashed in a ditch and he was thrown clear, uninjured, a miraculous escape that convinced him to ask my mother to marry him. And she got him to sing the song he sang to my mother when he proposed, which he'd heard the young Ethelyn Holman sing in the musical *My Dear Someone,* which he took Mother to see at the Pantages Theatre in Minneapolis in 1935, a daring venture for a young Brethren couple, so they wore capes and masks lest any Sanctified happened to be downtown at night, perhaps preaching on a street corner and singing "Come, Ye Wayward, God Is Calling" to the theatergoers. He did this so she'd know he loved her, went against Brethren principle to embrace worldly pleasure, she having read about Miss Holman's Charleston in the 1933 *Follies.* Dad had almost been killed by runaway horses, which made romance more urgent to him so he took her to the show. And there he was, sitting up in bed and telling Dorothy the whole story and how Mother was moved by the hit song, "My Dear Someone," and Dorothy said, "Sing it to her" and he did, in a whispery voice, Mother standing in the doorway, holding an oxygen bottle, the love of his life:

One little star knows where you are,
Shining tonight, steady and bright
Guiding me from afar.
And then tomorrow the sun
Will show me the way
To a brighter day with my dear someone.

Dorothy said, "Barbara Ann has an offer of a job with RedMedic—you know, what used to be Tomorrow Tomato—now they've decided that the lycopene in tomatoes improves male fertility or something, so she's writing it up, and Bill started work today for Universal Fire, as production manager, bringing in truckloads of logs from the Adirondacks. They season them in artificial ponds and cure them under gas lamps. It's amazing what people are willing to pay for nice firewood. Barbara Ann says they may sell their house in Minneapolis and put the money in Three Eyes, that's Indigenous Interactive Investment, which Alyssa founded. A way for the community to share in the prosperity. Myself, I wouldn't touch it with a ten-foot pole. Anyway, I saw her last night—Arlene, not Alyssa—and she's in good spirits, playing cribbage with Clarence. Pastor Liz dropped by and asked if she would like a prayer and Arlene said, 'No need. I'm winning.' She's told Clarence that she wants to be cremated and her ashes scattered at the ballpark, along the baseline from third to home plate. Anyway, I told her that you were seen looking around their old lake cabin and Arlene said, 'Tell him I never told anybody what went on with him and me at that cabin but if he puts it in a book he better get all the facts straight or I will come down and haunt him."

I told Dorothy I didn't want to invade the family's privacy and Dorothy said, "She's an old friend, for God's sake. What are you going to do when you're dying? Check into a Holiday Inn and watch old movies?"

So I went to Food Fair and bought a bouquet of daffodils and a "Lake Wobegon, Gateway To Central Minnesota" postcard and I wrote her a poem, *To a true Christian, Arlene, with love from an old Philistine,*

May you have pleasure and love beyond measure so long as you stay on the scene. Not bad, but I threw it away and wrote: *Here's to the wondrous Arlene. The best limericks aim for obscene, but I had nice parents and then there is Clarence, but I think it, if you know what I mean.*

I felt odd about comforting the dying, being a sightseer at someone's deathbed. What to say? What not to say? If it were me dying, I'd rather be alone in a dark room listening to Chopin than have to deal with other people's awkward obligatory sorrow. I'd be fine with Giselle sitting there, we could reminisce about our lustful sojourns in national parks where we couldn't keep our hands off each other as geysers blew and thermal pools bubbled and clouds of steam rose into the pines. Good to relive those days as dementia descends. My only deathbed comforting experience was on the phone with Arnie Goldman in hospice care and I told him the one about the ice fisherman who saw the funeral procession go down the road past the lake and he stood at attention by his fishing shack and his friend said, "That's awfully big of you to interrupt fishing to show respect to the deceased," and the fisherman said, "Well, we were married for thirty-five years." Arnie believed in jokes and the banishment of misery.

I went to see Arlene, of course. She and I were pals in our youth because it was easy to talk to her. She was curious. I talked and she wanted to know everything about us Sanctified Brethren, we were like an exotic tribe of forest dwellers to her. She asked me if I'd ever necked with a girl and I admitted I didn't know exactly what "necking" meant. She said, "Somebody should show you." In my family, when it came to sex, there were locked doors with yellow warning signs DO NOT ENTER: HIGH VOLTAGE but she and I sat in the car in her driveway under the Milky Way, and she asked if I knew what "going all the way" means, and I did not. "Oh," she said. I remember the tone of that "Oh." It was about as exciting as one syllable can be.

I headed for her house on Taft Street and then somehow got distracted by a new three-story apartment building where there shouldn't have been one—and came around a corner and there was a crowd of people in the parking lot behind the Lutheran church. Someone waved to me and I walked over. A woman whose name I should've known. It was their spring rummage sale, she said. Card tables, a dozen of them: stacks of magazines, boxes of sheet music, shoe trees, deer antlers, a mandolin, golf clubs, squirrel traps, chafing dishes, a Hamm's beer serving tray, a set of maroon goblets with painted flowers ugly as sin, a framed poster of the Northern Pacific Vista-Dome crossing the Rockies. She pointed me toward the tables of books. Art books. Klimt, Avedon, Jasper Johns. A book on self-healing. A stack of my *Lake Wobegon Days,* a buck apiece; they looked unread. A book called *Meditation: The Road from Darkness to Light* with a picture of a calm ocean on the cover. *The Joy of Naked Cooking.* I picked it up to see if someone's name was in it. It was a book with many photographs of naked people in their kitchens tossing salads or draining pasta, all looking joyful. And then I felt someone staring at me and it was my cousin Andrea and the look on her face said, *Oh grow up.* I thought of buying it for Arlene but Andrea had her eyes on me and I set it down. I hadn't seen her for ten years and now she knew I was interested in sex and would warn the others.

I walked in the house and Barbara Ann showed me into the dining room where the Queen was ensconced under a yellow quilt in a bank of cushions and she said, "I've lost five pounds this week and I figure if I lose any more, you won't be able to keep your hands off me. Anyway, I'm a tough old bird, and I'm tired of people with long mournful faces coming to console me. Your long mournful face is due to your Brethren upbringing, but I know that you just want to rip my clothes off." I said, "It's good to see you. You look terrific." She said, "Pancreatic cancer brings out the best in some people.

"Just ask me how I am. And I'll tell you. I'm fine. I have spent so much time worrying about death that it's a relief to have it here finally and now I can think about other things. Like that picture on the wall of the Living Flag on the Fourth of July. You were there. Remember that day? It was 1961, you and I stood in the crowd on Main Street forming the Living Flag, wearing red caps, part of a red stripe, and up above on the roof of the Central Building, Lowell the photographer crawled trembling out on a ladder sticking straight out from the roof, a hundred feet in the air, anchored by eight big men—Clarence my boyfriend was up there, holding the ladder, looking down and seeing you with me and getting jealous, Lowell terrified of heights, frozen in dread, and one of the anchormen yelled down *Squeeze in tighter, act like you know each other,* and the crowd contracted a little and you squeezed up close and I kissed you—what else was I going to do? Lowell was trembling and the picture turned out blurry, and I bought a copy and now it's hanging on the dining room wall, it's like an impressionist photo of a crowd impersonating a flag. They had to drag Lowell back off the ladder, his eyes shut, hanging on for dear life, and he never went above the ground floor for the rest of his life. He died at fifty-one or fifty-two from a bad heart valve that could've been repaired but he was afraid of surgery. Remember his funeral? His dog was there and it wept through the whole service, wept rather loudly and it was hard to keep a straight face and people had to leave the room to keep from laughing. Lowell never married, he slept with that dog who was so lonely without him that he had to be put down and his ashes were mingled with Lowell's and Pastor Tommerdahl refused to preside at the committal because he refused to believe in the resurrection of pets. Remember?"

She was in a talkative mood. She said, "I want a simple funeral with *It Is Well With My Soul* and that Mary Oliver poem about the grasshopper and tell Liz to read the passage about the loaves and fishes, and absolutely no eulogy or anything that sounds like one. And tell Mr. Lundberg he can skip the cosmetics because I want a closed casket. The way he did up my mother-in-law, he made her look like a ninety-year-old cocktail waitress.

"I'm eighty years old and for years I wondered if I'd make it to seventy because my grandmother Detmer didn't, you know, and then I wondered if I'd make it to seventy-three because my mother died at seventy-two from a state of conniptions. She worried about death night and day and she worried about what we'd do without her, and she spent months putting up jars of cream of mushroom soup so we wouldn't starve to death. God, we hated that soup. We wound up throwing it all away. She had us play the hymns she wanted for her funeral, *Asleep in Jesus, blessed sleep from which none ever wakes to weep* and *Blest be the tie that binds our hearts in Christian love*—over and over and over, *Asleep in Jesus* and *Blest be the tie,* and sometimes she'd ask me to sing one, and what could I say? She'd listen to them, weeping, and she never got tired of mourning for herself. When she finally died, my dad said, 'If I hear either of those goddamn hymns again, I'll shoot somebody and I don't care who.' So at her funeral we sang *O Happy Day* and *Praise God from Whom All Blessings Flow.* She imagined she had cancer but she died of a stroke from the anxiety. She worried herself sick imagining us lost and destitute without her and all in all it was something of a relief when she was finally gone. She was miserable right up to the end. She'd been a teetotaler all her life of course, having been brought up Baptist, and she confessed to me that she desperately wanted a mint julep before she died. She'd read about one in *Gone With The Wind* and she was curious but she also tortured herself with guilt for wanting it. Finally, close to the end, she gave me a look and I went and mixed one up for her with mint leaves, all nice and frosty, and she took a sip and she loved it and it made her miserable to discover what she'd been missing all her life and she died that night. Anxiety and regret killed her. So when I found out about the pancreas, I told myself, Don't go down like Mother did. Have a good time. So that's what I'm doing. Tell me a joke. Make me laugh. Tell the one about the rhubarb pie."

So I told that one. Ole is dying and then he smells Lena's rhubarb pie, fresh from the oven, and he manages to get down the stairs and go in the kitchen and he gets out a knife to cut himself a slice and Lena whacks him one upside the head and says, "Leave it alone, Ole, that's for the funeral."

"Don't stop now," she said, so I told the one about the man and his wife who died in a car crash and went to heaven and it was beautiful and he said, "You know, if you hadn't made me quit smoking, I could've been here years ago."

She still hadn't laughed. I told the one about the man dying of congestive heart failure and he looks up from his deathbed and says, "Joanne, forty-seven years you've stuck with me. You stayed with me through the two heart attacks, the stroke, the prostate cancer, the loss of my left lung, the brain tumor, and now this congestive heart failure, and you know something? I'm starting to think you're bad luck."

"Thanks for trying," she said. "This is the best morphine I ever had. Also the first. It's a good thing I didn't know about this stuff when I was young, I would've robbed banks to buy me a lifetime supply. But I didn't know. Maybe ignorance is the key to righteousness. How are you?" She didn't let me answer that question. "I was disappointed by your memoir. You didn't put me in it or most of the other kids you grew up with. You left out your Aunt Eleanor's pickup truck. She was the only woman in town who owned one. A Ford Ranger, five-speed, two-tone blue, box liner, with mag wheels. She hauled her firewood in it and after she butchered a beef cow, she hauled the meat to the locker plant. All the men in town admired it and she never let them drive it. You left out the New Year Polar Dip and all the fun we had in winter, the tobogganing and skating. And you made yourself out to be so lonely and misunderstood. Poor little you. You weren't lonely, and we were all misunderstood—what in hell was that all about? You were popular enough. Why portray yourself as the tortured artist? That's bullshit. We had a lot of fun. Our parents suffered through the Depression and the war and we did not. We used to drive around in my dad's old Model T and sing. Remember?" And she sang me an old song by the Four Aitches:

We used to park in
That Chevy of mine
And it felt divine
On a winter night
You held me tight.

O Cheryl, I need to know,
Did you only love me 'cause
It was 30 below?
I lay my heart at your feet
But you were only using me for heat.

69

Spring is a time for sweet amour
But I'm not sure.
Springtime is not my favorite season.
I miss back when you and I were freezin'.

She knew all the words and what's more, her voice was that of a young girl, not an old lady. We knew all the hit songs and sang them at parties. My grandkids don't know "My country, 'tis of thee" and couldn't sing it if you paid them.

And then she was worn out, and she pulled the covers up to her chin and adjusted her pillows and turned off the bedside lamp. She said, "Don't wait too long to come back. I have more to say." And I tiptoed out.

I walked down Lincoln Avenue and noticed how silent it was at three in the afternoon. And then it struck me: nobody was practicing piano. It was April and Mrs. Hoglund's spring recital was a month away. But dear Mrs. Hoglund is dead and evidently nobody is learning that Chopin étude she loved so much. She was a patient woman, her gray hair braided and piled high in a triple coil, her glasses hanging on a silver chain across the great promontory of her bosom as she listened to you attempt the Chopin and there was no way to conceal your mistakes. It was like the high jump: either you go over the bar or through it. Now, I'm told, the schools encourage creativity. Mrs. Hoglund did not. She believed in the virtue of careful imitation of virtue. You practiced sounding like the masters and thereby beauty is available to all, at least secondhand. I walked down the street and heard no music at all. No radios playing or phonographs. People wear earbuds. The world has turned inward. The triumph of individualism. It made me feel lonely.

Norm didn't care that the school no longer teaches cursive writing and the kids diddle with their thumbs on iPhones and send texts. He didn't care that, for the first time ever, no lutefisk was served at the Sons of Knute Christmas dinner and there was very little comment about it. But he cared that the Sons of Bernie Polar Plunge was gone, a New Year's Day ritual when the ice was cleared from around the town dock and on a bugle call a mob of men dropped their parkas and dove naked into the water, splashed around and whooped and yelled, and hauled themselves out, a rite of manly stoicism ushering in a new year. Norm said, "One year they voted to wear swimsuits and that killed the whole meaning of it and it died a quiet death. It was a dramatic event, like going to war. You didn't want to go but you didn't want to be the only one not going, so you went. A cruel surprise when you hit the water, but the rest of the day was brighter for it." The last rotary-dial telephone in town is in the Mist County Museum where kids go to learn about hitchhiking, 33⅓ LPs, road maps, knock-knock jokes, drive-in movies, song lyrics consisting of whole sentences, and rotary-dial telephones. "You and I are museum pieces, pal," he said. He didn't care about most of this but he was upset that his daughter-in-law was homeschooling her eight-year-old. "How do you learn about life if your teacher is your mom and you're the only kid in the class? Who will tell you dirty jokes? When do you learn swear words?"

I thought of him as I walked that quiet deChopined street and felt a wisp of affection for old times, for Fern and Estelle and LaVona and Helen and Lois, my old teachers, and Ruth our choir director. I never had Mrs. Hoglund. Her high standards scared me. So I wrote limericks instead of playing Chopin, it was more within my reach.

My youth is fading so fast,
The present leaves me aghast.
But I pull up my socks
And go for long walks
And smile as the doctor goes past.

4

MILLENNIALISM

The boom in Lake Wobegon began in June 2016, when Roger Hedlund's daughter Molly was a bridesmaid at a friend's wedding in Oshkosh, Wisconsin, and went outdoors during the rehearsal because her high heels hurt and she needed to walk barefoot in grass and she met Sam, a groomsman, who was taking a picture of the church for the wedding scrapbook though it was all concrete and rather ugly. He took his shoes off and they sat in the grass and he talked about worms. He knew the groom because they were partners in a company, LifeCycle, which breeds composting worms and maggots, which, he told her, can reduce a two-story home to a pile of dust in three weeks or less. She apologized for her ignorance of insects and explained that she had a headache from the stress of high heels and he said, "Let me show you something" and took her head in his arms and pressed on her temples and neck and talked about composting and climate change, meanwhile the headache simply vanished. Gone. His purposefulness combined with cranial care was a stunning contrast to the slackers she'd dated previously, and she was 25 and eager to stop Twittering and begin adulting, and here was Sam, for whom composting was a calling, and he showed her a corrugated cardboard box he designed called Floating Home. It folded up to the size of a briefcase and unfolded to make a boat with a paddle and then could be refolded to make a one-man tent, and when you die, it becomes your coffin and they put worms in with you and in a few months you are compost, ready to join the green vegetative world rather than be a pet-rified mummy. He was excited about this: he said, "The whole Western world is locked into a sentimental notion of the beautified corpse in a jewelry box, the body pumped full of poisonous chemicals leaking into the earth, enormous vast parks of little Victorian monuments of angels and sheep that nobody visits or cares about—or else they burn the body and poison the air. And this—THIS is the natural way that allows the body to return to the earth from which it came rather than pollute it! And the hundreds of square miles of marble monuments can be bull-dozed and made into playgrounds or farms or neighborhoods for the living—no need to treat the human body as a trophy animal—we can treat it as mortal flesh and let it return to dust as God intended." His passion about decomposition—and later his passion for tomatoes and their ingredient lycopene—she fell in love with it and with him. She could see that this idealist needed someone to make sure he had his phone on him and his car keys and wore a clean shirt.

Two months later they married in a helium balloon floating over the lake piloted by a minister who also played euphonium, and clouds of biodegradable confetti fell as the vows were said. They moved in with Roger and Cindy and got to work trying to conceive a child. Sam was a New Yorker who loved Lake Wobegon instantly. He'd lived with a weightlifter roommate, Lars, in a tiny studio apartment above a disco bar in Hoboken and commuted to work on a bus full of meatpacking workers on their way home from the night shift, and then, smelling of butchery, on a subway to SoHo packed with people giving him the evil eye, he went to work in a cubicle on the 35th floor writing commercials for thieves and scoundrels and now he was free to pursue his vision of making a better world. He dug two gigantic worm-breeding pits and turned the barn into a shipping center and hired a dozen workers. And the sales came flowing in: the world was eager to have composting worms to live in a small bin in your kitchen and devour garbage and turn it into excellent compost. Sales were brisk and got brisker. Roger and Cindy were delighted. Molly had almost married a 42-year-old unpublished writer who'd been working ten years on a novel set in 11th-century Iceland, who dressed in furs and played the lute and was gay and couldn't face up to it. Sam was a champ in their book. He was a good earner, he paid his rent, and he made Molly very happy. She even said so herself.

He talked Roger into planting tomatoes to make an energy pill called RedMedic, 90 percent lycopene, the source of life itself, the cure for diseases including many as yet unknown. It rid the body of poisons—*If you like peeing, you'll love lycopene*—it had been shown to decrease the risk of congenital pertussis, peripheral pancreatic insufficiency, developmental diabetes, systemic fatigue, chronic Carrion's disease, inflammatory reflux, parasitic chlamydia pinworm, flaccid keratitis, aggravated digression of the intraskeletal capillaries, obstructive microsporidia, traumatic clostridium of the lower extremities, and sexually transmitted sleeping sickness, a ghastly list of susceptibilities that RedMedic could suppress or relieve, using the common garden-variety tomato, the Love Fruit. RedMedic got a big boost when the rapper T-Gunnar raved about it on *Late Morning with Laura and Nate* and said it gave him an erection you could pound nails with and sales went through the roof and RedMedic stock jumped from $4 to $41 and wound up at $87 and LifeCycle took over the old St. Wendel's Brewery and a workforce of 200 Mexican families took up residence, and they brought with them a cousin named Fernando Flores who knew about the latest implements employing artificial intelligence. His English wasn't great but he knew AI upside down and backward and sold Sam on a precision sprayer ten rows wide that uses digital cameras to identify weeds and spray them with herbicide and identify tomato plants and spray them with fertilizer and insecticide. A drone scans the field as the season progresses and calculates the ripening of the crop and at the peak a robotic picker goes through and harvests.

Norm was not a farmer but he watched the whole spectacle in the fields and as an old Democrat, he was inspired by the sight: it was like a story in the *We Are All Neighbors* chapter of *American Civics*, a brown-skinned immigrant demonstrating a complex implement that enables you to grow delicate row crops rather than soybeans. He explained the

workings of the machine in Spanish, giving his compadres responsibility
for maintenance and repair. Old farmers stood and watched the sprayer
go through and saw how it distinguished pigweed from tomatoes and
instead of saturating the acreage spritzed the isolated targets and as Roger
said, "This changes farming. Everything you knew is now obsolete. Either
you go back to school or you go to work on your golf game." Those old
farmers weren't golfers though. They signed up with LifeCycle, soybean
farmers discouraged by sluggish prices, dairy farmers tired of looking
at udders. The next spring, tomato acreage in the county exploded a
hundredfold, surpassing corn and beans, and the rent check came from
RedMedic and robotic planters put in the tomatoes and the farmers
watched and went home and had breakfast with their wives. Farming had
been easy; the hard work was sitting around and making conversation
with your spouse and her relatives. They looked at their spouses and
words failed them. LifeCycle offered courses in conversational English
for native speakers. As a gift from RedMedic, each farmer received a
Lazy Man robotic lawn mower that after one manual pass memorizes
your yard, every tree and fence, and mows it while you sip your iced
tea. For the first time in their lives, men needed hobbies. Some took
up woodworking, or raised flowers, or took up the button accordion;
others took to the internet and learned a great deal about the deep-state
liberals running the federal government so as to obtain small children
and eat their brains and drink their blood. Pastor Liz got a few anguished
calls from wives contemplating desperate measures. More and more men
turned to fishing and that helped. A beer or two at lunch helped.

Dancing helped them lose weight, they fussed with their hair, they
felt seventeen again, out on a date, and found that they could rewind
the marriage back to its illustrious romantic origins and it was so much
better than all the foofaraw of lawyers and divorce and dating and remar-
riage, and out on the dance floor, after a cocktail, the merengue or tango
or conga could arouse dormant desires between mature grown-ups and
they'd pull into their driveway and walk away from the car without
locking it and two people with one mind head upstairs and close the
door and articles of clothing fall to the floor and the creak of bedsprings

and whispery voices and a woman making vocal sounds that would surely surprise the members of her Bible study group, not to mention her daughter-in-law and grandchildren.

5

MR. GONZÁLEZ

I asked Carl Krebsbach to come look at the cabin and give me an estimate and he said he had two months' work on the books and couldn't get to it until August but I pleaded—"Just come out and give me your opinion then. As an old friend." He said, "My opinion is that even though it was a gift, you paid too much. Old Man Gunderson threw that thing up around 1936 and he was no carpenter, it's a crackerbox of bare studs on a concrete slab, cheap siding, no insulation, bare rafters—it's nothing but a wooden tent with electricity, why not tear it down and start over, make something nice? Your wife isn't going to want to spend one night there. She'll get a hotel room in Sauk Centre, you'll be all alone. So you'll go back to New York with her and the cabin will be taken over by a family of raccoons. What's the point?"

"If I told you, you'd laugh, but I want to fix it up and put in plumbing," I said.

He said there was a Henry González who was a good carpenter looking for work, why not ask him?

I said, "What about Mike? Dorothy recommended him."

He said, "I didn't say this so you're not hearing it from me but what Dorothy knows about construction you could put in an eyedropper and have room left over, and the reason Mike is so available is that nobody who's hired him will ever hire him again. Henry's your man."

I said, "How about you be the contractor?" So we shook hands on that.

I wasn't putting in plumbing for Giselle's sake—she already has a family cabin on the Connecticut shore that her dad lent to Aaron Copland one fall and he wrote most of *Appalachian Spring* there. William Carlos Williams's poem about so much depending on a red wheelbarrow glazed with rainwater was written there and Ginsberg began "Howl" there except it began:

I saw the best minds of my generation sitting in the woods, eating bacon lettuce and tomato, looking for egrets and examining each other for deer ticks. And it was called "Owl." (It became "Howl" later in San Francisco.)

Giselle does not enjoy spending time in Lake Wobegon. Standing politely as people discuss the history of the Thanatopsis Society is not her idea of a good time. People tell the story of Wally and the Winnebago or Gladys and the bear in the bird feeder or the time the Flying Elvises parachuted into the Fourth of July picnic, and she pretends to look interested until her face turns wooden. She accepts a plate heaped with bad food and pushes stuff around with a fork until a dog shows interest and she sets it down where he can reach it. She doesn't disparage, she just disappears. Imagine a Buddhist trapped in a school board budget meeting in Butte, Montana. That's Giselle in my hometown. She floats along over the mishmash and gobbledygook.

Carl and Mr. González—Henry—appeared at my door the next morning and had a look around. Carl thought I was crazy. Henry said, "We can do it. You want it, it can be done." Carl pointed out about 27 things that might blow up the budget and said, "We can build you something twice as good for the same money you'd spend repairing this rat trap." Henry said, "He likes it. I can see why. It's got a good family feel to it." He put his hand on my arm. "You have good memories here." I nodded. He gave me a dazzling smile. "Tell me where they are." I got tears in my eyes. I led him out on the porch. I pointed to the swinging bed. I led him to the beach and the dock. I picked up a flat rock and threw it sidearm and it skipped two, four, six, eight times. He said, "There was love here. You loved someone." I said, "Yes." I was all choked up with memories of Arlene. Carl was crawling under the porch, inspecting cracks in the foundation. Henry said, "I can strip the shingles off and rip up the linoleum and you don't need interior walls. But you need a nice bathroom." Yes, of course, for Giselle. A fine big bathroom with a commodious shower, tile walls, and a tile bench where she can sit in the steam, then wrap a towel around her and walk out and sit with me on the porch.

Carl was muttering under his breath and I heard the word "ridiculous." Henry was upbeat. I gave him ten grand for a down payment. And that's all there was to it. Henry understood without my having to spell it out for him. This was a house where a door opened and a burden dropped and I tasted the tenderness of life. The plank table where I cleaned the catch of bass and sunfish, Arlene leaning in watching closely, me cutting off the heads and tails, filleting, disemboweling, scaling, working on the flesh of fish. Marj said to her, "Why do you keep going around in your swimsuit? Why don't you put on clothes?" Some bees buzzing around and I brushed one off Arlene's bare shoulder. It was very simple, we're hungry, we eat, we're curious, we look, we touch. We started to make love that night on the dock and on the Fourth of July the grown-ups went to town for the Living Flag and picnic and fireworks and we said we'd walk to town and meet them later and Marj had some serious words with her and then the grown-ups left and we climbed into an upper bunk and spent a delicious hour up there before caution caught up with us. "Live the life you dream about," Thoreau said, though he meant it in a spiritual way, not carnal, but I was high on Henry, he spoke clearly to me from the mid-19th century, I imagined a direct line connecting us. When he said, "Do not be too moral. You may cheat yourself out of much life so. Aim above morality. Be not simply good, be good for something," it went straight to my heart. I wanted to be good for Arlene, give her pleasure however she would accept it. My first venture into romantic devotion. History gives us no indication that Thoreau ever sat with a woman's head in his lap and stroked her hair, but it's not beyond possibility. When he said, "Our truest life is when we are in dreams awake," I can imagine him saying it to a woman, his arm around her, one hand on her breast.

Arlene sweetly offered me affection and I had dreams of being a writer and a person of consequence and I felt accepted in that cabin and I wrote large thoughts in my journal that sometimes I read aloud to Arlene. She said, "You are such a thinker. I never knew anyone like you." Now, looking back, I realize that "You are such a thinker" is not high praise but I pushed ahead and took big chances and I made myself a writer of sorts and this house was where some crucial transaction of self-esteem took place. Henry González, a complete stranger, understood this and Carl, whom I've known all my life, thought I should see a psychiatrist. He said, "Lock it up and let it sit for a year and come back and you'll see things more clearly."

So did Dorothy. She assumed my marriage was in trouble. She'd been single all her life and saw marital unhappiness wherever she looked. She thought I was building a cabin to escape from Giselle's fast life in Manhattan. She said, "You Brethren boys never figured out how to be happy with women. Your mothers had to keep silent and wear dark clothing and give the man priority. You couldn't go to movies lest your hands wander so you never learned about courtship. You couldn't dance or go to parties because it might lead to copulation and little bastards running around the house, so you married a woman without the least idea of what to do with her other than read the epistles to the Corinthians. You married a New York woman but deep down you're still Brethren through and through and the New York life of pleasure-seeking fills you with guilt and so you're looking for a cabin in the woods where you can sit and nurse your regrets." I love Dorothy but her mind does travel along narrow paths.

I said, "A few birch trees and spruce and a beach nearby and the neighbors a hundred feet away—I don't call that 'The Woods.'"

But she insisted I meet Mallory, the life coach. She moved to town to help her sister Wheely who started Conscious Lunch, which makes healthy meals that promote mindfulness. Oats and barley, banana, olives, that sort of thing. Wheely's boyfriend Stan owns Vanguard

Trucking. They buy diesel truck bodies and make them into customized luxury vans. A three-bedroom van that you can drive around the country and avoid state and local taxes by crossing state lines every fifteen days. Mallory wrote a book, *Make Your Bed, Make Your Life*, which sold a ton of copies and without meaning to, she became a life coach. She said, "People kept asking for advice and when I started charging money, they took the advice more seriously. And I'm a voyeur: I like to see people's secret lives. There are a great many successful people who have no idea how to clean a bathroom or make a bed. They earn a hundred grand a year and live like cave dwellers."

She had built a lake cabin three doors from the Gundersons' and one morning Dorothy dragged me over there to say hello. Mallory was a solidly built red-haired woman in a "No More Excuses" T-shirt sitting on her porch, eating bran flakes. Dorothy knocked and walked right in, which is her way, and Mallory looked up and Dorothy said, "This is our local writer. He used to have a radio show. He lives down the shore from you. He's trying to change his life or something. I thought he should meet you." The woman said, "What can I do for you?" I told her I was trying to get in touch with my past.

"I don't do the past," she said. "It doesn't interest me. I hear the words *Back in the day* and my brain goes to sleep. I start with now and I help people take charge of their lives by doing small things right. Making your bed. Folding your clothes. Creating clean surfaces. Disposing of the useless. Seeking to equalize your relationships. And flossing." She pointed to her upper incisors—"You have some egg in your teeth." I pried it out with my Medicare card.

She explained that people are easily overwhelmed by ordinary chaos and need to be taken through simple steps leading to order and order leads to clear thinking even for creative people like me. "I saw Dave Eggers's house once and it was a swamp whereas Joyce Carol Oates has a great cleaning lady. There's the difference. I had a writer client who was stuck on his memoir and was about to give up and get a day job and he discovered that when he walked two miles every morning at 7 a.m. after eating a bowl of bran flakes with sliced banana and sat down to work at exactly 9:15, out came pages and pages of excellent work like cars off an assembly line. And he learned to roll his socks into tight balls and line up the balls in a drawer and hand-wash his handkerchiefs and fold them and always carry a fresh one in his left pocket. It all adds up. He finished the memoir in two months." It was oddly appealing, her faith in the power of an orderly life to stimulate the brain. Who am I to disagree?

"The mundane leads to the monumental," she said. "Small steps lead to the top. Everything you need is in your head and believe it or not, repetitive routine helps unlock it."

I told her she should think about becoming a college counselor. She said, "I did that once. For three months. English majors living in squalor, trying to be writers, living in dorm rooms like feed pens, filthy clothing on the floor, underpants with skid marks in the seats, sinks full of beer bottles, stacks of pizza boxes four feet high in the corner. I took one look and suddenly understood the sad state of American fiction. I helped one kid. Persuaded him to quit creative writing and come home and get a job. I said, 'Why work twenty years writing and wake up in your mid-forties and realize Updike and Bellow and Morrison did it better? Why not make a life instead?' So I read to him a few pages of a story he was writing and he'd never heard himself out loud before and a light went on and he came home and got a job at LifeCycle."

Dorothy said, "That was Daryl's son Eric. And now he owns stock in the company and he and his girlfriend went to France on vacation this spring. He cooks meals, knows about nutrition, keeps a clean kitchen—no more stack of pizza boxes. And he writes thank-you notes. *Thank-you notes!* Name another male, twenty-two, who writes thank-you notes. Not texts. NOTES. He wrote a letter to Mallory, thanking her for giving him a life."

"Good work," I said. "I'm not working on a memoir and I don't order take-out pizza, but if I need help, I'll certainly think of you."

"I have nothing against writers," Dorothy said on our way over to my cabin. "My nephew Douglas's boy Jimmy is a songwriter. Seventeen. You met him, he washes dishes at the café."

"The kid with the earbuds." She nodded. "The earbuds with the shrieking and pounding." "Yes," she said, "those are the songs he writes."

She and I come from the era of "I've got sunshine on a cloudy day, when it's cold outside I got the month of May," and "My heart went boom when I crossed that room and I held her hand in mine," and at parties we stood around and sang songs, everybody knew the words, but Dorothy adapts to new things and she was excited about the kid's music because—she said—he had millions of followers on ToodiFy and Weezil and ConsterNation. She was proud of him. "It's not my cup of tea, nor yours, but he's building his brand and working hard and in five years, this kid is going to have himself an empire or die trying." She texted me a song of his and I had to listen to it five times before I understood the words. Our songs were about love; this was about money.

Jesus said not to worry,
That God's got your back,
But, baby, I am in a hurry
To stash my cash in a big stack
Talking trash gets me dough
The Golden Rule is pure B.S.
Give to the poor? Hell, no.
Keep it for myself, oh yes.

One week, you're a dishwasher pulling hot plates off a rack and next thing you turn your own angst into a big success story and create a flashy persona and buy reams of real estate and become a celebrity who, if you die from an overdose, it'll be front page, not back in the C section. A teenager's dream. Listening to that anguished child's voice, I couldn't imagine any sensate human being tuned to it for more than a moment, let alone singing along with it, but it was touching that Dorothy was proud of him. Like having a pet porcupine.

Henry and his son Orlando ripped up the green linoleum, which was eager to be ripped, having already worn itself out in many places, and Henry recommended hardwood flooring, but I voted for linoleum. "Not tiles?" he said. "Linoleum," I said. I wanted authenticity. So he found, in a surplus warehouse in St. Joseph, a roll of green linoleum somewhat brighter than the 1960 one, and that looked okay to me. He laid a 10-by-15 square on the floor and I felt like Arlene might walk in the door at any moment and take me in her arms. It made me happy.

But that morning I texted Giselle a picture of the green linoleum and she said it was the same green linoleum she remembered from the apartment of her old boyfriend Alfie. He was a would-be actor but he could only play one role, that of a raving lunatic. He threatened to jump out the window and she informed him that jumping from a second-floor window wouldn't necessarily be fatal, especially with the awning of the sidewalk café beneath, and she continued packing her bag, whereupon he dipped a fork in rat poison and stabbed himself in the chest, so she unpacked, and coaxed him into a therapy group for agitated artists. He tried out for the role of Wild Bill Malone in *Skin*, and during his audition he reached for a jelly doughnut on a plate and strained a hibiscus ligament in his lower back and fell to the floor screaming. He threatened to sue, and to save themselves the expense, the theater agreed to hire him as a stand-in so he'd qualify for workers' comp, which paid him $500 a week. He then got a job as a security guard in a Broadway musical museum, sitting at a desk and eyeballing the tourists as they came in and checking their bags and purses, which paid him another $500. Whereupon he was caught stealing from people's purses. A loser, in other words.

I texted Giselle: "I'm rather fond of green linoleum, for some reason. Are you sure this is the same as your boyfriend Alfie's?"—and she texted back, "Actually, it's the linoleum from the county jail he spent two months at after he was fired for stealing. When I look at that linoleum I can hear him pleading that he loves me and if I leave him, he will eat Ajax cleanser. Wood flooring would be so much better." So I scrapped the linoleum. I still wanted to preserve the outhouse in some form. I'd sat in there smoking and reading novels, maybe I could use the boards to line the walls of the toilet Carl and Henry were building. Carl said, "There is no way to treat the boards to disguise the fact of what they came from. Trust me." So one day when I was in town, he burned them. "Fire me if you like, but I've done you a favor," he said. Henry dug a septic tank out in the woods and a trench to the cabin. I agreed to hardwood flooring.

Orlando helped out with demolition, stopping to go for a run around the lake around noon while Henry and I sat on the porch and had our lunch. He ran barefoot two-thirds of the way around and then swam across the lake. Henry wanted him to go to college, Orlando wanted to try out for the Twins. He'd pitched for the Whippets the year before and the team was unbeatable with him on the mound. He was also a sterling shortstop. Lutherans never did make good shortstops or second basemen (too deliberate), but when Manuel and Chico or Orlando put on the uniforms, Norm told me, suddenly you saw double plays, which had been as rare as solar eclipses, now an everyday thing. Our slugger Lumbering Larson had twice been thrown out at first base by the left fielder and he was replaced by Carlos who was a doubles and triples hitter. Orlando had shoulder-length hair sticking out from under his cap, which would've given the Dutchman angina to see, but he was dead, died two years before from cigar smoke inhalation. Norm said the kid had a blazing fastball and a wicked slider and when he pitched a two-hitter last summer to beat the Willmar Wildcats and win the Central Minnesota championship, the Whippets dugout emptied and the players threw themselves into a big dogpile, and the fans stood up and yelled like crazy even though the game was in Willmar and the Wobegonians were outnumbered by sullen Willmarites, fifty to one, still they whooped and rang cowbells and honked horns, very atypical behavior for us. Wearing a Whippets T-shirt had been a badge of shame; we'd been losers so long we'd forgotten how to wave a banner and yell. I told Henry, "You must be proud of your boy, such a terrific competitor." Henry said, "He's not bad," which is exactly what a Wobegon dad would say. Exactly.

Henry's brother, Father Jorge González, had been brought in by Bishop Petters back in February to celebrate a 9 a.m. Spanish Mass at Our Lady of Perpetual Responsibility, given the influx of Latinos. Father Jorge was a charismatic Catholic who believed that dance opens our hearts to the Holy Spirit and brings us spiritual awakening not experienced by those who sit like stone statues and so the 9 a.m. was rather boisterous compared to the 10:30 in English where there were no joyful outcries or twirling with upraised arms, just plodding and plopping. The 9 a.m. had accordions and conga drums instead of the organ, sometimes a marimba and maracas, and people flocked into the aisles and danced the *Sanctus* and there was hugging and weeping and women prostrating themselves before the B.V.M. and when some of the old German Catholics joined them, out of curiosity, Father O'Connell moved the English Mass to Saturday night so as not to compete. He said, "I don't do Mardi Gras. You put on a show, pretty soon there'll be animals and acrobats."

More and more old Germans came to the Spanish Mass. It was exciting, what with the drums and the up-tempo *Sanctus*, and the Lord's Prayer sounded new to them (*Padre Nuestro que estás en el cielo, santificado sea tu Nombre*), and the Hoerschgens, Frauendiensts, Schoppenhorsts, Schmidts, Schrupps, and Jaegers were drawn to it, out of curiosity at first, then they got the feeling. Elation is contagious. You sit packed in a pew with strangers who are rocking back and forth and laughing and weeping and you—you—stoic though you be, you think back on your sainted mother, your beloved children, and you weep along with the others. And some Lutherans snuck in too, and the effect of the Spanish was to sort of wipe out the Reformation and take them back to the Middle Ages. Spanish released feelings not available to them in English. Some hard-core Lutherans came who believed Catholics sold the forgiveness of sins to raise money to buy jewelry for the pope and now they felt the Holy Spirit making them One with the Others, and they wept for joy, wept for Jesus's sacrifice for our sins, weeping that had never happened on Sunday morning at Lake Wobegon Lutheran except in the nursery, but it happened in Spanish at Our Lady, two- and three-handkerchief shedding of tears.

It was thrilling for the Lutherans to see people kissing the feet of statuary, a hundred candles flickering, the smoke pot swinging and holy water flying and the Gospel text where Jesus tells his disciples not to worry about what you will wear, and all around you are people in bright shirts and jeans and so next Sunday you leave your Sunday clothes at home and wear red and yellow and sandals and feel liberated and hold your arms in the air and sway to and fro, hoping nobody sees you and then, what the hell, you don't care. Once released from the bonds of English, the Holy Spirit took hold of them and they danced as best they could, which is all God asks of us, and language was no barrier, worship no longer literal, more improvidential, rocking out with the Hernándezes, Márquezes, and Aguilars, and Father O'Connell's Saturday night Mass became a retreat for a dwindling crowd of grumblers, and he contemplated retirement. "I went to seminary," he said. "They didn't offer dance classes. We knelt in prayer, we didn't do the rhumba. Jesus fed the multitude, he didn't teach them new steps. But who am I? Just a cranky old Celt with a leather jockstrap. In a year, I'll go to the Perished Priests Home and sit and read Graham Greene. If the sheep want to salsa, who gives a shit? Let God deal with it."

I asked Henry if he missed Mexico and he said, "Certainly. Not all of it, but the Sierra Madre and Veracruz and my mother's village in Oaxaca. But this is home now." He said, "Your people are good workers and my family are workers so we fit in okay because most people here aren't big talkers so English isn't so important. You can get along fine on a few words." He certainly read us right. We're okay with silence. It's considered a virtue. People do well to talk less. Clarence Bunsen once stood up at Memorial Day in the cemetery and said, "If ever there were a time for silence, this is it. How much better than a speech would be two minutes of silence in which we think about those who lie here and what they did for us." And everyone stood in silence and after a minute you heard people weeping. The honor guard wept, the members of the Ladies Sextet, the American Legion guys. Nobody suspected the truth, that Clarence had forgotten he was supposed to give the annual speech. Ever since then, they've skipped the speech and just observe silence.

This is not a town where you can talk your way to the top. We're suspicious of salesmen, politicians, big woofers. Plenty of preachers have discovered that here, substituting for our Lutheran pastors, young men fresh out of seminary, eager to bestow their learning on us country pumpkins, and they soon realized they were talking to a stone wall. Some of our kids went to liberal arts colleges and became progressive ideologues and impressed others of their ilk but found no audience here, just friendly faces, all blank. The Mexicans were, like us, respectful of those who dig in and get the job done. We could see that. The robotic machinery required close supervision. The workers had plenty on their hands and when robotics went awry they gathered round and dealt with the problem. Their kids went to work mowing lawns and cleaning houses for Wobegonians working at Aunt Mildred's Meatloaf or NutriSoft or Universal Fire. They opened a car wash that played *conjunto* rock 'n' roll and the kids sang and danced as they washed and waxed. Dorothy said, "I get my car washed every day, it costs five bucks, and it makes me feel young. Cheap at the price."

6

—

BECOMING

My remodeling the Gunderson cabin was a hot topic of gossip in town, no surprise to me. I had a wife and an apartment in New York—why did I need a rundown cabin with an outhouse? Who was I seeing on the side? Were Dorothy and I an item? Was I running a sex ring?

No, it was a history project, pure and simple. I was reliving the summer of 1960, I was eighteen, six-foot-three, 168 pounds, I had a moustache because Arlene liked it. I woke up in the morning and looked down at the sleeping Arlene and put on pants and a shirt. Marj Gunderson was drinking coffee out on the porch and I poured myself a cup and joined her. She was an Eisenhower Republican but she was fascinated by John F. Kennedy and read about him in the *Tribune* and asked what I thought of him. Brethren parents didn't solicit their children's opinions; children were supposed to fall into line. I told her that Kennedy was a war hero, an author, and his wife, Jackie, spoke excellent French, and I thought they would bring wit and style to the White House. (I had picked up the phrase "wit and style" somewhere, it wasn't a phrase that came naturally.) "But do you think he's a good man?" she asked. I said, "When his PT boat sank, he was willing to give his life for his men." (I'd read that somewhere too.) There were rumors about Kennedy's love life, she said, and then Harold came out with his coffee and she changed the subject; she didn't want to get him riled up and talking about Democrats and their weakness on communism. "Sleep okay?" he said to me and I said, "Yep. You?" And then we talked about how we wanted our eggs, scrambled or poached.

They were easy to listen to. They had stories about odd relatives, the bachelor uncle who drove around the Midwest with his tux looking for tap dance contests to compete in and the glitter he put in his hair, the grandma who believed that the bourbon on her breath would kill the aphids on her houseplants, the bigwig city-councilman cousin who was dehorsed by a bad case of the croup that unaccountably raised his voice from baritone to contralto, the clownish brother who trained rats to race and jump hurdles and exhibited them at county fairs, the saintly brother who died at Normandy—he looked up from his trench to see what was going on and in a flash he was gone—the runaway cousin Kathleen who raced motorcycles in a thrill show, the Catholic nun who could curse like a sailor, the aunt who sat at the piano practicing Wagner while the house filled with smoke from dinner burning on the stove. They poured themselves fresh coffee and Story Time began and they told the same ones over and over and added new details, the glitter was rainbow-colored, the houseplants died but not the aphids, the rats wore cowboy hats, Kathleen raced her bike up a ramp and through a hoop of fire and landed in a water tank and rose from it wearing only a tiny bikini.

I was content in their world but had my eye on the future, maybe writing for the *Tribune* like Will Jones in his "After Last Night" column, or for *The New Yorker* like the great A.J. Liebling who knew about food, war, boxing, and France, or writing humor like Thurber or Twain. No poetry for me: too easy and it didn't pay. I wanted to earn a living as a writer. *The New Yorker* was Mount Everest, and such ambition couldn't be admitted to just anybody but I admitted it to Arlene and she was sure I'd make it there. Sometimes I was too. Kennedy was the future, a new decade beginning, the country advancing confidently in the direction of its dreams, and I imagined I'd marry Arlene, write a funny book, move to New York, and be friends with Joe and Jim and Sid. It all seemed highly possible and then I drove the 1956 Ford to Minneapolis and what happened happened.

Now, sitting in the empty authentic cabin at the yellow table, I contemplated the happenstance of my life. A big adventure like putting a canoe in an unmapped river, no idea what rapids and surprising waterfalls lie ahead, dense forests, hostile denizens wary of intruders. A sobering subject for a former idealist. Somehow it all began here in this cabin. I was advancing confidently through Thoreau, dreaming airy dreams, and I walked with her through the dark to the dock, and she stuck her hand in my shorts and one thing might've led to another and I might've married into the trash-hauling business, become a partner of Norm, and instead I wrote books and did shows. Once or twice this summer, I opened the cabin door and imagined I'd find them sitting around the yellow table and it'd be then again and all of now would be fiction.

The millennials were transcendentalists too, I suppose, in pursuit of dreams, though maybe more *dental* than *transcendent*.

Alyssa and Prairie started Becoming Press, which specialized in memoirs by people who had reinvented themselves. A woman who identified as a man and then became pregnant but as a father, not a mother, and raised his daughter as a boy in order to offer him a choice and the boy identified as a primate, an orangutan, and underwent a hair-planting procedure called fermentation and was donated to a zoo. There were memoirs by dummies who had self-sophisticated and stockbrokers who became singer-songwriters and a Baptist dentist who became a Buddhist nudist. Prairie wrote *The Middle Child's Tale: How I Stepped Up and Found Primacy,* and Alyssa wrote *Standing Tall,* which began,

I was a six-foot Amazon by the age of fourteen and already learning to slouch and slump so as to minimize myself and one day I slipped on an apple peel and sprained my back and was laced up tight in a back brace, and that was when I determined to be myself and if I towered over others, let it be their problem, not mine. With height came self-assurance and when classmates called me "pushy," I pushed harder. I spoke up, made eye contact, no meaningless smiling. Thus you eliminate a lot of pointless friendships that only clutter up your life and you eliminate short and self-conscious men, which is good for all concerned.

They published *Seeing In The Dark* about America's first blind ophthalmologist and *Doctor Demented* about a schizophrenic psychiatrist and *Father No* about an atheist priest and *Heather The Head-Hunter*, about a lady linebacker who passed for a male in the NFL for three years, thanks to her bone-cracking tackles.

One morning Giselle called and said she missed me too much and the Appalachian hike had been postponed a week on account of a rockslide and would I please meet her in Minneapolis? She had an unused Delta ticket she wanted to cash in and how could I say no, so I drove to Minneapolis and picked her up at the airport. I told her the green linoleum had been replaced by hardwood flooring, but she wasn't interested, she wanted to take my clothes off. I come from a culture of tongue-biters and would never express such desires outright, we would lurk and intimate, then be resentful if it didn't happen, but she is a New Yorker. We got a room at a hotel by the Mississippi, and Giselle took a shower and walked out with a towel wrapped around her and I said, "When do you want to have supper?" and she said, "I didn't fly out here to have supper" and dropped the towel. That's the New York way. So I performed my husbandly duty and we ordered room service and looked at the falls of St. Anthony and she said, "Tell me what you want with this cabin on the lake."

"Nancy couldn't bear to deal with Norm's stuff so I'm throwing it out."

"You're not expecting me to spend a summer there?" I shook my head. "No, I'm turning it into a capsule of the summer of 1960. Maybe we'll turn it over to the local museum."

"The whole town is a museum."

"No more." I told her about the boom economy and how LifeCycle was selling almost a hundred thousand Floating Homes a month: "It's a national phenomenon and it's happening in Lake Wobegon, people deciding they want to recycle Grandma rather than preserve her.

"Let's not talk about death," said Giselle. "Let's go back to bed." So I sang her the old HighTops song,

All I want to do is be with you
In a hotel on Fifth Avenue
My arm around you and my finger hooked in
The belt loop of your pants
The sweet vibrations
Of your hip gyrations
This is the sensation of romance.

I sang it, our reflection in the window, the big river rolling by over the dam, it felt for a minute like we were on a ship heading upstream, and she said, "I'm not done with you yet" and we fell into bed together. "You're my best friend in the world," she said. "I am married to you forever. I don't want to be without you. Put that in the front window of your museum so they can see the past is over. No do-overs. No seconds."

The next day she flew back to New York. She promised she'd come to Lake Wobegon and look at the cabin when the work was done, and she kissed me goodbye. It was a real kiss, not an ex-wife kiss, not a motherly kiss, but a sustained smooch with erotic overtones. I didn't want to see her go and the night before I'd considered stealing her driver's license so she couldn't pass airport security, but wisely did not, she being an independent spirit who does not care to be cornered, so I watched her disappear into the terminal and the anonymous concourse. I felt mournful in the car and drove around Lake of the Isles and Cedar Lake and Loring Park and then got the idea to drop in at Groveland Home, a care center by St. Mark's Cathedral, which I've visited whenever I'm in the neighborhood to give a little show in the memory unit. With an audience of the demented, there's no need to schedule ahead, every day is today. I walk in through the double locked doors into the dayroom where a couple dozen of them sit quietly and I sing "Tishomingo Blues," my old theme song, and they brighten up, and I sing the coffee jingle and they clap along *(Coffee stimulates your urges, it is served in Lutheran churches, keeps the Swedes and the Germans awake through the sermons. Have a pot of it today, I'm sure you'll say it's awfully good coffee)* and then I go into my limericks, the young fellow from Pocatello, the Baptist lady of Aspen, and so on. It's the rhythm of the limerick that makes them laugh, not the joke. They don't get jokes, but they love the beat and the rhymes. They can hear that it's funny though they don't know why. This is not so different from a normal audience, if the truth be told.

Every show is the same. After the limericks I sing "How Great Thou Art" in an operatic style and lay it on pretty heavy, and they're highly amused. If I forget to do it, some of them will call out, "Great Art," and I cry, "Aha!" and do it. Some of my old heroes live there, old radio celebrities, like Hugh Mongous the newscaster, the morning drive-time stars Ben Dover and Rhoda Dendron, who now cannot remember their own names and they're delighted to see me though they don't know who I am. It's a great audience, maybe the best.

Thanks to memory loss they all live in the moment: I stand among the wheelchairs and tell the story about the dog Buster who dove into a hole in the ice to catch a walleye that got off the hook and swam under the ice and finally, on the verge of suffocation, he burst up through the fishing hole in Bob Bauer's fishing shack. Bob was on his fourth brandy Alexander and listening to Beethoven's Fifth. He leaped up and knocked over his kerosene heater and flames burst up all around him and the shack burned and Buster ran away and the volunteer firemen raced to put out the fire and pumped water on it and turned Bob into an ice statue and he walked out of the fish house, glittering with ice, and the firemen jumped on the truck but the fire had weakened the ice and it cracked and broke and the truck went through and Buster saw the walleye and dove in and got it in his teeth and took it home. To my demented it's all happening *now* in this instant, not secondhand. I tell the same story every time I go there, which the inmates enjoy to the hilt and laugh and clap—*The best stories are the ones you've always known:* that's my credo. Dementia liberates them from the addiction to novelty. And if they're having an especially good time, I toss in the midnight ride of Paul Revere or the wreck of the Hesperus or Frankie and Johnny. They love it all. It was not about ingenuity but familiarity. I end the show by reciting the 87 counties of Minnesota in alphabetical order, a real showstopper, and then "The Star-Spangled Banner" for a standing ovation. For me, it's a spiritual experience, a ritual of selflessness. I saw my old friends Sam and Janet Evening in the midst of them, laughing and clapping. When I was a kid, their 11 p.m. "After Hours" show was the height of sophistication and I'd sneak a radio up to my room and listen to it under the covers, Sam and Janet talking about the parties they'd been to and hobnobbed with Cedric Adams and Arthur Godfrey and Lyle Bradley. I thought of asking for their autographs, and thought, "No, we're way, way beyond that now."

The attention span of the demented is short. Half an hour is long enough. They enjoy my show and then they go back to watching golf tournaments. It's a lesson in the transitory nature of fame. One year you're the ace of spades and then you're a pair of twos. Sam and Janet used to fly off to New York regularly and be wined and dined by publishers hoping to place their authors on "After Hours" and now they're thrilled if someone brings them a Coke and a cookie.

Scripture warns that the high shall be brought low, and Norm and I used to talk about Wobegonians who flew too high and came crashing down to earth. Pastor Phil Fuller, host of *The Friendly Gospel Hour* who resigned in disgrace after suggestive material was found on his laptop in a motel room in Omaha. We knew Phil from Youth For Christ in high school and followed his career, rising to the top of the radio gospel charts, invited to the Reagan White House and got his picture taken with the First Couple, everyone smiling. He palled around with Rush Limbaugh who advised him on investments, he was a celebrity guest on Caribbean cruises—why did he feel it necessary to get a motel room in order to look at pictures of young women in tiny thongs? Firm female ovoid buttocks evidently excited him, and so what? But shame drove him into a dark corner and his attempt to conceal his interest—he registered under a made-up name and paid for the room in cash—made his attraction seem perverse and the secrecy of the whole matter—the bishop using the word "inappropriate," no mention of cheeks and thighs, which let people imagine groping and grabbing though it was only gazing and grunting. It made no sense. His wife tracked him down, suspecting he was seeing another woman, and he was, her name was Candy, she was eighteen, posing in a thong bikini on video. "Now the poor klutz is pumping gas in Kansas City," Norm said. "How can one person be that dumb?"

And Phil's brother Merlin, the valedictorian of his class, a *summa* graduate of the St. Clarence College of Law, lieutenant governor of South Dakota, a big kahuna in conservative circles, and he attended his niece's confirmation in a Lutheran church in Pierre, and went forward to read from Paul's Epistle to the Colossians, and out of his Bible dropped a racing form with a picture of rats on it. It landed at the feet of a reporter for the Sioux Falls *Argus Leader* who handed it to Mr. Fuller who denied it was his and cursed the reporter and accidentally dropped his Bible and a brochure dropped out for a rat racing track in Nebraska where you could bet big money on critters with names like Blackie, Odin, Roofer, Potent Rodent, the Green Bay Pack Rat, and Marshall Boggs, and there were dozens of receipts for Merlin's bets. The reporter wrote a simple factual story and the idea of a believing Christian spending thousands of dollars on racing rodents made Merlin Fuller unmentionable and his network went dead. The lights were out. The car wouldn't start. The dog wouldn't hunt. He called Norm and asked if Norm knew of any job openings in Lake Wobegon. Norm said, "How do you tell a former celebrity that he has to change his name and grow a beard and get a night job and start over again?"

As J.P. Peterson, the Scandinavian Hank Williams, sang:

You know it says so
In the Holy Word:
Those who were low
Are gonna fly like a bird.
Those who sat high
And got a big slice of pie,
Lived in silk and in satin
With a place in Manhattan,
Trouble-free, high in the tree,

King of the hill, talk of the town:
Remember: what goes up is bound to come down.

I had once been a sort of celebrity, not a *celebrated* celebrity, just a public radio guy, which is no great feat—you speak low and slow in a British accent, saying *colour* for "color" and *theatre* for "theater," pronounce French through the nose and try to sound thoughtful and mildly troubled, grow a moustache, wear dark clothes, carry a pipe and you're in like Flynn. I became the host of *A Prairie Home Companion,* an oddball show on Saturday nights, live, with loon calls and singing dogs and tap dancers and songs about going back to dear old Piscacadawadaquoddymoggin and stories about the beauty of winter, the passing of youth, the ordinary miracles of love and loyalty, whose goofy amateurism appealed to some people, a show with no marketing, no creative consultants sitting around a whiteboard discussing the narrative arc. People discovered the show while twiddling the dial and it became a secret shared by thousands, then a few million. It was an inexplicable hit based on less planning than would go into the average high school prom and it kept rolling along for forty years because I didn't know what else to do. At one point, they threatened to put me in the Broadcasting Hall of Fame and I declined: fatuity in perpetuity is not my brand of cornflakes. I'm from Minnesota. And then, one Saturday night, I recited a fine limerick, one of the best I ever wrote:

There was an old lady named Jude
Who, imagining her solitude,
In warm weather chose
To take off her clothes
And walk around town in the nude
And old men and rubes
Would stare at her boobs
And think thoughts licentious and lewd
She was eighty, Miss Jude,
And not a great beauty
But O how she lightened the mood.

A tidal wave of email came in, decrying the immaturity, the lowering of standards, the catering to base instincts. Listeners accused me of abusive cartoonification, hierarchical dehumanization, and malicious crudity, and the Hall of Fame executive committee voted to rescind my nomination, which I had already declined, and the rescinding got into the paper (*KEILLOR DENIED PLAQUE*), but who cares?—Norm called me that weekend to say it was a great limerick and hearing the word "boobs" on public radio gave him hope for the future of the country. "You're a brave man," he said. I said, "Every so often you've got to break the rules and exercise a little common humanity."

A Seventh-day Adventist preacher in Minneapolis said it was depraved and filthy, A minister condemned me for writing "I'd be pissed if I were a Methodist," and the local public radio station sent an investigative team who found a limerick of mine (*There was a young woman named Jane who avoided gin and champagne and consorting with men but now and again she was thrilled to take walks in the rain*) that had made a number of women named Jane feel dismissed and diminished, all of which reminded me of the clown at the Mist County Fair who sat on a bench suspended over a tank of water and tried to get people to pay a buck to throw three baseballs at a bull's-eye and drop him into the tank. He called them hayseeds, rumdums, sad sacks, creampuffs, bozos, fruit flies, dumbos, insulted their wives and mothers, got them worked up, and men kept plunking down money to throw baseballs at the bull's-eye and they got so angry they couldn't throw straight. You learned from it: don't respond to life's insults. There is a kick in the pants waiting for you around every corner and the best thing is to tip your hat and walk on by.

The angry letter-writers took themselves too seriously. Midwesterners are brought up on modesty. *Don't think you're somebody because, believe me, you're not.* That was gospel in Lake Wobegon. We said that all the children are above average—not some, All. It was illogical but illogic didn't bother us whatsoever. Thoreau said to advance confidently and expect success, and our parents said to sit down, do as told, wait to be called on, and for God's sake, don't show off. The letter-writers were simply showing off. In a world of hatred and injustice and terrible cruelty, they threw the book at a jaywalker.

This is where the millennial tycoons differed from us. I googled Alyssa and found an interview on YouTube where she told a guy: "Nuts to equality, it only means mediocrity. It means men pretending to think I'm okay. Fake respect is an insult: I say, crush them underfoot and move on. A boss at Google put an arm around me and said I had a great future in front of me and he was looking down the front of my shirt at my necklace and I wrote him up in a report and he was out the door two days later, heading for a new job managing a Tastee-Freeze in Tuscaloosa. If you have the power, use it. You whack a CEO good and hard and it shows the messenger boys they better keep their eyes on the floor and not ogle the women. I don't believe in the 'women's movement,' I believe in me. I am my own best supporter. I used to be too emotionally available and I got into some relationships that opened a hole in the dike and needed plugging. My biggest investment is me and my own self-sufficiency. The love you give yourself can never be taken away. Grow your following, build connections, personalize the brand, stay on track. Win, win, win. And I do. Believe in your own worth and worthy means wealthy. Go for it."

It was out in the open, selfishness as a matter of principle—I come from self-effacing people who fend off compliments and avoid self-promotion at all costs and embrace meekness lest we be struck down dead by bolts of lightning or by a flaming six-pound hailstone or a berserk buzzard, something out of the sky. Alyssa and the others were smart and hardworking and dedicated to earning buckets of money while many good Christians were teaching small children to color within the lines—the millennials were prospering because they embrace the digital world that flummoxes the rest of us and also they are focused, which is another word for "heartless." It seemed to me that they are the future. They thought so too.

I liked them, their language, the word "sketchy"—*That's sketchy.* A girl says to a guy: *Just man up. Sweet.* Which is like cool but not exactly. Instead of dating, they *hang out.* An old man tries to confide in them:

Too much information. T.M.I. Things get too heavy, they say *Drama.* You bullshit them, they say, *Shut up. (No way.) Whatever. Take a chill pill. Get a life. Get over yourself.* I love that. We didn't have that, back in the day. I am now actually over myself. Totally. But I am over. I know it. The town as it was when I grew up held no interest for them, nor should it. You can't steer the car by looking in the rearview mirror. Onward. I wish them well. Someday, God willing, they'll discover it's more fun to be old and free and irresponsible and forget your troubles along with your PIN numbers and be stunned by wonder when the grasshopper lands in your hand and feasts on the sugar left in the crevices from the glazed doughnut you ate for breakfast. An old man sees this and is delighted. An old man sees the bare shoulder of the woman he's been married to forever and he cannot help himself, he reaches over and puts his hand on it and she smiles. Someday this will happen to them.

7

CURRENT AFFAIRS

Mine was a simple life. I went into town for breakfast at the Chatterbox. I glanced at the paper. I said hello to Darlene and asked how her daughter is and Darlene said, "Fine." Henry and Orlando came to work. I talked to Giselle every day; the hiking was hard, she felt good, she missed me. I made another attempt to read *Moby-Dick*, lost interest, and put it down. I am not a serious person. I think of the sea and I remember the words to "Who Left The Halibut Sitting On The Poop Deck?" It's where my mind goes, it's in my head.

When Henry got to cutting lumber for the partitions, I hiked around town and was struck by the number of unfamiliar faces. *How to say this gracefully?* I used to be a celebrity in Lake Wobegon, having written books about the town, and whenever I returned, people'd grab my elbow and say, "I've been meaning to tell you that your story about my cousin Kyle flying his parasail to drop the green bowling ball that contained his grandma's ashes in the lake and the speedboat towing him swerved to avoid a pontoon boat with a load of Lutheran ministers and suddenly he was on a collision course with a hot-air balloon—you were wrong about the pontoon boat, it was called the *Agnes B* not the *Agnes D*, as you said, and the ministers didn't all fall off the boat, only six of them did, and the grandma's boyfriend's name was not Raoul, it was Ramon, and it wasn't a hot-air balloon, it was helium." I couldn't walk a block down

Main Street without being corrected about some little detail—Pastor Ingqvist's name was David, not William—Jack of Jack's Auto Repair wanted "How Long Blues" played at his funeral, not "My Father, How Long"—the so-called "Unknown Norwegian" statue was not unknown at all, it was somebody's great-great-uncle Gunnar—the story about the "talking toilet seat" was true except the talking was not in Norwegian, it was "Hey! Cut it out! I'm working down here!"—but now the people who cared about the facts were dead or had moved away, accuracy didn't matter, and in a few years I'd be free to invent any nonsense I wanted. People glanced at me, no glimmer of recognition, and walked by. They had other things on their minds, mainly involving money. History was of little interest to them. History is an old man's specialty. Ask me about Quaker Puffed Rice shot from guns, ask me what hero rode the West in search of truth and justice, ask me about the plastic bag of white margarine with the orange bellybutton, ask me to recite the starting five of the Minneapolis Lakers or Truman's vice president—I was there, I saw, I remember. I remember when kids rode bikes around town as free as birds and nobody knew where we went and what we did and who with. And I remember Lake Wobegon when some men farmed with horses and the Knutes marched *en masse* on May 17, *Syttende Mai,* and the Living Flag assembled on the Fourth, and the whole town filled Main Street on Christmas Eve for the singing of "Silent Night"—ask and I shall tell. I may not even wait to be asked.

The three surviving Norwegian bachelor farmers stared at me, two of whom, I'm told, are Trumpers, Mr. Hauge and Mr. Berge, both in their nineties, old friends who argued for years about whose ancestor was the first Grand Oya of the Sons of Knute, and they were delighted by Trump because he drove Democrats batty, and they put on red caps and sat on the bench by the bank and when Democrats looked at them and shook their heads in disgust, it warmed their ancient desiccated hearts. Mr. Berge has memory lapses and forgets why he hates Democrats but his dementia never weakened his principles. He even continued hating people whose names he'd forgotten. Me, for example. He thinks of me as Kohler, which is the company that makes toilets, but he can't remember the word so when he saw me and looked confused, I made a flushing sound and it came back to him, and he sneered and said, "Beat it, Kohler." It confused him that so many new people lived in town whom he had no grudge against; he was glad to see me, someone he loathed on sight, even though he couldn't say why.

I got a phone call from Larry Becker's wife, Becky, sobbing, sitting at his bedside, saying he had asked for me. Larry was in my class but we hardly knew each other and I hadn't seen him since our 25th class reunion but I drove to the hospital in St. Cloud where he lay, babbling unintelligibly though I thought I heard him say "Diana" or "Indiana," trying to tell me something. Though he taught high school geography for thirty years, we knew him as a man who'd never traveled anywhere— gas was too expensive, or he had a garden to weed, and also he loved his 1967 Chev that was in pristine condition, a fifty-year-old car with 47,000 miles on the odometer. He was quite proud of it. His four kids grew up and moved to far-flung places and seldom returned.

I asked her what happened; "I heard it was a stroke," I said. She shook her head. "Larry was proud of being able to still put his pants on standing up, and he'd just taken a shower and he was stepping into his underpants and—" she broke down and sobbed. "I bought him the wrong kind of underwear, not the briefs but the undershorts, and—" she sobbed and put her hand over her mouth—"he caught his big toe on the elastic band. I was there. I tried to help him but he hopped away and he fell and banged his head hard against the side of the tub." She put her arms around me. "Oh my God. If he'd just sat down to put on his underwear like I told him a hundred times to do, he'd be okay. Why couldn't he listen to me? He was seventy-nine years old. What do you have to prove to yourself when you're seventy-nine years old?" And she put her face down on the bed and wept, Larry apparently unaware of her.

The Beckers were a hard-luck family. They were the last family in town to keep chickens and they had a rooster who crowed every morning, eight crows, the famous first eight notes of Beethoven's Fifth. Someone got a video of it and sent it to the TV show *Amazing Animals* and they sent a talent scout and a camera crew and even though the Beckers waved their arms and tossed cracked corn and oats on the ground, the rooster wouldn't crow, and the camera crew went back to Chicago and the big opportunity was lost. They killed Ludwig that night and ate him the next day. Becky sat and wept on my shoulder, saying that they were planning to take a cruise in the Caribbean but Larry wanted to wait until the week before it sailed to see if the price wouldn't go down and it didn't and then he died. She seemed to think that if they'd bought the tickets back in February, they'd have sailed away and he wouldn't have fallen and hit his head. I tried to comfort her, which wasn't easy. "He always looked up to you," she said. I said I had always admired him for his garden, his beautiful tomatoes, his beautiful car, his fathering of those four children. She said, "We never hear from them. They're scattered to the four winds." I asked if she wanted a priest to come. Or Pastor Liz. "Any port in a storm," I said. "I don't think it matters," she said. "I used to think so but I gave up thinking about it."

That day Henry González was ripping out some rotted boards on the porch and then he stopped and came into the cabin holding a little steel box. A label on the top said: *MY LIFE.* "I found it in the kindling box," he said. I opened it. There were a couple dozen index cards and I recognized Norm's handwriting on them.

We were Lutherans, born to suffer, suffering was its own reward. Don't baby yourself. Your leg hurts? Don't think about it and it'll go away. If you can stand up on it, it isn't broken, just put ice on it. A number of people died, thanks to this principle. Nobody knows how many; they don't want to know. Mom slaved over a hot stove, Dad did backbreaking construction and hauling. He pulled his own teeth, lived with massive hemorrhoids. God sends us illness and pain and misery in order to draw us closer to Him. "Those whom God loveth, He chasteneth." I quit believing around the age of ten. But I still went to church so people wouldn't think less of me. It wasn't worship, it's Roll Call, and unlike the Savior Himself we avoid unbelievers, even abhor them. I look around the church and it is full of unbelief. I can see it in their eyes, they want to believe, wish they did, but it just isn't there. That's why people move to California, to free up their Sundays and go to the beach. In California, people believe in the ocean and the sun, not Middle Eastern mystics.

Evidently, he was writing a memoir. I'd written one and he'd asked me how to do it. "For my kids," he said. "They don't know me at all. They know cartoon characters better than they know their own father." And I told him to do exactly what he'd done, write down on cards what you want to say and when you have 50 or 60 cards, look at them and see if some order suggests itself and fill in between them. He'd called me on the phone, I was in New York, he was thinking about retirement. He said, "There's a lot of time to think on this job because you're not dealing with people much at all, because when you haul trash for a living, nobody ever asks for your opinion about anything except maybe the weather. Nobody. And why would they? So I've saved up a lot to say."

We believed in middleness, the happy medium, avoid extremes. Hold your horses. Don't make a big fuss. Keep a lid on it. Wear navy blue. Don't be unusual or the neighbors will talk. Stick with the crowd. And that's why we love storms so much and when the sky turns black we go out on the lawn and stare at it coming in, we'd like to be able to cause trouble like that too.

We recited the Lord's Prayer and remembered our debtors and tried to forgive them, rotten bastards though they were, even some who attended our church, and they prayed to forgive us, so it was a standoff.

My folks worried about illness and imagined their aches were cancerous and dizziness meant a coronary was imminent, so that they never really enjoyed their good health. They were seldom ill but were always prepared to be.

107

We believed the world is out to deceive us. The better it looks, the worse it is down deep. Some people were fooled but not us. There is always more than meets the eye. So we couldn't appreciate beauty, we were looking underneath and trying to figure out what is the hitch.

"If you can't say something nice, don't say anything at all" is our motto. This means that stupid people have the floor, they bore us to tears talking about things they know nothing about and nobody dares tell them to shut up.

I couldn't roast meat or fry eggs without my mother's critical supervision. "Don't run the mixer so fast, or you'll get potatoes all over." I couldn't hang tinsel on a Christmas tree or paint a flat surface without her watching, pointing out the unevenness. Maybe this is how I wound up in the trash business: you just throw it in the truck and dump it in the dump, no art to it at all, just a strong back and a small brain.

Marital conversation wears out after a few years and so you have this.
Nancy: Why the gloomy look?
Me: I'm fine.
Nancy: But you're so quiet.
Me: I'm thinking.
Nancy: About what?
Me: Everything.
Nancy: Are you mad at me?
Me: Of course not.
Nancy: You seem like you are. What did I do? Did I say something wrong?
Me: No, you're perfect.
Nancy: Don't be sarcastic.

I bought Nancy a pearl necklace and a pair of gold earrings for our

25th anniversary and she never wore them. "For fear I might lose them," she said. "Here? In the house?" "You never can tell. Most accidents happen in the home," she said. "Then put them on when we go out," I said. She said, "I don't want to show off and make other people envious." This makes me so sad, the reluctance to show happiness. I gave them to her out of gratitude for a nice marriage and she felt this should be kept a secret.

I walked into the living room where she sat reading the paper. She said, "Norm? As long as you're up, would you mind—
I said, "What?"
She said, "Oh, never mind. I'll do it myself."
Me: What? I'll do it.
She went into the kitchen and came back with two cookies on a plate.
Me: I could've gotten you a couple cookies.
Her: But you wouldn't have put them on a plate.
Me: If you asked me to, I would've.
Her: I didn't want to bother you.

I used to like people more back before I got into the trash-hauling business. It's a necessary job and yet people look down on you. They don't look down on choir directors, talk about useless, my God—why interrupt a worship service to give a performance? I think I could be happy living alone. I can go for days without hearing anybody say anything that interests me. They're talking trash. Who needs it? I don't. Let me out of here.

It was quite a document for a guy who drove truck for a living. I didn't know what to do with it. I didn't want Norm's kids to read it and get upset that their sweet old man had all this darkness in him. It didn't sound like the Norm they knew, and why should they have to worry about him after he's gone? They'd likely blame themselves. He wasn't unhappy, just blowing off steam. The man was dead; let him rest. So I went to the hardware store and bought a tube of Liqui-Steel and glued the lid of the box shut and put it back under the porch. Let it sit and if someone in the 22nd century wants to power-drill it open and look at it, let them.

That night I had a dream that I died. I heard it on the radio while driving along the River Road in Minneapolis, a man said I was dead, so I pulled over to the curb and then the car died and wouldn't start. I got out and walked. Several people asked if I was okay, and I said, "No, I'm dead." And they didn't seem surprised or alarmed. I walked down to the riverside and saw angels, holy men and martyrs, visionaries, blessed children, prophets, saints, reference librarians, blues harpists, cleaning ladies. And a maiden singing, "I dreamt that I dwelt in marble halls." I said to a prophet, "This is great! If my wife hadn't made me give up White Castle hamburgers, I'd've been here years ago." He stared at me. It's an old joke but I realized that there is no irony in heaven. Because everything is perfection. I asked him, "Why do I not feel blissful? I should be enjoying this infinitely more than I do." He told me to be patient. I tried to walk back up the hill to Minneapolis but I couldn't. I tied three logs together to make a raft and got aboard and floated down the river. It was hard for me to wrap my mind around the idea of Eternity. Boats passed me, people singing joyously, and I didn't feel blissful at all. The river got wider and wider until I could hardly see either shore. Shiploads of happy singers passed by. I thought, "I don't belong here at all." A voice called to me from a canoe and it was Julie Christensen, my old friend from sixth grade. She threw me a rope and pulled me to shore and I got off onto dry land. She had been very beautiful, fair-skinned, and now she was angelic. She danced and jumped rope and sang an old jump-rope song:

Betty, Betty, are you ready?
Pretend the rope is hot spaghetti.
Who'd you kiss? Was he sweet?
Make your heart skip a beat?
You're so cool and in the groove,
How much clothing did he remove?
One, two, three, four, five

She wrestled with me on the shore just as we did when we were kids. She fought with all her holy might but she could not pin my shoulders to the ground, holy as she was. And then she sat up and blessed me and said, "You will return to the world you left and you will have one more chance to make good." I said, "What if I don't know what to do?" She said, "You know." My mother used to say that often. The burden of knowledge. I woke up at 4 a.m. in the cabin and walked down to the shore in the dark and watched the sunrise. I wanted to call Giselle and tell her I loved her but she's a late sleeper and a dream about death is not a good enough reason to wake up the woman you love. The meaning of the dream seemed childishly simple. Each day is a new chance. You descend into sleep at night and you are awakened by the gift of daylight. Make good what you can and hope it's good enough, which it won't be so forgive yourself.

8

119TH

Back in April, Mr. Bell from the high school had called and asked me to hold a date in late May because they wanted to give me a Distinguished Alumnus award at high school graduation. He said, "It's in recognition of your radio monologues, which unfortunately I'm not familiar with but I'm told they were pretty good. Somebody said they were heard around the country. I wasn't aware of that. I had your younger sister in my class and she was awfully smart. What's she up to these days?"

I was going to tell him that, due to my poem about Jude and her boobs, I was damaged goods, but I decided to say Thank you and let it go at that. I held the date and a week later he called to say that they'd decided to give the award to Sam of LifeCycle instead though he wasn't an alum. "Fine," I said. "I understand." He explained that a school board member had objected to my receiving the award on grounds that I was anti-business, which isn't so, it's only that I'm no good at business, but the real reason was a front-page story in the New York *Times—The Little Town That Made It Big*—all about Lake Wobegon and LifeCycle and Universal Fire and AuntMildred's.com. Front page with a picture of Alyssa and Prairie and another picture inside of Lutherans Anonymous, a group that Alyssa had started, recovering Christians discussing their issues of guilt and reticence and abstinence from pleasure. Alyssa drove to Minneapolis the night before and bought six bundles of *Times*es and brought them back and sold them for ten bucks apiece. It was the talk of the town, of course, and so Mr. Bell tacked downwind and selected Sam who was quoted in the story saying that in Lake Wobegon the welcome mat was out and people were glad to hear new ideas. I went to graduation to show I had no hard feelings and there was Sam on the dais and the Class of 2021 marched in, looking very serious, feeling the gravity, knowing that there would be no more food fights, no more flames bursting from someone's pants as he farts into a cigarette lighter, never again will someone laugh so loud that milk comes out his nose, life is now turning away from the friendly coastal inlets and heading out to sea. I suddenly wished I were the speaker and that I would say, "Never let yourself be shamed out of masturbation. It is a good and reliable old friend. Many unwise relationships have thus been avoided that otherwise could've wasted years of a person's life." Just a thought. Of course I wouldn't have said it because people would remember it for years and guys would come up and say, "Hey, J.O., how's it going?" Guys whose admiration I don't want.

I listened to the valedictorian's speech ("Stronger United") and the school board president's remarks and it was clear from the way Mr. Halvorson the principal handed the plaque to Sam that Mr. Halvorson expected him to smile and bow and sit down but Sam went to the podium and gave a speech, which I recorded on my cellphone:

Everyone has the power of choice, which is the difference between us and muskrats and raccoons. So get your shit together. Your first goal should be $100K per year and get there before you're twenty-five. All it means is selling a $100 product or service three times a day. Quit your job. Working five days so you can be free for two is bad shit. Turn your hobby into income. I did it with composting worms and maggots. Weird, right? It doesn't matter. Don't try to fit in. Get serious. Be self-validating. Refill your energies by prioritizing things that matter. Dare to be a different you. Listening to other people's bullshit is the first step toward failure. Network only with people who have something you need. Bear down and get your life together. Get your shit done. Thanks for listening.

It was fun watching Mr. Halvorson and the superintendent twitch every time he said "shit" and how the same word thrilled the students, especially the boys. I could see how Trump got elected president by saying a string of irrelevant things that made no sense and saying them with complete confidence and tossing in some truck driver language to show he was a regular guy. The Class of 2021 gave Sam a standing ovation and what struck me was how he was so much like me at age eighteen, reading Thoreau with my hand on Arlene's thigh. A painful thought.

Our oldest resident, Senator K. Thorvaldson, was sitting in my row, dozing through Sam's talk. He is slowing down now that it's been discovered he is 107 and not 102 as had been thought—the date of 1918 on his birth certificate turns out to be 1913, the eight was a three, and this sudden rush of aging was tough on him. He sat, eyes closed, and when his niece Mavis said, "Are you okay?" he muttered, "What do you think?"

It's good to have him out in public, a living illustration of life span, available for observation, not hidden in a care center. He has accepted wheelchair living and you can see the prune juice in his saddlebag, within easy reach, and a ginger ale bottle full of bourbon and as Mavis pushed him to the car, he was talking to some people who weren't physically present. I heard him mention Harry S. Truman with deep loathing. Senator K. was a Dewey man and his contempt for Truman is rich and deep, for being soft on communists in the State Department and for handing over eastern Europe to the Reds. Senator K. is still standing fast on Republican principles, despite dementia or because of it. This is Living History and you could bring the graduates over to ask Senator K. about the New Deal and they'd get some of the flavor of the past, not just an outline. And someday, sooner than I think, I will be a similar educational resource. The young are watching China, thinking about economics, about the high cost of our antiquated health care system, about the degradation of the planet due to invincible ignorance, and it would be good for them to meet an old ditzy Democrat who is fueled by self-righteousness.

So I avoid comment when some old codger complains about the high price of artisanal firewood. I was not brought up to complain.

Avoid other people's arguments. The town feels lively and prosperous and so what if the old culture is dying off. The Sidetrack Tap has two competitors, Trott Brook and Vino Court. The Sidetrack is for grumpy people, Trott Brook for those who enjoy group singing, and Vino Court for contemplative dialogue. So be it. The Chatterbox Café coexists with La Plaza Populo and Sunny Gardens, a vegan café, no eggs, no dairy, they serve oat milk and cheese made from cashews, the employees are committed vegans, even the janitor, so the danger of inhaling meat microbes is minimal.

Once it was "the little town that time forgot" and now it has caught up with time and is getting ahead of it. Our Lady of Perpetual Responsibility is busier than ever and offers ESL classes, and at Lake Wobegon Lutheran I found the old green hymnal stacked on a table in back and in the pews was a new *Praise, You People* paperback in which God is mother, not father, and the Bach chorales are gone, replaced by "Hallelujah" and "Here Comes The Sun" and "I'm A Believer" and I took one to Pastor Liz and she said, "Don't ask. Just don't ask. I have no comment. I work under a church council, freely elected. I am only a janitor or usher, here to keep up appearances." And then a group called Lutherans Anonymous started meeting on Tuesday right in the church basement—"We're a full-service church, we're here for everybody, even heretics are welcome," said Liz. She showed me a list of their Twelve Rules.

1. *I am descended from Lutherans and am powerless to change this.*
2. *I have faith that God does not see me as Lutheran but as a creature capable of deep feeling, even ecstasy.*
3. *I believe I have become imprisoned in a culture of restrictive manners that do not serve my Higher Calling.*
4. *I have examined myself and found where inherited Lutheran behavior has made me judgmental rather than loving.*
5. *I have confessed my shortcomings to another Lutheran.*
6. *I have apologized to my children.*
7. *I am prepared to follow God's leading even if it should lead me out of the Lutheran Church and embarrass my relatives.*

8. I have asked God to allow me to speak honestly and openly when this is needful.

9. I have stopped the fetishization of neatness, rule-following, and other herd tendencies.

10. I begin every day with the hope of attempting to do something I've never done before, such as offer up exclamations of joy or tell stories that don't shy away from the vulgar truth.

11. I kneel and pray, openly, verbally, at any time during the day when I need to confess my shortcomings or seek divine guidance, even if I am in the midst of others.

12. I am determined to maintain a positive and cheerful outlook every day of my life, even to the point of silliness and extravagance and full expression of personal idiosyncrasy.

"It's a club for people who haven't been to church for a long time and want to attach a Higher Purpose to it rather than just sleeping late on Sunday and reading the paper in your pajamas," she said. "The church doesn't miss those people much but maybe L.A. is their way back to God, so what the hell, let them meet here, it's better than going to the Sidetrack Tap." As an old Brethren boy, I know that childhood is when they make a mark on you that you carry all your life, but if some Lutherans wish to be anonymous and believe in redemption—as we once redeemed Green Stamps to get a set of TV trays—then God bless their hearts. It's a long hard road for a believer to gain unbelief, believe me. I worked at agnosticism for a number of years and came to believe that God didn't care one way or the other, and so I returned to the faith and here I am, a Brethrener fallen into Anglicanism, a quasi-Catholic, on my knees, doing what I can.

Over the years, the Lake Wobegon Chamber of Commerce had tried, halfheartedly, to lure industry to town but our inbred modesty worked against us. We were brought up to avoid vanity—we're like elm trees in that regard. Describing our town to others, we hesitated to go beyond "not that bad" or "pretty much okay." But LifeCycle arrived under cover of romance, and then RedMedic and AuntMildred's.com, and suddenly the town was growing and feeling lively.

It's simple economics. Minneapolis got the big head in the Sixties and imagined it was Major League and built office towers charging insane rents and got written up in the New York *Times* as an Up & Comer and cultural oasis and it fostered companies that made enormous air-cooled computers the size of pickup trucks so Minneapolis thought it was cutting edge but the bubble burst when Silicon Valley made millions of personal computers and ate the monster computers' lunch and as for the arts, sweetheart, they are nothing but window dressing, and young entrepreneurs found that if they leased 2,000 sq. ft. with a 34th-floor view of the Mississippi, the rent would wipe them out and they'd have to sleep on a bench in the bus depot and get their meals at the Union Mission, so they left—they didn't need civic pride, just good Wi-Fi and a lavatory and a place to plug in a coffeemaker. Some found their way to Lake Wobegon and where some trendsetters go, others will follow. A house here costs less than you'd pay for a cardboard box in Minneapolis. All it took was for a few bright persons to make the jump and soon others followed, and the town filled up with ambitious kids determined to beat the big guys.

That spring, Lake Wobegon suffered the indignity of placing 119th in the Most Iconic Minnesota Small Town contest, losing out to crappy towns like Bagley and Sleepy Eye, shithole towns like Le Sueur and Shakopee, boring towns like Plainview and Rockville, and Eveleth, a hotbed of hockey players and prostitutes, and International Falls, full of undocumented Canadians. It was a terrible shock after being Page One in the New York *Times* (*Strong Women Lift Lake To Prominence*) and the *Wall Street Journal* (*Nuts To Manhattan, Heeeeeeeere's Minnesota!*), and now—119th? It felt like a typographical error. But the prize went to Westwood Hills, which is not a small town at all (pop. 21,817) but a suburb with no Main Street, only a shopping mall, no newspaper, an encampment of blocks of four-story condos designed by robots whose occupants don't know their neighbors from a bale of hay. Zero history: twenty years ago it was all cornfields. The town motto is "Home of the Cougars," the Cougars being the high school team. It should be "Home of the Spaniels." The high school looks like your standard penitentiary.

The water tower has no name on it. Few people are out walking and if you asked one of them, "Which way is north?" they'd have to pull out their phone to find out. It's Nowheresville. It's not iconic unless you're being ironic.

It won because the novelist Pete Pistollero lived there (birth name: Pete Peterson) whose murder mysteries are set there, thirteen of them, featuring a serial pet killer who has yet to be nabbed by the veterinarian/sleuth Polly Amoroso—suspects include the town's demented dentist, the disbarred lawyer-turned-gardener, the rapturous Baptist chiropractor, one book after another leaps to No. 1 on the list—*The Case of the Lost Retriever*, *The Assassination of Lassie*, *The Case of the Terrorized Terrier*, and many more, *The Broken Pointer*, *The Squashed Chihuahua*, *The Dalmatian Cremation*, *The Toxic Dachshund*, *Orgy of Corgis*, *Slaughtered Rottweiler*, and somehow Pete Peterson keeps the pot boiling. People have theorized that the books are given by dog haters to dog lovers but the killer is undoubtedly sinister, and Polly provides therapy to the bereaved owners and that is the heart of the story, the large role of a beloved animal in human lives. Pete P. lives on a 10,000-acre ranch in Montana and employs three full-time copy editors because he doesn't know "lay" from "lie" and can't spell "cat." The copy editors are rumored to be copywriters as well. He owns a sheepdog, raises thoroughbred horses, is heavily invested in Buddy Boy gluten-free dog food, every year a new book, sometimes two, and it's never reviewed in the New York *Times* and the first printing is a million copies and there is always a second or third.

People have told me, as my book sales have dwindled from five digits to four, that I should try my hand at murder mysteries but the truth is that there is nobody in Lake Wobegon whom I have murderous feelings about. I have sometimes wished I could injure someone but the personal-injury mystery is a nonstarter. The injured party knows the injurer— Lake Wobegon is a small town—and after the spill or the slip, the poke, the collision, there is an immediate insincere apology and then a long period of wariness on the part of the victim. In other words, there's no story, just the suspicion of a story. Pistollero's latest, *Are Newfoundlands*

Fireproof?, is an e-book, selling like crazy from behind a $15 paywall, a million readers weeping into their Kindles, the author adding to his acreage. When I google him, I get nothing about his private life except one snippet of a story in a Montana weekly, in which the sheriff was called to the ranch to rescue the owner from high in a tree where he'd climbed to escape his own dog who'd turned on him. The sheriff shot the dog with a tranquilizer dart and he was sent away to a pet center for compliance training and medicated for aggression relief. "Mr. Peterson suffered flesh wounds for which he was treated at the scene by EMTs." I'd love to know more but that's all there is.

I loathe the man, as I loathe most wildly successful authors, and it hurt me when my hometown pals pointed out what Pistollero had done for Westwood Hills and that my Lake Wobegon books had done zero, zilch, nada, noogies, to create a positive image of our town. "Humorists are lousy salesmen," they pointed out. "It took decades after Mark Twain died for Hannibal, Missouri, to become a tourist mecca, but thanks to *West Side Story* rents on Manhattan's Upper West Side have risen steadily."

I went to my class reunion and one after another old classmates approached and said, "So I guess you heard how we lost out on being Iconic Small Town of the Year?" as if it were my doing, and Alvin Osterhus stuck his face into mine and said, "Your book *Lake Wobegon Virus* certainly did us no good. Not that anybody read it but the title alone does cast aspersions, you have to admit." He said, "I never got around to reading your books but I understand they portrayed us in a very poor light. I do know your father was disappointed in you. He told my Uncle Luke that he wished you'd change your name and if you didn't, he might have to change his."

I accept insults from some people but not from Alvin. Alvin is my age and drives a car with rags for a gas cap and a garbage bag for the window on the driver's side because he broke it throwing out the beer bottles. He is my age and still loves blowing up stuff. He has no eyebrows from when a cherry bomb went off in his face. Violence is his second language. I sat next to him once at the Sidetrack, watching a Vikings game, and what thrilled him was the sack of the quarterback, his arm back to throw deep and three 250-pounders blindsided him and his helmet flew off and he fumbled and was carried from the field, crumpled and broken, never to be the same man again—Alvin creamed in his pants to see it, not realizing that was *our guy* who got sacked. The man is not normal. But when he brings my dad into it, he crosses a line. I looked him in the eye and said, "Your retinas are all yellowish just like your cousin Howard's the time I saw him the week before he died of kidney failure and I told him to go to an ER and he laughed at me and not only that but he also had let his life insurance lapse and so he left Cynthia to deal with his profligacy. Stupidity and disease are a dangerous combination." I gave the man something to think about, namely mortality. He went straight home and called an oculist.

But word got around town that my books were to blame for the town's reputation as Loserville. Someone started a Facebook page, *Pack Up GK And Send Him Away,* that asked people to sign a petition declaring me an environmental hazard. "He has portrayed us as rubes and yahoos and philistines, a bastion of ignorance and intolerance. He has exaggerated our weather, our reticence, our fondness for Jell-O and luau hotdish with Spam and pineapple. He has made Lutherans into an Ole and Lena joke so now people in New York and L.A. chortle at the mention of Lutherans. That's on account of him."

I did not try to defend myself. I tried to be above it but it cut me. It cut me deep. I found comfort visiting Arlene.

She and I have some stories in common that cheer us up. We love to remember our old friend Corinne who died of despair at age 43. She put rocks in her pockets and canoed out on a lake around midnight under a new moon and threw herself overboard. We never understood why. She kept her despair private, a common habit in the Midwest. What we remembered was her sitting at the piano and playing "Whaddaya Mean Ya Lost Your Dog?" *(Who put the rove in Rover? Where's that doggone dog of mine?)* and while still singing she did a tap dance and during the chorus juggled a tennis ball, a stuffed dog, and a corned beef sandwich. She played it for each of us when we were down in the dumps. She dressed up as her hero Elizabeth Cady Stanton for Halloween and said suggestive things to the fathers of trick-or-treaters. She was a Buddhist economist who believed that contentment is wealth. She also believed that civilization is based on good plumbing. Her other friends remember the canoe and the rocks in the pockets. But we remember her singing, *He's a hunting dog all right, keeps me hunting day and night. Here, Rover, come, Rover. I'm looking for him now all over* and we remember the tap dance. She'd taken tap as a kid and still had the lightness of being. We were there, we saw it. We didn't see her paddle out on the lake in the dark.

We both remembered our English teacher Miss Hardin who hit her head on a cupboard door and suffered bouts of dementia— what we referred to it as "a loose screw." Once while reciting Matthew Arnold's "Dover Beach" by heart, she launched into some Whitman, and then asked us to write a hundred words about the "themes and motifs" and we did our very best, though "Dover Beach" is about death and Whitman was celebrating life, and the correct answer would've been "You're out of your mind" but we didn't want her to feel bad so we hog-tied Matt and Walt together and Arlene and I both got a C-minus on the quiz. We agreed that a C-minus for B.S. is certainly better than getting an A or a B. It was Miss Hardin's last year of teaching. Arlene and I cooked up an imaginary 18th-century English novel, *Waverly Fields,* by the Brontës' aunt Thallis, that didn't exist and we each wrote our term paper on it and each got an A-plus, quite an achievement—to invent a work of literature and to be its best critic, pointing out how it anticipated Trollope, whom we hadn't read and only knew from the *Literary Digest Synopses of Classic Novels* that we found in the school library. Miss Hardin wrote on my paper, "I always knew you were capable of more," which I took as a compliment.

We both remembered the famous Reverend F. Huston Youngdahl whose Sunday morning service was broadcast on WCCO. He'd been chosen to speak at Wendell Willkie's funeral, a high honor for a Minnesotan, to eulogize a loser. He came to town and baptized three young people after Frankie Renquist drowned. It took place down at the lake. He stood on a dock and spoke to a big crowd about Jesus calming the waters of the Sea of Galilee that day when the apostles were scared because this lunatic came shrieking out of a cemetery and Jesus got him calmed down and then the apostles got in the boat and a big storm arose and Jesus was asleep in the boat and the apostles were thinking, this guy isn't the Messiah, this guy is bad luck. And then Jesus woke up and he said, "Storm, be still," and he stilled the waters. I was standing nearby, paying close attention, when the Reverend got so excited, he dropped his Bible on the dock and bent down to pick it up and a blast came out of him like trombone blats at the clown show, two longs and a short, and the smell of it was strong enough to strip bark off the trees, and the Reverend did not acknowledge it whatsoever. Anybody else would've said, "Oh my goodness, P.U." But he pretended that nothing had happened. Arlene was one of the baptizees and she heard him. When a man refuses to take ownership of his own farts, he loses his moral authority. They were not little whispers but big boomers. It made an impression on us both at the time, to be skeptical of authority. Others were present who insisted they heard nothing of the sort; they were unable to hold conflicting ideas in the mind—Man of God Lets Big Smelly Poots. We, however, heard the sounds precisely because it happened and it was loud. Arlene's mother accused her of making it up, but you cannot invent two longs and a short that smell as bad as those did. Arlene lost her faith for a few years on his account but seems to have it back now, and when I visit her, she likes to take my hand and we say Psalm 23 together with the valley of the shadow of death and the table prepared in the midst of enemies. It's a beautiful contrary pair: dying while surrounded by goodness and beauty.

She felt well enough to accompany me to Larry Becker's funeral. He'd been a baptizee that day along with her and now he was an old coot in a coffin, rouged and combed, looking like the maître d' of a bad restaurant. His cousin Judy was playing the electric organ (it was at Lundberg's mortuary, Larry had given up on God a long time ago) and the organ made an oozy sound like someone wringing out a wet mop. His brother Gary talked about Larry's countless little unsung acts of kindness to others, which, frankly, I felt were unsung because they didn't exist. I felt a tap on my shoulder and there was the grandpa of my classmate Alan Davis, except it wasn't his grandpa, it was Alan himself. He was the drum major in the high school band, dressed in gleaming white, big grenadier's hat, high-strutting, pumping the big baton, as the marching band swung around the corner playing *Stars and Stripes Forever* and a wave of exhilaration swept through the crowd, and here he was, shrunken and shaky and gray. Life had betrayed him, poor guy. He had to give up the big baton and pick up a dentist's drill and it didn't suit him so he dropped out of dentistry and took up barbering. Apparently he is his own barber and it's not a good look, especially in the back and on the sides. The front was okay, what there was of it. He said, "The old gang is fading away and pretty soon there won't be any of us left." He said this as a great revelation that had just come to him. A late-breaking news bulletin: *Mortality is reported in the suburbs.*

Norm knew Larry Becker, who'd flunked out of divinity school due to hard partying but used a fake diploma to obtain a job as a Methodist youth minister in Boston, but Methodist youth were scarce so he bartended for a living and drove cab. One night a nice kid named Mark ordered a rum and coke and told Larry that he'd created a fantastic computer program called Digital Directory Terminal (DDT) and Larry told him, "DDT is a terrible name, why not call it Facebook?" And Mark said, "That's it!" and wrote up a slip of paper that said "Facebook, ⅛ of common stock to Larry Becker, signed M.Z." And Larry took it home, not thinking, and a few years later when he heard about Facebook, he couldn't find the paper. He was apparently worth millions but he couldn't prove it and when he spoke to a lawyer about it, the lawyer said, "Take a number and get in line" and laughed long and hard. He ransacked his apartment, tore apart his clothing, searching for the scrap of paper. Larry saw Mark's picture in the paper and tried to track him down, hung around on street corners, looked up people who knew him, befriended him on Facebook, then was blocked. The fact of his enormous wealth haunted him. He had dreams at night of a mansion, a stable of horses, a schooner, a summerhouse in Connecticut. One day he encountered Mark on a sidewalk in Boston, followed him fifteen feet from a doorway to a limo, and said, "I gave you the name Facebook" and Mark said, "Thank you." The limo pulled away and Larry pursued it and was run down by a bicyclist and after that, he gave up on God and everything became blurry. He came back to Minnesota. Becky introduced him to gardening. He took up fishing. He calmed down a little. Then he became one of the first guys in town to wear a *Make America Great Again* cap. You looked at the *MAGA* folks and you saw all the slowest thinkers in town and in a small town everybody knows who you are, you don't need to wear a red cap for identification. He died with delusions of having been cheated, like the other *MAGA* men, except his delusion was real, Facebook was his idea.

None of this got mentioned at the funeral, of course. Liz delivered her homily about each of us being a clay jar filled with God's light, hard-pressed on every side, and perplexed, but still our mission is to let our light shine. I did not see how this applied to Larry at all, but I don't claim to be smart. I am still trying to comprehend the woman I've been married to for twenty-six years, her passionate eye for art, her restlessness, her perfectionism that forbids her to sing because she can't bear bad notes, and her love of gardening. My old mother was wary of my marrying a New Yorker and all that that implies, but Giselle came to our house and after a big hug and some small talk she excused herself and went out back and weeded the flower beds for an hour, three wheelbarrowsful, and thanked Mother for the pleasure, and because she let her light shine, she was welcomed into the family.

Arlene and I sat through Larry's funeral and hung with his grandchildren and she explained to them that this white temple with its classic columns and stained-glass arch over the door, *Fugit irreparable tempus* (Time flies and cannot be retrieved), before it became Lundberg Mortuary, was the home of the Thanatopsis Society, founded in 1880, a women's club that didn't seek women's equality because it believed in women's superiority. They sponsored lectures by learned persons, celebrated World Federalism Day and held a sonnet contest on Shakespeare's birthday and some of the women formed a club, the Proust Roost, that read Proust à la française. The Thanatopsians believed a person should live life so well that she will not fear death, which is not the same as Lutheranism, not even close, but there were Lutheran Thanatopsis women who synthesized the two. The club dwindled in the Thirties and the temple was sold to Mr. Lundberg in 1946. A few Thanatopsians continued to meet in various homes but it leaked away around 1974. A sad loss. Integration into male society didn't work for many women: they got swallowed up by mediocrity and never shone so brightly as when they were with other women as Thanatopsians.

The grandchildren find this hard to believe: small-town women enjoying Proust in French, women who married football players and duck hunters, but those children don't know about the magnetic influence of our old high school French teacher, Eleanor McDonald, a smart stylish woman who presided over the club for fifty years. Most towns didn't have an Eleanor and the only French they knew was *filet mignon*, but she was a dynamo and whoever sat in her class came away infected with her enthusiasm. Or my eighth-grade English teacher, Frayne Anderson, who admired *The New Yorker* and read us stories by Salinger and Cheever and Updike but never told his own story, how he'd served in France in the 82nd Airborne, landed on the beach at Normandy, a stoic Norwegian, received the Purple Heart, but nobody knew it until after he died. We were taught by giants. All you need is two or three inspiring teachers and you're ready to get in the game and give it your best.

I pushed Arlene home in her wheelchair, she was exhausted from the outing, but still spunky. "You didn't have the advantage of learning French," she said. "The Brethren thought French was worldly but a new language gives you an interesting perspective of being an outsider and from that you learn a few social skills. I remember that about you, how naive you were. No wonder you married the first woman who showed interest. You had no idea you could break off a romance that doesn't make sense. French would teach you that. Eventually you found the woman you love, or rather she found you. But I worry about you. Your mother loved comedians so that led you to find gainful employment, but you still don't have the social skills a man your age ought to have. I worry that you might take up with some floozy who sprinkles sparkle dust on you. I feel like I don't dare die until you're safely back in New York with Giselle so maybe you shouldn't wait around for my funeral but fly back so it's safe for me to expire." She was kidding, but not entirely. I wheeled her up the ramp that Barbara Ann's Bill had built on the steps to the front porch and Clarence came out to accept delivery of his wife.

"How was the funeral?" he said. "Fun?"

"Endless," she said. "Don't you do that for me or I'll haunt the hell out of you. I'll follow you around like a bad habit."

9

THE IMPROVEMENT MOVEMENT

The millennial crowd took up the cause of civic improvement that summer as the money poured in, to wipe out the embarrassment of being 119th, inferior to Le Sueur and Shakopee. Some people started to talk about changing the name, Lake Wobegon, to something more positive. Someone suggested "Paradise," someone else suggested "Golden Valley," but there already is one, a Minneapolis suburb. "Okay, Golden Fields then, or Golden Plateau," he said.

Alyssa had organized a task force of millennials, Moving Forward Together (MFT), and they took up the renaming cause—put an ad in the *Herald Star,* pointing out that Bob Dylan wouldn't have risen to such great heights as Bob Zimmerman, that Nina Simone became High Priestess of Soul because she set aside Eunice Waymon, Norma Jeane Baker needed to be Marilyn Monroe and Elton John had to bury Reginald Dwight. They discussed classy alternatives such as Shoreview and Lakeville and MeadowWood. And then someone came up with an Ojibwe name, Manaadjitowaawin, which means "to treat all creation with respect," and how could a person argue against respect for creation, never mind that the word is not melodious to the non-Ojibwe ear, and soon there was a formal petition requesting a vote on Manaadjitowaawin, a name that few could pronounce and nobody could spell, but the millennials saw it as their way of taking ownership of the town and Wobegon would be gone once and for all, and they enjoyed saying "Manaadjitowaawin" and saying it at every opportunity, showing off their superior language skill, and so a referendum on the question: *Shall the municipality of Lake Wobegon change its name to Manaadjitowaawin? Yes or No.* Someone said they got the name from a children's book. "Good they don't want to name it Pooh Corner," said Mayor Alice. Myrtle Krebsbach was in favor of Manaadjitowaawin; she said, "I've wanted to live somewhere else for years, now I can do it and not have to sell the house." Alyssa and Sam presented the petition. They said "Lake Wobegon" was "loaded with negative connotations" and Manaadjitowaawin would give us a fresh start in life while also honoring the native people whose land we had taken, their culture that our ancestors had abused. "Revision means Revitalization." Alyssa offered to compensate local businesses for any expenses incurred by the change.

Alice hemmed and hawed and suggested she appoint a commission to study the matter but the Manaadjitowaawin proponents had the signatures to force a vote. Margie Krebsbach suggested a compromise, such as Nelson Grove (in honor of Stan Nelson our old football coach and veteran of Normandy) or Bradley Park (for Lyle Bradley, Korean War combat pilot and biology teacher and leader of the local birdwatchers), but MFT considered that a racist diversionary tactic and wanted an up-or-down vote on Manaadjitowaawin. And so the vote was set for June. Their motto was "Respect for Creation is Our Obligation" and Alyssa printed up signs, "Manaadjitowaawin" or We Be Gone," a clear threat. They circulated a letter from a realty broker, saying that people under 45 strongly favor a spirit of inclusivity and respect for diversity suggested by an Ojibwe name and the end result of the name change would be to boost property values by 10 to 15 percent, maybe more. They got a judge to order the council to allow all residents to vote, not only registered voters. They distributed leaflets: *Manaadjitowaawin ¡Sí! ¡Bueno! Lake Wobegon ¡No! ¡Malo!*

I didn't weigh in on the Manaadjitowaawin question because, as

Dorothy pointed out to me, I was a divisive figure in town—people over sixty liked me, people under forty, not so much, and those in the middle were reserving judgment. I felt bad about that, of course. I wanted to be liked by young people, our heirs and assigns, our prosecutors in the court of history. On the other hand, why seek the approval of people who love horseshit music?

Alyssa started a book club, *Advancing Books Means Gaining Knowledge*, ABMGK, which Dorothy said also stands for Anything But Mr. Garrison Keillor, which I thought was something of an honor, serving as a scarecrow on the feminist bonfire. Dorothy said, "Don't let it upset you. You still have friends in town, old friends, and they may not like everything you stand for and there have been times they had to close their eyes and look away but they're fond of your family and you seem to have straightened out somewhat."

"Thanks," I said. "Thanks a lot."

The first selection of the ABMGK was *I Am Woman, I Am Unlimited* by a writer named Juicy Lucy Gambucci and 300 folks gathered in the high school auditorium for it. She weighed 677 pounds, stood 6'6" tall and had big hair piled high on her head, tied with a gold chain around it and made her entrance to *Thus Sprach Zarathustra*, wrapped in a purple cape as big as a ten-man tent, gold sandals on her size 24 feet, and there was no *I'm so happy to be here* or *Thank you for coming*, she let them know from the get-go what was what: *You bought this book because you wanted an excuse to come to a freak show and you still feel guilty about how you treated fat girls in school and you wonder what happened to them, Dolly and Dotty and Polly and Molly, those tubbybutts who got excused from gym because nobody dared look at all that flesh, those friendless fattycakes everyone avoided and nobody sat next to in the cafeteria for fear somebody'd think you were their friend. Racism is no joke but smart black girls were popular and admired compared to the open cruelty bestowed on us victims of weightism. My mama was a big woman and she was helpless to protect me. We ate to ameliorate the pain and the pain only got worse and finally I gave up on weight loss entirely and decided to make as much of myself as I could. My legs got powerful carrying this load and I went into pro wrestling as*

Hungry Hilda the World's Widest Woman, and I fought a couple hundred matches, traveling the country with a troupe of other giantesses, six of us in two comfortable semi-trailers and it felt good to walk out of the ring all sweaty and smelly and my belly bouncing, and to see the weird little men who were powerfully attracted to us and who paid extra money to go into a little room where we would lie down on them and jiggle. They wished to be enveloped and we obliged. For a while I loathed them and joined the Women's Defense Force, which gathers outside bars at closing time and waits for the men who're trying to talk girls into coming home with them and we jump the men and grab their car keys and lock them in the trunk and roll it down a hill. But what we discovered is that most men are terrified of big women because we are powerful. I come from a big family or large people: I look around and I see the genetics of the situation. So why should I fear what I was born to be. I'm a fatso and I'm going to be the biggest meanest fatso in town, the Obese Who Must Be Obeyed, Avoirdupois in Action. And Juicy Lucy stood grinning in rapture and opened her cape and stood in her octuple-X green bikini, a bra big as a two-man hammock. She leaned down slightly to fold her enormous flaps and folds into different patterns. *I live alone in Chicago. My house is an old fire barn so the front door is big. I go running in Grant Park every day, three miles, and people feel the ground shake as I approach and they clear a way and they all have cellphones but nobody ever takes a picture because they are terrified of what I might do. The mounted cops all know me and wave and say hello but the foot cops don't. I eat two meals a day that're delivered by six men on bicycles and my goal is to become the fattest woman in America, nine hundred pounds, and donate my body to the Field Museum to lie in a golden sarcophagus and to enlarge people's imagination of what is possible. Thank you for coming. It gives me pleasure to observe the wonder and horror and guilt and curiosity in your eyes. When you are me, you see people in an entirely different way.* And the music played and she wrapped her tent around her and strode out, her footsteps were felt throughout the room, and she was loaded into her van and driven away.

The next book they read was *Crossing The Great Divide* by She Who Knows Ericson, a bestseller that summer, and Alyssa put up the fifteen grand to bring the author to town for a reading. The book is a memoir of a person growing up in Tulsa, Oklahoma, who was identified as a white biological male at birth and named Steve but who now knows herself as a trans woman who is Cherokee. The book argues that racial identity is no more definitive than biological and that she identifies as Indian and anyone who can't accept her as such has a serious problem. "When we limit others, we limit ourselves," she says. "I know who I am and when you tell me I'm wrong, I can see clearly who you are. You're a bunch of ignorant assholes. You invited me here to show how tolerant you are and I can see through you like I see through a screen door. You're no better than anyone else. In fact, you're worse because you don't know how bad you are."

She Who Knows accused the audience of "benevolent sexism and soft racism," and said, "I don't let anybody dictate who I am, not even my brothers and sisters. I was Steve and now I'm She Who Knows. Deal with it." She used the F-word frequently except she didn't say "F-word," she said the word itself, and after a few hundred F-words and F-variants, it loses whatever oomph it had and becomes a sound like a racquet punching a tennis ball, and finally Alyssa said, "I think you're trying to provoke me into rejecting you and I refuse to do it," and She Who Knows used the word again, and Alyssa asked her if she'd feel better if the members of the book club left the room, and she repeated the phrase, and they left, and she drove back to Minneapolis with a pocket full of cash. The club's Advisory Board met with Alyssa and suggested that the next author they invite be someone—they couldn't come up with the word, so Alyssa said it. "Normal?" Some women nodded. One said, "I don't think we should avoid controversy, but it'd be nice to have an author whom we actually like, at least once in a while." Alyssa promised to keep that in mind.

Alyssa saw me on the street the afternoon after the She Who Knows event and she walked right up and said, "You hate me, don't you. I know you do, so don't bother to say you don't."

I said, "I have no basis for hating you."

"You think I'm selfish and insensitive, and you know something? I don't care."

I said, "I don't hate you, I'm worried about you." I leaned up close to her and said, "Your retinas are very yellowish, a strange orange-yellowish tinge and I've read that that's a serious indication of traumatic trichinosis, a stress-related disease that's often malignant. You should check it out." She laughed at me but it was a shallow forced laugh, and I knew she was going to go google it and find references to diseases that would keep her awake at night, dreading. Google gives you a couple dozen diseases to worry about, from Alzheimer's to jaundice to yellow fever.

The next day she was slightly nice to me and said, "Hello, how are you?" like a regular person, and gave me a half smile. She looked like she was thinking of inviting me to lunch and then thought, "Maybe next week." There was a definite change. Not a come-to-Jesus moment but a gesture of civility. A sense of mortality makes us better people. Me, for example. I am 79 and have numerous underlying conditions and back when I was young and fascinating and furiously busy, I was capable of monumental negligence and treating people like furniture and then I spent some time in a hospital ER ward among the crazed and dying and desperate and now I'm nice as I can be. When I was a big shot, I was a jerk half the time and a fool the other half, but in old age, we accept our essential equality. I was at Mayo once for a routine checkup and a man in a wheelchair approached, pushed by his wife, the richest man in Minnesota, and we spoke as friends, though we'd never met, and a month later his obituary was on the front page of the paper. The obit devoted ten paragraphs to his business acumen and acquisition of other companies and it left out our talk at Mayo. I didn't ask him how he was doing, I could see, but he told me, "I'm eighty-five and I'm dying and I think about my life and this good woman and how can I be anything but grateful. God bless you." It was kind of him. My people are dying, so kindness is very much on my mind. Though my eyes are quite clear, not yellow at all, I check them regularly.

Margie Krebsbach came to my defense, for which I was grateful. She wrote a letter to the *Herald Star* saying that people can like what books they like and that she, for one, had liked several of my books, though she didn't name any in particular. She was a doer, leading the Great Books group, which was reading *Oliver Twist*, a group of six compared to the three hundred of ABMGK, and she invited me to come talk about Dickens, which I was grateful for but declined. Dickens was a good-natured writer and so he's been on the back shelf for ages. He created heroes you'd enjoy having dinner with, which is practically unknown in modern fiction. These days the reader dines alone in a cave and the waiters are weird with guttural voices and the food tastes like someone spit in it and there is never dessert.

Alyssa and I had lunch two days later. She was eating at the Chatterbox and I sat down with her and she didn't tell me to go away. I said, "Jesus said to love your enemies so here I am in case you're tempted." She laughed, a good sign.

She said, "You're not an enemy, just a sort of a civic liability. You celebrate defeat and humiliation, and demonize success. It travels under cover of Minnesota modesty, which is a variant of chronic depression." She said, "In the annals of history, there are dreamers and doubters. You're a scoffer. You may call it satire but what it does is nail people's shoes to the floor and poke fun at those who dare to think big." But she pronounced *annals* "anals." I said, "I've never been in the anals of history. Some people were and it pretty much wrecked 'em." She was not the butt of the joke but I must admit that her animosity hurt me. My wife can cut me more deeply since she knows more, which makes the casual animosity of a stranger seem so ridiculous and unnecessary. Like gum wrappers dropped on a beautiful golf green. Why? In God's name, what were you thinking?

The enmity of men is nothing to me but I have always craved the approval of women. I've done plenty of shows before crowds of happy women and their sullen men who'd been dragged there by wives and resented it, and I didn't care. Women were enough. My closest pals are women. My producers were women: I took orders from them, I resented bossy men. But I secretly wanted Alyssa to like me. Isn't that pitiful? But it's the truth.

Sam proposed building a golf course for civic improvement but one day, hitting golf balls on the football field, he shanked one and the ball whacked a cockapoo that Kaylee the child care dog trainer was teaching to push a stroller and the mutt flew at Sam and leaped up and bit his ear and one of its fangs hooked his earring and ripped the lobe and he fell down, screeching in pain, his eyes crossed and little stars and planets orbiting his head. EMTs were called and he declined first aid but the man was in shock. To be hurt so bad by a small gentle creature.

I met him a week later, walking with Roger, his father-in-law, who'd flown in from La Jolla, and Sam was very nice, his ear bandaged under his Minnesota Twins cap, and he offered me a piece of his Pearson's Salted Nut Roll. Just stuck it out and I broke off a chunk. He had been an English major at NYU but could not force himself to read Henry James's *The Frozen Duchess* and paid a woman $500 to write the term paper for him and her paper took a feminist route that brought his authorship into question and he was kicked out with a permanent red P for Plagiarism on his record, which closed the door to any and all professions except for advertising.

He said, "If I'd loved Henry James I might've spent ten years getting a Ph.D. and written a thesis, *Men's Lapels As Emotional Signifiers in The Ambassadors,* and gotten a job at a state college and become fond of martinis and instead I got into composting and married Molly and learned to enjoy life." Maybe so, but he didn't look right to me and his earlobe was tattered. I got the feeling that the cockapoo attack had done deeper damage. His eyes flickered and darted to and fro, his *Uhh*s were elongated. He hadn't trimmed his nasal hair, very unusual for him, and he was presenting two tusks of hair from his nostrils. A man doesn't point out this sort of thing to another man—that's his wife's job. Perhaps she'd been traumatized too.

"Sam just put down a half million to buy the old asparagus cannery," said Roger. "It's going to be the new Floating Homes factory. We outgrew the barn." I congratulated them, but the nose hair bothered me. It's a bachelor farmer trait. Would he be taking up snoose and spitting and manual nose-blowing too?

"Roger tells me you've written some books," said Sam. I admitted that I had.

"I'd like to write one about LifeCycle but I can't seem to concentrate. I keep forgetting things. My mind is all over the place. Molly says I should get me a ghostwriter but I'm not sure they'd get the tone right. The whole thing came to me in a dream, people dying and sailing away in a boat, floating home, the naturalness of it. But how do you ever find the time to write?"

I was about to tell him—"I write because I have nothing better to do"—and then I thought of Mallory. "I know someone who could help you," I said. "She's a life coach. Everybody needs a boss, even a boss needs one. The higher up you go, the more you need someone to remind you to trim your nose hair." He flinched and reached for his nostril and got the point. "Thanks for the advice," he said, "Got to run." He turned to go and then turned back. "What's her name?" "Mallory," I said. I thought his eyes looked definitely yellowish.

Sam and Molly weren't dummies. I'd known her since she was an infant and followed her career as a star field hockey player and photographer of elderly relatives and trees and now she was riding high with LifeCycle and RedMedic and though Sam was the guy who dreamed up the concepts, Molly was the operational brains of the company, flying off to Dallas and L.A., Boston, Washington, to manage their extensive archipelago of subsidiaries, meanwhile I saw Sam more and more in the company of Mallory the life coach. Mallory's voice is authoritative: it's the voice you hear on the airport tram saying, "Stand Back, The Doors Are About to Close" and when people hear it, they stand back. When she told him to pull up his pants, his crack was showing, he promptly did as told. She'd hand him a napkin and say, "Right cheek" and he'd reach up and there it was, a chunk of crabcake and a crouton. The man was in some ways a genius and in others a four-year-old and Mallory's job was to bring him up to speed. When I saw her tending to him, it always made me take a look at myself in a mirror to make sure bodily fluids weren't leaking out. Once, in a casual moment, standing outside the former Bon Marché, I asked him what Mallory charges and he said, "Three grand a month."

"Does she travel with you?" "Nope, When I'm on the road, I FaceTime her morning and afternoon."

"So she's made a difference?"

He told me that he'd been in the habit of not changing his underwear and Molly had given up on telling him and now Mallory asked him, "Clean underwear?" And if the answer was no, he found a clean pair and a lavatory to change in. She also sent him to a health resort to go on an all-flower blossom diet for a day and cleanse himself of toxic fibers. He said it made him feel childlike and sweetened his breath and Molly loved it when he blew on her.

After the embarrassment of the 119th-place finish, Alyssa tried to reason with me. "You're writing a book about us, aren't you. I know you are so don't bother to deny it. You're going to write an old grampa book about how good it was Back In The Day and how we ruined it. I wish you wouldn't. What's the pleasure in being an obstruction and frustrating people who are trying to get things done?"

I told her I was only an observer, a mere stenographer recording the modest modern history of my little town.

"Bullshit," she said, but she said it with a smile.

I thought it was sweet of her, the wistfulness of *I wish you wouldn't* and the cheerful *Bullshit.* I was starting to like her.

She patronized the Chatterbox, as did I, and sometimes we sat near each other. Our eyes met and we didn't blink. We ate the mushroom soup from the same pot. The town is too small for hatred unless you are Norwegian and senile. You cannot hate people you eat with on a regular basis. That is the principle on which France and Italy operate and other great civilizations. You can hate with gay abandon on the internet and cable TV but not around the same table.

They were fourth-wave feminists, out to rule the world and I am a last vestige of colonialism, a descendent of DeSoto, an heir of arrogance, but I don't hate them. I reserve that for the good gray warriors of the Lost Cause that is the Republican Party, who've seized the Supreme Court in their insurrection against democracy. I spend all my animosity there and this makes me a prince and sweetheart to everyone else.

And then one day Alyssa and Prairie approached me, all charming and exuding good will, and asked, "Do you know Cole Lehrer?" I said, "Sure." He is the most famous native of Lake Wobegon. In *Time*'s list of *Top Two Thousand Influencers*, he's the only one we can lay claim to. We knew him as Larry Kohler, but he became Cole Lehrer when he produced *Self-Conversations*, a series of six audio books hailed in the Eighties as the first wave of post-literate, or reductionist, writing, addressing the reader directly, sweeping aside the old elaborative writers such as I. His audio recordings sold 17 million copies worldwide, mostly to women who suffer from nameless anxiety and need help falling asleep. In the tapes, as in the books, Larry talks directly to the reader:

Don't worry about it. Let it go entirely. So he broke your heart. That's because you are capable of love and he isn't. You'll come out of this kinder and more loving as a result and he will always be clueless. You have friends and that means you'll be able to find love. He won't. One day you'll feel a lightness of spirit, a lifting of cloud cover, a straight shot to the stars. Meanwhile, go for good walks and let your heart sway where it will. Talk yourself up. Don't regret a single thing. Look down the road. Wear bright colors, yellows and pinks. You are beloved by a great many people, more than you'll ever know. Strangers look at you and are inspired to live larger. You've been bruised and wounded but your heart is full. I'm here, my arm around your back. Accept my love and honor. We're at the Petersons' house, Lois and Jim. She raises irises and hydrangeas and he has a nice tomato patch with netting over it to protect against squirrels. They are very nice people and they introduced me to you because they knew you were lonely. Jim plays "Moon River" on the ukulele and they sing a duet and we have iced tea and vanilla wafers and then we'll see a video of their cats Snowball and Midnight.

It was an endless loop of a monologue and people found it comforting and calming and Larry got rich and also got addicted to methamphetamines, wrote crazy threatening letters to former girlfriends and therapists, went through a Zen yoga program along with a mountaintop isolation program and recovered mostly, married a Little Rock model named Jocelyn who took him for half his dough plus his gigantic glass-block home in Malibu with a river running through the master bathroom, and Larry moved to northern Minnesota, a cabin on the upper Mississippi, started writing books about interpersonal harmony, but those didn't do as well as the Lake Wobegon tapes, so he went back to the original formula that helped jittery women get some shut-eye.

Alyssa wondered if I might have his email address or phone number. I don't. Larry and I aren't pals; we never even made it to Nodding Acquaintance. "I love his tapes, they're so peaceful. I love the repetition," Alyssa said. And then it hit me: Larry has eight million followers on Twitter and they wanted his mailing list. I told them I'd try to get to Cole. Alyssa said, "I think he has some obligation to do something for the town, don't you?" "Of course," I said. It felt good, her asking my help. When people need you, they forget they don't like you. It pays to be necessary.

LifeCycle prospered and Molly's parents, Roger and Cindy, bought a beach house in La Jolla. Being Lutheran, they felt uneasy about ease and luxury but, to work off their guilt, they volunteered at a food shelf for mentally ill and homeless elderly. The food shelf was in the midst of a bitter battle between the organic healthful non-GMO faction and the Whatever people and Roger and Cindy tried to be peacemakers but did not see why the mentally ill should be deprived of chicken nuggets if they were used to that—they had worse problems, such as schizophrenia. Roger developed gastric spasms from the stress and started sleeping days and lying awake nights. Cindy got addicted to running and became skeletal. They went into counseling with a therapist they both despised and that brought them together.

Sam and Molly restored the family farmhouse to its 1870 simplicity and held a big garden party to celebrate LifeCycle's record-breaking year. I was not invited, nor was Arlene, so I wheeled her to the Chatterbox for lunch, and a couple old classmates joined us and got to complaining about the changes in town. "I don't have anything against Mexicans, but they're awfully clannish," said one, and they were offended that, instead of American history, the school was introducing History of Our Continent, which then led to jokes about incontinence. We were grateful when they left.

"Why do people get so whiny and resentful?" she said. "Life is good. We have Chinese takeout now, did you know that? We had chow mein in school, but now you can text CHI on your phone and there's a family named Chin who live in the old Thorvaldson place who'll deliver Kung Pao chicken or the Seven Joys of General Tso pork in little white containers. My God, what a pleasure after all those years of mac and cheese. I'm glad I lived long enough to see it.

"And language. There's so much more than what we had. *Totally.* We never used that word. Ever. We didn't dare think in terms of totality. We allowed ourselves to be 'sort of happy,' or 'kind of interested,' we didn't want to commit. And now young people are totally into it. It's awesome. We never were awesome. Awe was what you'd feel if Jesus appeared to you in person and placed a hand on your forehead and made you intelligent, you would be awestruck, so you couldn't use the same word for, say, the way someone's hair looks."

She said, "But you are awesome. I couldn't have said that ten years ago. And I've seen more of you this month than I have in the past ten years. I tell you, if cancer is what it takes to revive friendships, I wish I'd gotten it more often."

She said she'd decided I was awesome in ninth grade when I performed a magic trick in the school talent show. I recited Robert Frost's "Fire and Ice" while inserting a flaming match into my right ear and extracting an ice cube from my left ear. She was dazzled by this. And two years later, I sort of asked her to the prom. She remembered that spring day clearly. She sat next to me on the iron railing in front of school, lightly perspiring in her white blouse and wool skirt, and I said without looking at her, "I was meaning to ask you if you were going to the prom and if you weren't going with anyone else, if you might like to go with me. I don't know. Whatever. You don't need to tell me now or anything.

It's just an idea I had." She remembered this, word for word. Not an actual invitation so much as discussing the theory of one and then turning it down in her behalf. She said, "Let me think about it" and waited for me to ask again and I never did. And now here I was, an old has-been, and we were good friends again and life had turned out all right.

"Life is good. It's good I didn't marry you," she said. "I considered it, but you were too confused for me. And if I'd married you, I'd've hung onto you and you never would've met Giselle and that would be a shame. So you have me to thank for your happy life, just so you know. How did you meet her anyway?"

"She came to my show in New York with a handsome guy with big hair who I assumed was her boyfriend and we talked for a few minutes and she was very lively and I liked her a lot, then found out he wasn't her boyfriend and I was overjoyed and invited her to lunch."

"You didn't tell her you were thinking of maybe inviting her but maybe not if she had other plans, so whatever?"

"Nope. I said, 'Lunch. Tuesday. What do you say?' Or words to that effect."

"So why don't you ever bring her out here to visit us?"

"She's a New Yorker, a coastal person, and she gets very quiet when she leaves the city behind. She loses her bearings and she misses the rumble of the subway, the salt air. Not to be poetic or anything but a deep breath of it reminds you how happy you could be when you were twelve. Discouragement is dissipated by salt air. People in despair have gone to Far Rockaway intending to swim out past the surf and not return but the air revived them and they came back to town and had a good dinner and resumed life." I said that cornfields do not have the same effect.

"Bring her to see me, she has a right to know what I know about you. But don't wait too long." She looked happy at the thought of befriending the woman I married instead of her. That's Arlene. Bighearted all the way. She extends herself to the anxious and needy. Even as death approaches, she cares about us all. She is reading to her granddaughter Annabelle the poems of Mary Oliver, a real investment in the future. The little girl loves the line—

You do not have to be good.
You only have to let the soft animal of your body
love what it loves.

She wakes her grandma from a nap, whispering—

Tell me, what is it you plan to do
With your one wild and precious life?

And Arlene says, "I love you, my little soft animal."

10

THE KING OF NORWAY

"Life is good," Arlene said. "Think of all those years we got along without Google and if we wanted to know something, we had to go down to the library and page through encyclopedias or search through newspaper files but now I google my cousin Helen in Boston and find a long article by her about taking ballet in classes taught by militant instructors and learning pliés and pirouettes useless in normal life and it was like the Marines except you longed to be a snowflake and then become Clara in *The Nutcracker,* which meant you'd go to Mount Holyoke and become a prize-winning poet and get a pedicure every weekend but instead she got a pair of antlers because her butt was too big, which predicted she'd go to Boston U and marry a hockey player. But she divorced him and became a therapist working with depression in the arts. All this information from googling her name. Way back when, I met her at a family reunion and asked what Boston was like, she said, 'Okay' but she's much more interesting than that and now you can know that, thanks to Google."

She googled King Haakon VII of Norway and read about his visit to Minnesota in May 1926 when her grandpa Arne Holm was Grand Oya of the Sons of Knute and chairman of the welcoming committee. Other Norwegians resented Arne being so distinguished—the Holms had come to America as the Hoels but the implications of "hole" convinced them to switch to Holm, a Swedish name, and many Norwegians resented them as social climbers, but nevertheless when the royal visit was announced, the town threw itself into a fury of beautification and removal of crab-grass, which up to then had been considered merely another grass species but the king's visit raised people's standards. All because word came down from the palace that His Royal Highness needed exercise and couldn't just sit for hours being admired so Arne announced a Beautiful Lawn Contest, the king to walk around and judge, and people went to work trimming and planting and laying sod, weeks of furious labor, and then the palace announced that the visit would be a rest stop due to the king's busy schedule: breakfast in Minneapolis, a school in Rushford, a concert in Starbuck, lunch in Spring Grove, tea with us, dinner in Twin Valley, a play in Hawley, dessert in Grand Forks, and could we please as an act of Christian charity let the poor man take a nap? No speeches, no children's choir singing songs they don't understand, no presentation of useless homemade gifts—the king had spent his life attending cere-monies and we would distinguish ourselves by giving the poor man a bed to lie down on and a chance to wash his face and use a toilet.

"Of course," Arne said, and it threw the town into shock. The king's visit was a sign that they'd made good in America. They'd been brushing up on their Norwegian for weeks. And now the king would come to town to sleep and use the toilet? *Why didn't Arne stand up for us? The man could sleep in the car, take a dump at a gas station.* The hard feelings lasted for years, even though, the day before the king's visit, he got sick from a bad batch of herring and the trip was canceled. Haakon had been in America one week and already had attended eleven dinners. Word had been passed to please avoid herring since he was a Danish prince who'd been elected king of Norway when the country gained indepen-dence in 1905, and he had no stomach for herring, a fishy dish preferred by peasants; Danish aristocracy would no more eat herring than they'd swallow grasshoppers. But in Decorah, Iowa, he ate what was put before him as a children's choir sang "Kan Du Glemme Gamle Norge?" And he rose and headed for the exit though the choir had five more songs to sing and was violently ill on the sidewalk, as dignitaries averted their eyes, and was driven to the hotel and put to bed, next to a basin, and he spent most of the day emptying his stomach. When a monarch upchucks, it is no mere leakage, it is a major eruption.

The Ringnes family never forgave this insult. Florence Ringnes was Mrs. Holm's cousin and expected to join the king for tea though she wasn't a tea drinker and they didn't speak to each other until shortly before Mrs. Holm died. Florence gained vengeance by taking over the Ladies Circle at church and was so domineering that younger women literally could not butter bread or boil water in her presence. She was so fiercely superior, she made others incompetent. It all began with being left out of the king's visit, though the visit didn't occur. And many years later, Arlene, googling Haakon, read all about the canceled visit and the hard feelings it caused, and she realized that her marriage to Clarence in 1964 was a sign that peace was restored, the Bunsens having been furious at the Holms in 1925 because they'd gone to great expense making their yard into a showplace. "Now all the people involved in the feud are dead, but now and then, in the years we've been married, Clarence sings a few bars of 'Kan Du Glemme' just to remind me I'm descended from a Holm who married a Gunderson but nonetheless he's true Norwegian, and I have some Holm in me and come from a line of pretenders."

I know something about pretenders myself, having tried to deBrethrenize myself by reading Thoreau and Hemingway and skinny-dipping with Arlene and running away to the U to major in pessimism and try to write dark surrealist fiction in which moody men in black turtlenecks drank absinthe cocktails and thought dark thoughts and tried to think them in French, but then I had to earn a living and surrealism wasn't paying even a minimum wage so I went on the radio and told stories about the friends and neighbors in my hometown, and that worked out okay, but it also gave Lake Wobegon a reputation for naivete, and now I was blamed by many for our finishing 119th.

I still feel loyal to the hometown and when the choir at graduation stood and sang the school anthem, I got teary-eyed at the part about

When you walk down Oak or Main,
Everybody knows your name,

They ask you how you are,
You say, "Not bad,
All right, I guess about the same."

I love that: it's not true anymore but it used to be. I see the letters to the editor of the *Herald Star* and note how carefully they tiptoe around the edges of controversy to avoid giving offense: that's my people. I love old friends, even the known Trumpers, and the secret ones. Friendship is truth and truth stays true, even if some friends bought a bag of horse hockey thinking it was golden apples.

I am a loyal Minnesotan and liked being back among modest people with much to be modest about. The food is unremarkable, the scenery doesn't draw foreign visitors, and the people, though polite, are not particularly friendly. We seldom raise our voices in anger, except to loved ones. We will pull your car out of a snowdrift but more to demonstrate superiority than out of charity. We are a smug, self-righteous people but we care terribly what outsiders think of us and if the New York *Times* refers to Minneapolis as a cultural mecca, they close the schools and people hug each other in the streets. Minneapolis imagines itself as a major city (New York, Los Angeles, Chicago, Minneapolis), which amuses us outstaters, like if your brother Gerald got a hair transplant and changed his name to Jeremiah. There is a reluctance to have too good a time lest your dark Lutherans see us as frivolous, but there is a generosity of spirit, a willingness to serve on committees, not that we would ever compliment ourselves, but I can because I don't live here anymore.

I feel loyal to the Sidetrack Tap, even though I quit drinking years ago, and when a new bar opened across the alley and offered ten varieties of nonalcoholic beer and ale, I didn't set foot in it. The new bar, Trott Brook, owned by Ben Trott, a brewmaster who served a citrus ale and a brown beer with chocolate malt and a white beer with coriander, and he liked to gather his musician friends and get the crowd singing Irish drinking songs and sea chanteys, and it was irritating, non-Irish Minnesotans pretending to be hearty and jovial and clapping their hands and bellowing *With me too-ry-ay fol-de-diddle-ay,* just because some bully with a banjo told them to be boisterous.

Men go in the Sidetrack to brood, not to be make-pretend seafarers. It isn't Dublin, it's Minnesota, for God's sake. It's an old man's saloon. As long as you can make it down to the Sidetrack and order a beer and a bump, you're still living and capable of mischief, and if you can't, then you're packed off to a sanitized room with intravenous tubes stuck in you and some TV talk show is on and you can't get out of bed to turn it off and after a while you don't even care anymore and then you die while some woman on TV with three-inch eyelashes is talking about the pressures of celebrity. But if you can haul yourself up on a barstool and hold a glass in your hand and bellyache about the old lady, you've got a slice of the good life: so be content with your lot. You hope and pray to be talking and making sense until your last day when you enjoy a beer and a brandy and win a couple bucks at cribbage and head for your car and there is the jealous husband of the drum majorette you've been seeing on the side at the Clover Motel and he shoots you cleanly in the frontal lobe and down you go, no suffering whatsoever, just a moment of regret that you had the cheap brandy and not the Courvoisier.

And when you die, your Sidetrack pals will sing "For He's a Jolly Good Fellow," including the second verse: "Will there be beer in heaven, or should we bring our own?" and the third, "The fish have peed in the water, so drink your whiskey straight." But no banjo, thank you very much.

Mr. Trott tried to be friendly and brought his beers over for Wally to taste and Wally tried to be friendly in return but the beers didn't fizz or taste beery. Then one day Trott came over and made Wally an offer for the Sidetrack. It was a large sum of money. "Let me think about it," said Wally. It was almost midnight and Trott was thoroughly soused (but how do you get drunk on coriander beer?) and Wally thought, "What the hell, the offer might disappear by daylight" so he said, "I've thought about it. It's yours. But toss in two grand for the player organ and five for the billiard table, okay?" And they shook on it and Wally wrote it down on paper and Trott signed it and, by golly, he made good on it a few days later, and Wally handed over the keys and sold his patrons down the brook. Mr. Trott promised to preserve the Sidetrack exactly as it was, which is impossible, what with mortality and all, and so I dropped in for Wally's last night behind the bar. He looked quite pleased with himself. He said, "I am going to take a shower tonight and throw away these clothes and take four more showers tomorrow until I get the smell of this place out of me and then the Missus and I are going to move to Flagstaff and never associate with beer drinkers ever again. It is the beverage of ignorance. I have heard enough stupidity for one lifetime. Alcohol is what turns sensible Democrats into raging Republicans." Nobody else heard him say it. The place was packed with all the old regulars, tossing back stiff drinks, deep into grief and diving deeper.

They knew the banjo bastard would be arriving in time and the chorus of deckhands and their *folderay* and various $10 beers made from parsnips or mushrooms seasoned with sawdust, so from now on they'd have to drink at home with the old lady glaring at them, wishing she could blow the man down *diddle-ay-diddle-ay*. A sad day indeed, me boys.

I haven't had a drink in twenty years and of course a sober man makes the drunks resentful so I had a ginger ale on the rocks that looked like Scotch. And there was J.P. (Jack) Peterson who had brought his guitar and was singing all the sad songs he knows. "Look what the cat dragged in," he said. "The famous author. What brings you to town? Somebody die?" I know Jack too well to take offense: he was jilted by three different women, all of them alert and discerning, and when a man's been rejected three times on reliable authority, there must be a reason. He was a housepainter for years and probably inhaled a good deal of lead. He lives half-time in a trailer on what's left of his grandfather's farm and the other half at his uncle's cabin on the Upper Peninsula. His resentments run deep. He had a hit song when he was in college, a novelty song that was quite hot in 1964:

I knew a Mister Larson,
A good old Swede named Sven
He was the greatest felon that there had ever been
He wore a fake moustache and said, "Give me the cash"

He robbed them daily, not just now and then.
Had a wonderful time and lived a life of crime
Stealin', stealin',
Stuck up banks and Brink's
Bought his honey diamonds, minks,
And she loved her darling Swede
Who gave her all a girl could need,
Took her to the best resorts
Where he got into her shorts
And made her shout for glee
'Cause Larson lived by downright larceny.

He didn't sing "Sven Larson" tonight. He sang an old sad song, "I'm going to North Dakota and I don't expect to see you anymore" and he was going to sing another and noticed that I was the only person listening to him so he put the guitar down. I bought him a beer and a bump and he thanked me. He said, "Did I ever tell you the story about me and the skunk?" This is one thing I enjoy about Lake Wobegon, the old chums who love their stories so much they forget how often they've told them and so they tell them again and it's remarkable how the stories improve with repetition. "No," I said.

J.P. was a deer hunter. He did it out of ignorance, because his dad had done it, and like his dad, he wrapped a deer hide around himself and wore a pair of antlers and sat in a blind with his back to a tree and watched the stump where he had set a bowl of raspberry Jell-O covered with Miracle Whip for bait. Deer love Miracle Whip especially with chopped walnuts and raisins. He attached a brown string to the bowl and tied the other end around his ankle, in case he fell asleep. Which he did.

He slept peacefully until he felt a slight tug on his ankle and jumped up, gun cocked, and saw a skunk with its nose in the Miracle Whip crunching on walnuts. For this skunk, the sight of a man with antlers was too much excitement for one day. The skunk raised his tail and cut loose. He was a teenage skunk full of hormones, and the aroma almost knocked J.P. off his feet. He dropped his gun and staggered out of the clearing, tearing clothing off him as he stumbled blindly ahead through the underbrush, and that was what the family in the Winnebago saw as they drove up the highway, a naked man with a shotgun who smelled bad, towing a bowl of Jell-O.

They didn't stop to help him. They couldn't imagine what help would be helpful. They called the sheriff and a couple of deputies responded and found him in the ditch. They tossed him a blanket to wrap himself in and they sprayed him with Hi-lex, which they keep in the squad car for just this sort of thing, and he recovered to where he could point in the direction of his car. They drove across the field, J.P. walking fifty feet ahead, and they saw his pants, which had his car keys in them, and they got a quart of sparkling water and threw it in his face to wash out his eyes, and asked him if he was okay. In Lake Wobegon, we are brought up to say yes to this question.

So the deputies were glad to leave him there and eventually he found the car and made his way home. He soaked himself for a couple days and then resumed his life, but you never completely recover after an experience like that. He went to Bill the barber who shaved his head but his hair grew back smelling skunky so he had it done again. When his friends ran into him in town, they didn't ask, "How's it going?" because they could see for themselves. The people in the Winnebago posted a picture of him on Instagram, naked, armed, somewhat crazed, with the caption, "Somewhere someone is having a worse day than you," which someone saw in a book of trending memes and showed to J.P.—he'd become a joke to media managers and content specialists—and it broke his heart and he took up residence in the Upper Peninsula. It happened three years ago but, standing near me in the Sidetrack, he still smelled faintly acrid and looked unwell.

He told me the whole story, except for the Instagram part, and said, "One good thing about getting skunked is that deerflies never bother you again. Up on the U.P. they got deerflies the size of hummingbirds. Bug repellent only irritates them. But they smell skunk and they leave you alone."

It was sad to think of the Sidetrack coming to an end, even to a guy stuck in sobriety. Mr. Trott was all about innovation, as if by making mushroom beer you had achieved enlightenment. The Sidetrack was about getting a little buzz and sitting among friends. Life is complicated, your car is experiencing seizures, your wife is tired of your nonsense, and your urinary tract feels leaky so sit down and have a bump with the boys, deal out the cards, maybe you'll come up with a plan. One step at a time. You can't plant corn and deal with women at the same time. It doesn't work. The simple life suits us best. Dreadful things befall the rich and powerful. Nobody is meant to be a star. Charisma is fiction. It's the dummies who stand up on stage and it's the smart people who sit in the dark near the exits. Everybody knows it's true.

The urge to be top dog is a bad urge. You learn this at the Sidetrack Tap. Inevitable tragedy. J.P. had a hit song when he was 22 and his life fell apart, three separate handsome women showed him the door. And I suppose he looks at me and sees a onetime radio host who said "boobs" on the air and came tumbling down the slippery slope. The raccoon is a swashbuckling animal who goes screaming into battle one spring night to win a mate, carries on a heroic raccoon career, only to be driven from the creek bed the next spring by a young stud who leaves teeth marks on his butt and takes away the girlfriend, and the loser lies wounded and weeping in the ditch and later hurls himself into the path of oncoming headlights and his carcass lies on the hot asphalt to be picked at by crows. Nobody misses him at all. Nothing is learned. This is not a life for sensible people. A sensible person seeks to know the neighbors, enjoy his portion, live a long life, and feel a little wistful when the coronary slugs you hard but you joke with the ambulance guys who try to save your life, you say, "My wife pounded on my chest like that once but that was because I was seeing another woman." And then everything goes dark. Thank God you get to miss your funeral and the weird eulogies. The cremation might be interesting but not the funeral. That is the Lake Wobegon view of life. In Mr. Trott's bar, drinking his specialty brews, you get to thinking you're something special yourself, and that, as we know, is the doorway to the coal chute and the long slide to the cellar.

The next morning Henry said, "I heard you were at the saloon last night. Is everything okay?" I told him I appreciated his looking after me and, yes, everything was okay. He said, "I don't want you to go down a road you'd regret later. We're all here to look after each other." So there was one more thing I have in common with him: we're not strangers on a lonesome highway, we're village people at heart and feel a responsibility to save a neighbor from going over a cliff.

He asked if I was sure about the oak flooring, should he return the green linoleum sample? I said yes, that Giselle didn't want to be reminded of her old boyfriend.

I went to the Chatterbox for breakfast and Dorothy said, "I hear it was quite the party last night. They said you and Jack Peterson were drinking together." I told her he was drinking for the both of us and if I'd had half of what J.P. drank I'd still be in bed.

Giselle called from New York and said, "Where were you? I tried to call you twice last night." She said she missed me and wished I'd come East and meet her along the Susquehanna where she and Russ and Kerry were walking the trail. I said, "I've got to make sure my workers stay on the job. There are millionaires waving hundred-dollar bills in their faces. And I'd be miserable on the trail. I know nothing about nature. I don't know a pine from a spruce from a fir tree. I don't know a bobcat from a bobolink."

She'd just walked through a Pennsylvania town past the ballfields and remembered her dad teaching her to hit a baseball. "We lived on Grove Street and his office was around the corner and we often saw Andy Warhol at the grocery and, yes, he was buying Campbell soup and Brillo pads. Andy played second base on the Village Indians team Sunday afternoons in Central Park. Dad managed the team and a lot of his patients played on it, many of them immigrants, like George Balanchine and W.H. Auden and Nabokov and Stravinsky. They looked on baseball as ultimate proof of Americanness, and they wanted to pass for natives and so they took speech classes from Minnesotans, not New Yorkers. Dad tried to tell them: in the arts it's a big plus to have an accent, you don't want to sound like you come from the prairie. Yes, many Americans suspect aliens of being communists, but mainly farmers from Iowa. The rich people who'll support your work love those accents, especially French and Russian. If you sound like you're from Duluth, forget it.

"Nabokov loved Disney and wanted to write comic books, Balanchine wanted to sing in the movies like Fred Astaire, and both were proud of their baseball prowess, Balanchine of his shortstopping, Nabokov of his knuckleball, and my dad had to persuade them to recover their foreignness and stop trying to walk and talk like regular guy guys. And Isaac Bashevis (Ike) Singer who played first and wanted to write the Great American Trucking Novel—Dad said, 'What's with the Mack Truck mishegoss? You're a Semite, not a semi!' Jascha (Huffer) Heifetz was the catcher and Dad shut down the team rather than let Heifetz destroy his hands catching Nabokov's knuckler: 'God meant you to be a violinist, not a backstop,' he said. They were crazy about baseball and they wanted to be 100 percent Americans. Jackie Pollock wanted painting to be a normal manly aspiration, same as baseball, and the Huffer felt similarly about violinism, but clearly America expected artists to be way out in left field, so I grew up around people who practiced eccentricity as a professional obligation. Huffer couldn't wear a crewcut and play violin, he had to have wild cyclone hair, and Pollock couldn't attend church suppers, he had to be dissolute and smell bad.

"I loved growing up among geniuses. I walked down the street with Balanchine once and I jumped over a mud puddle and he said, 'Do that again' and he made me do it over and over, as he studied it and sketched it on a pad, and months later I saw it in *Les Sylphides*. Bernstein heard me whistling and wrote it down and made it into 'I Feel Pretty' in *West Side Story*. There was brilliance everywhere you looked and it made me long for the ordinary and that's how I fell in love with you. I never knew a Minnesotan before I met you. You loved vanilla shakes and you didn't go to a movie and rip it to shreds afterward. You had nice hair. You were a good listener. You didn't mind that I beat you at chess. Do you remember that?"

I did indeed. We played on a bench in Central Park around 98th Street and a bagpiper was walking around and keening and two ballet dancers were stretching and Giselle took two pawns and then a bishop and a little boy stopped and looked and said, "She's got you, mister," and two moves later it was checkmate. We went for a walk along 103rd and she pointed out the building where George and Ira Gershwin lived and she sang, *'S wonderful. 'S marvelous, that you should care for me* and I sang back to her, *You've made my life so glamorous, you can't blame me for feeling amorous.* And so we got the consensual part out of the way early and went back to 102nd and became lovers. We lay in bed and I whispered, "Being naked and having you in my arms are the start of a new life." She said, "I think it should be '*is* the start of a new life,' even with two gerunds as subject, especially since the *having* and the *being* are one joy."

"I never knew a woman who talked about gerunds while making love," I said.

"You never knew a woman *before* who talked about gerunds while making love," she replied.

"That too."

I had failed twice at marriage, failed badly—each time, a big overture and then no more songs, just aimless dialogue to pass the time and long silences waiting for a shoe to drop—and she had had various boyfriends to occupy her time and go to movies with and then came that Great Shining Lunch when we discovered that we have a lifetime of things to say to each other. Which so far turns out to be true.

11

CREAM OF HAPPINESS

Dorothy came by the cabin to return the copy of the *Times* I'd left at the café. I told her I was done reading it. "Well, how was I to know?" she said. She said she'd gotten a phenomenal offer to buy the café that morning. "How much?" I asked. She said, "Six figures." "High six or low six?" I asked. "Low medium," she said. She had turned it down and now she needed to know if she was crazy. I told her she was. She said, "The town needs this café. La Plaza Populo is all very nice but twenty-three bucks for a plate of spaghetti? Really?—and Sunny Gardens is so religious about vegetarianism, the clientele knows that everyone at the tables around them feels the same way about most things and it's like being in a club for people named Joe Smith. But at the Chatterbox, there is no like-minded membership requirement. There is more—What's the word I'm trying to think of?"

"Inclusivity," I said. "Diversity."

"Thank you. I'm all in favor of vegans and designer spaghetti and if somebody starts a Tibetan barbecue or a Finnish fish restaurant, more power to them, but I'm keeping my place open as an outpost of democracy. Come to the Chatterbox and meet people of many flavors, including some you disapprove of. Fishermen or fashion models or fascists, they're all welcome."

I asked her who made the big cash offer.

"You're not going to believe this," she said. "A family who came through town last winter. Pulled up in front of the café in a black BMW SUV and a man and woman got out and a teenage boy who was not happy to be seen with them and the man was furious with his son and hissing at him and the woman was aware that people were staring at them—for one thing, they were terribly overdressed, like *Vogue* models, not a wrinkle on them, and they wafted delicate odors of deodorants not available to the general public and here they were in a family fight, the boy was using the roughest language, the F-word was flying—the father said to him, 'One more word and I'll choke you to death with my bare hands here and now'—and the mother was embarrassed and trying to smile and shrug—and I led them to a far corner table and they quieted down a little and looked at the menu and I brought them each a bowl of my grandma's potato soup. I don't know if you ever had it, we seldom serve it because there is no recipe, it's just potato and onion and milk and corn meal and anything else you have around. Poverty soup. She said it was the soup that got them through the Depression. And the moment those three put a spoonful in their mouths, homicide was gone from their hearts, peace was restored. The father spoke in a friendly voice to his son, the mother put her hand on her husband's arm, they even laughed once or twice. They each had an entrée—I forget what—and then they ordered a cup of potato soup for dessert, and when they finished it, they were happy. The mother asked me for the recipe and I said, 'There is none, you have to reinvent it every time, it's all leftovers.' And the man said, 'If you ever want to sell your café, let me know and I'll buy it so long as it includes rights to the soup.' And he gave me a business card and he called me yesterday and made me an offer. And I'm still considering it, sort of."

"So it's the soup that he wants to buy?" I said. "Why not whip up a batch of it and pay a laboratory to come up with a recipe and sell him the Cream of Happiness soup and make yourself rich?"

And she told me pretty much what I expected her to say, that she'd given up making it because it never tasted quite right. She remembered how her grandma's soup tasted and sometimes her soup came close to the mark but it never was the same. She'd made a batch now and then that other people thought was good but she didn't. The artist lost faith in the art. "Sometimes it was too creamy, other times it was too potatoey, and eventually I gave up on it. The plain truth is, I lack the motivation. I'm not unhappy enough. You've got to get pretty low to be uplifted by potatoes. And I'm not ready to sell the joint. Speaking of which—did I ever tell you where I got the money to buy the café?"

She had told me numerous times but I shook my head. A person has a right to tell their story and if you tried to bar everything you'd heard a dozen times before, what would be left? Solomon said there is nothing new under the sun but did that mean he was tired of life and looking for a new solar system? Not at all. People who think baseball is boring then go out on a lake and look at the water with a fishing line hanging in it: does this make any sense whatever? You play a recording of that Chopin étude you love so well and do you wish the pianist would add his own variations or maybe toss in a German drinking song or stop and share a reminiscence of his childhood? No, you do not, you want Chopin. A man reaches over to his wife and accidentally puts his hand in a place that makes her sigh in an interesting way and though she pretends to be coy and says, "I was just about to go to sleep," she goes along with him and soon they are exposed to each other and making love and do they bother to invent some new ingenious techniques such as bringing an inflatable swimming pool into bed and a hairdryer to blow bubbles and spread peanut butter on each other and maybe insert bratwursts willy-nilly? No, they go about making love in a manner that has served them well for decades and it is even more thrilling now than ever, repetition has not dimmed its luster, because what's important is what's in their hearts, not what they're doing with their hands. And when her pleasure is suddenly unbearable and she lets out a cry and pushes him away while also embracing him closely, it is a very familiar conclusion. But now I forget what my point was. What were we talking about?

Dorothy said, "It was with money I got from a dying man. I was in Minneapolis, I was a cleaning lady in the Foshay Tower and I got tired of cranky lawyers demanding this and that and one day a big-shot lawyer told me his office smelled musty, which it didn't, and he insisted I clean it all over again, and I told him to shove it up his ass, and he complained to the Foshays and Wilma Foshay hired me to look after her dad who was fading fast, so I did that. I tried to make him happy. Why should a person waste his last days on earth feeling miserable? Grief is for the survivors, not the dying one. So I sang him songs from *Music Man* and I did a striptease to "O What A Beautiful Morning" from *Oklahoma* and that opened his eyes—I went all out for that man—and he left me $70,000 in his will and meanwhile Jack of Jack's Café was looking to retire. He had inhaled so much grease that whenever he coughed, you could smell hamburgers. I put the money on the counter and two days later the *Chatterbox Café* sign went up. 'Chatterbox' was my nickname in grade school. I did the usual—pot roast, burgers, fried chicken, tuna casserole, fish sticks, Spanish rice—and added some of my mother's dishes—cauliflower bacon gumbo, Perfection salad, Hawaiian chicken curry, Shrimp Wiggle, BLT with green tomatoes, pork medallions with cranberry glaze, grilled walleye in tortilla shells, a pickle sandwich— well, you know the menu—the Minneapolis paper said we were the last café in Minnesota to serve sloppy joes, a gravy sandwich that holds fond memories for some people, so why not? I wanted to run a nice café, not a hash house, and that's why I put that verse on the window by the front door. *Glory to God in the highest, and peace to his people on earth. Let us delight in his will and walk in his ways. Enter his gates with thanksgiving; go into his courts with praise.* People thought maybe it meant I was Baptist. No way. But I hated dirty talk. I'd heard enough for a lifetime. So I put up the verses and we seldom had a problem with bad language. Anyway, I'm going to turn down the most money I've ever seen in my life because I think there needs to be someplace in town where everyone is welcome. It's not about money, it's about feeling at home in your own skin, if you ask me."

I said, "You got a six-figure offer for the Chatterbox Café in American dollars, right? Not Italian lire or Mexican pesos?"

She said, "This is my hometown, I'm happy here. I like the new-comers, Sam and Alyssa and Prairie and Rob McCarter and Mr. Trott.

I know you disapprove of them because you're set in your ways, but these are good kids. None of them is adrift. They want meaningful work, careers with a purpose, working in a collaborative and empowered environment. So they aren't big fans of yours—you were a big deal when your book came out in 1985 but now it's thirty-six years later and the world moves on. Get over it."

I had never heard Dorothy say the word "empowered" before. I pointed this out to her.

She said, "You come from the narcissistic hippie generation and these kids are entrepreneurs. They're passionate about work, they want it to mean something. They think they can be whatever they want to be. They're in no rush to get married and make babies. They want to enjoy their freedom. Rather than own stuff, they want to travel around, learn about the world—and they have time to do it because they're smart about digital stuff and they can pull down big bucks for less work. Maybe they spend too much time on Twitter and Instagram, maybe they overthink their every move, but I like them. They're outgoing, interesting, they like to be around other people. They're not loners like you."

Much as she liked them, Dorothy was strict—no cellphone usage in her café, no texting, no glancing at email. If Darlene or any other waitress saw a phone in use, the offender got a tap on the shoulder and an eye-roll. Dorothy said, "If you go out to lunch, be with the people you're with, don't be open worldwide for business."

I was at the Chatterbox for lunch that day and sat at a table that hadn't been cleared and a sheet of paper lay beside the plate. Written in a small, neat hand: *Every morning I wake up and lie very still being mindful of myself, reminding me that I am loved by myself and so I put on my running clothes and go out and do my three miles. I believe that if I skip the run, I will burn in hell. A three-mile run makes me feel worthy. So I do it even if I'm feverish and nauseated. Discipline and Execution are my dependable strengths, I am weak on Empathy. I do not do Regret. I never cared for poetry because it lacks accountability. Poets always blame someone else. I can't live like that.*

It wasn't signed and I set it aside and then a hand reached over my shoulder and snatched it up. It was Alyssa's partner, Prairie. "Find something interesting to read?" she said.

"Sorry," I said. "I was looking for a signature so I could return it."

"Sure you were. Ha." She smirked. I was willing to give my opinion of her writing, but she didn't ask for it so I didn't. I frankly think lack of regret is inhuman. It makes me think of the Nazis, not that she'd know who they were.

Like Prairie, Alyssa was a mover and a shaker. The millennial entrepreneurs had started their own Chamber of Commerce, Moving Forward Together, but it moved too slowly for her, and she organized a women's task force, Women's Enterprise Committee for Affirmative Nurture (WECAN), which set out to turn the town upside down. They brought up the issue of loitering with the town council one day, an issue that never had been an issue before, and of course everyone knew it was aimed at the three remaining Norwegian bachelor farmers and the bench by the bank where they liked to perch, and their habit of spitting and also their unique manner of blowing their noses, using the so-called "farmer honk," pressing one nostril tight with a finger and snorting snot out the other. All of us who'd grown up in Lake Wobegon were familiar with the honk, though of course we'd never do it barehanded, we'd use hankies, but the newcomers felt that Something Must Be Done, a law passed, as a public health measure, though their objection was about aesthetics.

"We run some major businesses here," said Prairie, "and we have investors who come to town, and often we take them to lunch downtown, and you'd be surprised at the number of them who, after a day of planning meetings and marketing conferences, their most vivid memory from the visit was the sight of grizzled old men bending forward on a bench and blowing snot out their noses. I realize that it takes all kinds, and to each to his own, and so forth, but this is disgusting. These people are like animals except they're antisocial. They want no part of anything, but there they are in the middle of everything, making themselves the unavoidable center of attention. What will they do next? Public defecation?" The room was quiet, people visualizing that possibility, and then

Mayor Alice suggested that a simple loitering law would take care of the problem. She happened to have one before her and she read it: *It shall be unlawful for any person to stand, sit, recline, or otherwise occupy space on any street or sidewalk without a clear purpose, e.g., awaiting the arrival of a friend or relative, or an appointment, or the completion of a task, and unlawful to fail to disclose this purpose upon the request of a city police officer. In addition, it shall be unlawful for any person, whether stationary or in motion, to engage in acts of expectoration or nasal clearance upon a city sidewalk.*

Mayor Alice ordered the proposed ordinance to be included in the record and be available for sixty days for public comment. The men in the room stared at the ceiling, avoiding comment. The idea of needing a demonstrable purpose in order to legally occupy public space struck them as tyranny, for married men as well as old bachelors. Lake Wobegon males are committed to conflict avoidance by evacuating the premises and finding something elsewhere to occupy them, which may have no reasonable purpose, such as photography, general hanging out, or fishing. The expense of fishing—boat, gas, license, gear—is such that the cost per pound of the bass and walleyes is more than what you'd pay for premium pompano, but it offers a safe getaway at moments of conflict. Car repair is another: if a man crawls under a car to examine its undercarriage and perhaps thump or tap or tinker with it, no woman is going to crawl under there to supervise him. Of course a man can lock himself in a bathroom and wait for the shouting to die down, but it's best to get out of the house, and an anti-loitering law would give her a chance to have you arrested. No fair.

Women win arguments, but men win standoffs. Play for a tie. This is the thinking of men in Lake Wobegon. And make an issue of unimportant things so you can concede and win points, then fight seriously for the important stuff. Women decorate the house and raise the kids and have the right to inflict good nutrition. Men grill the meat and have a voice in American foreign policy.

The anti-loitering law sat in the town council minutes and nobody mentioned it ever again after Pastor Liz said she felt the law might be used to prohibit outdoor wedding receptions. And WECAN had more important things in mind. They asked the town council to cancel the noon and 5 p.m. siren, which, "while it was intended simply to indicate time, it truly is an alarm and creates an atmosphere of anxiety and serves no reasonable purpose. If people need an alarm at those hours, they can set one on their phones." Mayor Alice took the idea under advisement. The noon and 5 p.m. siren was a regular feature of life to us who had grown up here, but of course we could do without it, so the volunteer fire department turned off the timer and that was that. The MFT also protested the sign on the highway south of town:

LAKE WOBEGON
Where the women are strong,
The men are good-looking,
And all the children are above average.

They considered it "stereotyping" and the line about women "patronizing," the line about men "sexually aggressive," and the line about children was "causing undue anxiety." The sign had been up so long, nobody could remember whose idea it had been: it was just a sign. Nobody took it as a guide to life. But WECAN got up a petition to remove it as "abusive speech on public property." Alyssa said, "The sign is terribly out of touch with our values and who we aspire to be. How about if the women are independent, the men are supportive, and the children are respectful of differences?"

Sam suggested "Lake Wobegon: Town On The Go." He also said the town needed an arts center. He wanted to bring great art to rural Minnesota, opera and orchestras and theater and an art gallery. "The sooner kids are exposed to the classics, the better. You grow up with great art and it just seems natural as can be. And it's for everyone, not just privileged people. You hear Beethoven when you're little and you can feel the beauty of it, you don't need to have it explained. I want my kids to have the chance to fall in love with beautiful things." He was serious. What was interesting to me was the fact that, as he talked about art and beauty, I noticed that his barn doors were unzipped. One advantage of a cold climate is that you have a 50 percent chance of knowing if your fly is open, but unfortunately it was May. Knowing your fly is open may not seem crucial, but I would rather know than not know. This may be irrelevant in the matter of creativity but not entirely. Unzipped is not the same as brilliance, no matter what your children may believe.

12

SISTERHOOD

Pastor Liz loathed her sister Alyssa, though of course she wasn't free to say so. I discovered the depth of loathing when I said, not thinking, "It must be nice for you, having your sister in town and see her doing so well," and she said, "My sister and I haven't exchanged a civil word in months and the last time we spoke, she told me I needed to lose weight and the vestments make me look like a Russian empress and not in a good way. 'What do you have against makeup? Who is doing your hair?' she says. She does it, hoping to piss me off, meanwhile she's donated eighty-five grand to the Altar Guild so they're fawning all over her and invited her to speak at their May luncheon and she talked about Believing In Yourself, which is pretty much opposite to what Christ taught, and they gushed about it and how confident she is and they want her to give a guest sermon during Lent. That woman never shows her face in church but she's got a small retinue of devoted fans like Britta Ingqvist and Donna Andresen and Tibby Marklund who follow her around like dogs on a leash."

"Tibby Marklund the organist?" I said.

"Right. She's been led to believe we might be getting a half-million bucks for a new pipe organ. No, my sister can smell vulnerability. She's got them thinking about a Women's Self-Care Caribbean cruise in March. And her one and only motive is to irk me so I make an issue of it and get her fan club upset with me. While I was in seminary, she was at a Lutheran ashram in Bolinas run by a guru from Fargo, the Rama Lama Rasmussen, which met in a large yurt, and the Sunday service was on Saturday night and was celebratory and clothing-optional and there were pictures of multiheaded deities. She earned her living as a therapist: she maintained that dyslexic children could be helped by having them read aloud to cats. Anyway, don't tell me about my sister. I know her and she's a monster. Listen to this." Liz pulled a slip of paper out of her pocket. "This is from her Twitter page: *Be true to yourself. Don't be afraid to irritate people. Don't try to 'Fit In'—Fitting in is like trying to wear someone else's clothes. So you're odd. Good for you. Embrace your oddity. Don't let the herd drive you. Head for the hills.* There's a lot more."

"I'm sorry I mentioned her," I said.

"I'm sorry I talked your head off. How is Giselle?"

"Giselle is hiking the Adirondacks with her hiking cousins Russ and Kerry and having the time of her life and she is giving me the freedom to not march with her but to renew old acquaintances here at home."

"Do you have cousins left around here?"

"Benny, Janice, Susie, Sharon, Wayne, and Randy."

"I don't believe I know any of them."

"They're good at that," I said. "Invisibility is their specialty. They're gardeners and they repair things and clean up. No need for publicity, there's already enough work to do."

"I wish my sister were like your cousins. I wish she weren't such an asshole."

"I don't think I ever heard a Lutheran pastor use that word," I said.

"Well, I try to save it for special occasions. In her case, it fits. I think she came here for the express purpose of driving me berserk. My sermons are online on Zoom and she critiques them. Facial expressions, body language, she says I look so glum. I want to wring her goddamn neck."

WECAN met at the town library and I slipped in the door and sat in back and listened. We Keillors are patient and can sit quietly for long periods and be unobtrusive and thereby witness the world working freely and not responding to us, a useful talent for a writer. So I sat in the back of the Women's Enterprise Committee for Affirmative Nurture and listened to Alyssa give a speech on authentic relationships. She said, "I believe in making a habit of self-reinforcement, making every day my best day, making Monday my day for charging and Saturday for self-care. It's what makes me feel I belong in my own skin. It's not easy. There are friendships that need to be tossed out the back door. Bad habits, like self-doubt. Kiss them goodbye. We need to own our truth, explore new terrain, and look for meaningful horizons while leaning into our own authentic experience, staying grounded but also finding our own space to innovate more creatively and ditch that whole old/young dichotomy— age is a metaphor, not a definition—and our habit of othering those who aren't keyed into our vocabulary of values."

I'd never heard anyone speak in sentences like those. My people spoke in single sentences like "If ifs and ands were pots and pans, there'd be no trade for tinkers." That stood by itself. And so did "Listen too hard and you'll always hear something bad about yourself. To a poor sailor, all wind is against him. Do your best and leave the rest. It's a foolish goose who goes to the fox's church." On the other hand, "In silk and scarlet walks many a harlot."

It was odd to hear her talk about owning your truth, having overheard her now and then with Mallory at her side saying, "That seethrough blouse lets people see the word Onward tattooed on your back and also your bra straps. They are very visible."

"Should I not wear a bra then?"

"Honey, you've got nipples the size of walnuts. I can see them half a block away. You need a padded bra. But that skirt is too tight and its riding up into your crack."

I heard Mallory at a distance, reminding her not to pick her teeth, not to say the F-word in the vicinity of older people, not to adjust her crotch. Alyssa was paying the woman a fancy price to correct flaws that should've been dealt with in junior high school, which seemed to me to show the problem with truth-owning and leaning into your own experience, you don't notice that people are staring at you and laughing.

She gave a TED Talk from the Aspen Institute about self-care— Dorothy sent me the link, and it was more of the same: "We're on a journey and as it takes shape, we set our course, recognize challenges, envision the transformations of mindset that need to be realized and the process of accessing insights and avoiding platforms of negativity and the need to create your brand, find your lane, and align yourself against the flow."

Pastor Liz saw the same talk and she hated it, the idea of avoiding negativity and getting out of negative space, and the next Sunday she gave a stink bomb of a sermon titled "God, I'm Hungry" and as she read it Sunday morning, she could see how dumb it was, and she cut out half of it, and afterward, three people came up and said it was the best sermon they'd ever heard her give. Liz was depressed. She'd seen her picture in the church directory and she looked as if she was heavily medicated and should not be allowed to operate a motor vehicle. Alyssa was in church that morning, looking glamorous, surrounded by admirers. Smiling, a dark blue blouse, no sign of walnuts. She told Liz it was an awesome sermon and asked for a copy of it.

13

SYTTENDE MAI

It was a fine month I spent, visiting with Arlene. You go home for a funeral and stick around and wind up learning more than you bargained for. I made a career out of talking on the radio and hardly remember what I said but I'll remember the weeks with Arlene as she lay dying. She said, "I've left instructions for no eulogy at my funeral. If people don't have any clear memory of me, why should someone try to convince them I was a good person. I'm not advertising myself for employment. That was a nice eulogy you gave for my brother but if you should outlive me—and I emphasize the IF—remember: no eulogy and if they call it a Celebration of Life, I'm going to climb out of the coffin and tell them to go fuck themselves."

"I never heard you say that word before," I said.

"Sorry to keep you waiting. I learned it from my granddaughter. No, I hate funerals. People die who nobody bothered to visit because they were boring and they die and suddenly become beloved and four hundred come to the funeral to hear how wonderful they were. It's non-sense. I had a wonderful life. Thank you very much. Goodbye and good luck. That's my eulogy."

She said, "What's more, I never fit in here. Just like my dad didn't. He loved to sing and he sounded horrendous but he didn't realize it, all he knew was that people in front of him in church winced when he sang and whispered among each other so he stifled himself, but he had a hunting shack in the woods where he went to raise his voice in song. I went for a walk once and heard moaning like someone dying of trichinosis and peeked through a crack in the boards and it was Daddy with pure pleasure in his face, singing,

Keep us, Lord, O keep us cleaving
To Thyself, and still believing,
Till the hour of our receiving
Promised joys with Thee.
Then we shall be where we would be,
Then we shall be what we should be,
Things that are not now, nor could be,
Soon shall be our own.

"It was agonizing to hear but it was beautiful to see the joy in his eyes. My dad. Musically, he was from some other planet. Same with me: I'm a pessimist. All my life I've imagined catastrophe, it's just how my mind works. I go for a walk and imagine a sniper shooting at me or a car pulling up and a masked man hauling me into the back seat and taking me to a cabin and tying me up and holding me for ransom. I've had an easy fortunate life and I keep imagining a meteor smashing into the house and killing us all or Clarence leaving me for a truckstop waitress or my grandchildren dying in a plane crash and it never happened."

She asked if I remembered the Whippets' game against the Uppsala Uftas when Ernie threw a beanball at Hammerhead Hansen's head, and of course I did. It was the top of the ninth, two out, bases loaded, Hammerhead came to bat, and Ernie was mad at himself and he threw a hard one, high and inside, but he was a knuckleball pitcher and when you throw the knuckleball hard, the ball doesn't hop and flutter, it's just a rather slow fastball, and Hammerhead swung and hit a long high fly ball deep to left center and Ronnie in center and Fred in left both went hard for it and you could see what was going to happen, two men dashing straight at each other, looking up into the sky, and the crack of their heads was audible in the bleachers, and down they went, both unconscious, and when the umpire got out there, he found the ball in Ronnie's right pants pocket, and called the batter out. The Uftas said he'd trapped the ball, and Ronnie wasn't saying anything, he thought it was Wednesday, not Sunday.

"But what's your point?" I said.

"You told about the miraculous catch and the Whippets' fans happiness that Hammerhead had flied out, but you never said that the Whippets were behind 16-3 at the time and that they lost the ball game 16-4. You always took a sunny view of life on the basis of incomplete evidence. And now? I think you were right. For me, the worst is here and I'm sort of enjoying it. Isn't that perverse? I've dreaded death and now as it approaches I'm enjoying each day like never before."

"No," I said. "We just see things differently. And as a result of the collision, Fred remembered a passage from 1ˢᵗ Corinthians about faith, hope, and love that he'd learned as a child, and Ronnie remembered the words to 'Today I Started Loving You Again,' which he used to know and he went home and sang it to Sandy, so some good came of the whole thing."

"Anyway," she said. "I must say I'm curious about death. My mother believed she would go to be with the Lord but if so, will our minds comprehend this? Will we keep our identity or will we join clouds of brilliant molecules drifting in the stars? I don't know. What do you think?"

I said, "My dad was a believer and he had no doubt about a life after death. We asked him where he wanted to be buried and he said, 'Surprise me.'"

"You are terrible," she said. "I don't believe in a hell. I think God put that out there as a way to inhibit the evil but He also terrified the righteous, and the wicked went ahead without much hesitation so far as I can see. It's like the man who lay dying and he said to his wife, 'Honey, before I'm gone, there's something I need to confess to you,' and she said, 'I already know all about it. That's why I poisoned you.'"

The joke made her thirsty so I got her a glass of ice water. She drank it slowly. She said, "Clarence thinks it's sick to joke about this but I think it's funny. I told him the other day about the woman dying who asked her husband if he thought he might marry again after she was gone. He said, 'Maybe.' She said, 'Would she live in this house and sleep in our bed?' He said, 'I don't know. Maybe.' She said, 'Would she wear my clothes?' He said, 'No, she's a size two.' Clarence didn't think it was funny. I pray for him. I prayed for you all those years you were living the wild life and getting your name in the papers. I prayed for you every night."

I asked her, "What wild life are you talking about? All I remember is walking fast in airport terminals."

"You moved six times in eight years. You had girlfriends. You went to Rome with a young woman and everybody was talking about it. You were talking on the radio about our town and we had no idea where you were. You were singing gospel songs while sleeping around. Luckily you married a forgiving woman."

"Whatever you were worried about, it's all over. I'm done with the fast life. It was a simple problem of too much too soon and a recurrence of adolescence. I'm okay now."

"I know and thank God. My prayers were answered."

Norwegian Constitution Day, *Syttende Mai,* arrived right on time on May 17th and people were glad to see it, a happy holiday like the Fourth of July used to be before it was taken over by motorcycle gangs and Trumpers and NRA people and QAnon and Oath Keepers and all manner of riffraff. It happened in 2017, word went around on the internet that Lake Wobegon was where the big rally would take place and there were rumors that Trump himself would fly in, and about ten thousand people descended on the town and pitched tents around the lake and parked their campers wherever there was an empty field, and monster bikes roared around and drunken parties raged all night and some motley bands of aging men with thin ponytails played angry rock 'n' roll at the ballpark and the citizens locked their doors and stayed home and guarded their daughters and the same thing happened in 2018 and 2019 and so May 17th took the place of the Fourth as a friendly celebration where a crowd gathers to sing the five songs that everyone knows by heart, *America, A the B, The SSB, GBA, The BHR,* and your heart is lifted by good Lutheran singing and even the agnostics get carried away. The sun shines, the honeybees buzz, you can hear the corn growing, the radishes come in. Rose bushes are in full bloom and a few of those make even a shabby little house look classy. A truckload of sweet corn is hauled in from Missouri. In a few weeks, strawberries will come in, pale red, and you pop one in your mouth straight off the plant and it makes you feel beautiful. Briefly. The last of the rhubarb is being picked to make strawberry-rhubarb pie, a great innovation, the marriage of tenderness and persistence, which is what makes a marriage work, obstinate kindness, and marriage, as we know, is the true test of character. I was allowed to retake the test until I got it right, for which I'm grateful.

For years the Fourth of July (and Toast 'N Jelly Days and *Syttende Mai*) were run by Clint Bunsen and run capably, no snafus, but he stepped down this year. He was a peacemaker, good at nudging people toward consensus; it was Clint who came up with the idea of the Living Flag—people united in a common purpose. Most Wobegonians dreaded having to jam together cheek to jowl in their red, white, and blue hats, and Clint loved it. Unity was his passion. He loved meetings and went to them the way other men go fishing. But he was resented by some people who've had car problems and called him to come rescue them with the wrecker and he got there and opened the hood and reached in and turned something, and the car started. They had fussed with it for thirty-five minutes and worked themselves into a fury of frustration and he clicked a switch and solved the problem and they handed him a ten for his trouble and he said, "No, no, no. My pleasure," thereby dramatizing his superiority. Clint's motto was "Make it work." He says it often, or used to: "Let's make it work." "We can make it work." Irene told me she planned to put it on his tombstone.

The millennials were pleased when the celebration moved to May 17 and the patriotism was toned down though the Living Flag was maintained though it shrank as old people died off and the younger ones found other things to do, but there still was a nice parade with an accordion band playing *Stars and Stripes Forever* as well as *Ja, vi elsker dette landet* and the Hermansons who had always dressed up as George and Martha now came as King Haakon and Queen Maud and to satisfy the millennials' need for diversity, Crown Prince Olav was Mexican and the parade marshal was Barry Halper whose dad had a dairy farm and who moved to L.A. and went into comedy and hosted *The Barry Halper Show* on CBS for fifteen years, a handsome man in a white suit standing up in a white convertible, waving, and he shouted my name, loud, very loud, and instantly I could feel my stock rise. The Farmers Union float with the 4-H'ers on it, singing:

> *We raise the crops that make your kids grow tall.*
> *Plant in the spring and harvest in the fall.*
> *Work late at night and rise at early morn.*
> *We plant the beans, we plant the corn.*

An ocarina band from Our Lady of Perpetual Responsibility played "Dona Nobis Pacem" followed by Miss Liberty in her greenish gown, holding up her torch and also a Norwegian flag. A few years ago she stepped on the hem of her gown and walked up it and tore it from her body and there she was in a bright red bra and panties and people remember how she simply picked up the gown and put it over her arm and kept marching, torch held high, five-pointed star on her head, unashamed, just as a French woman would do. Except she was Marilyn Pedersen, a good Norwegian, a woman of tremendous poise, marching on, torch high, unperplexed. I looked for Barry after and he was getting into a limo. "Liked your show," he said. "Gotta dash. Let's catch up sometime." And off he went, the man who gave me my first job in radio, my godfather and patron, the first guy who thought I had some style and pizzazz. I got a glimpse and then (*poof!*) he was gone.

It turned into a nice street party, with Ralph's crew roasting bratwursts and herring rings and Wally's old beer wagon operated by his nephew Neil and the 4-H'ers' Kool-Aid stand and Mayor Alice, after downing a glass of aquavit, stood up on the bed of a pickup and gave an impromptu speech and said that it's not a perfect country, not even close, not Norway or America, but it's come a long way and it was surely improved by the immigrants who came, Norwegians or Germans or Swedes, and most of us love it and it'd be a shame if we didn't stand shoulder to shoulder and sing the songs we've known since we were little, and she blew on a pitch pipe and sang "My country, 'tis of thee" and the crowd joined in and then the spacious skies and amber waves of grain and "God Bless America" and then the big one went up like a rocket, the sopranos full-voice on "the land of the free" and everybody cheered and it was all good and if you didn't like it, well, let the rest of us enjoy it and you can find some other malcontents and complain among yourselves.

For *Syttende Mai,* Pastor Liz gave a speech at the cemetery about the early Norwegian immigrants, all about how they came to America for their children's sake, sacrificing the pleasures of today to secure the promise of the future, and I couldn't help noticing that she stood on the grave of my classmate Orvie Asmussen who drowned a week before our graduation, diving off a high bridge into the Mississippi in order to impress our homecoming queen Marilyn Ingqvist. He was so excited about diving for her, he forgot that he could not swim, and he dove headfirst and never came up. She married Bill Paulson and she has never set foot in a body of water since and is fearful of flying. Orvie gave his life for love, a noble idea, but what he gave us is the fear of water. Liz talked about bravery and selflessness but we could all see where she was standing and so we thought about boneheaded stupidity.

To encourage attendance at *Syttende Mai,* Lundberg Mortuary held a raffle: first prize, a free funeral. An urn filled up with ticket stubs and Lundberg drew the winner and the winner was—Arlene Bunsen. "I tell you," Dorothy said, "If you put that in a book, nobody'd believe it."

Arlene was properly amazed and grateful. "I didn't even know I was entered!" she said. She told Clarence, "Now that we saved all that money on my funeral, you can buy that king-size bed we've been wanting all these years instead of our old double bed. But maybe after I'm gone, a big bed would feel strange." She patted his arm. "So find a good hefty woman and marry her."

I wrote in my journal that day: *A is luminous. Honestly, she gives off light. Clarence says, "It's so good of you to visit." No, it's not, I come for selfish reasons, to be blessed. Dying is so degrading—you need someone else to wipe your butt and floss your teeth—but Jesus teaches us to accept degradation in order to find freedom. The opposite of how we thought the game works. But I don't tell A this. She doesn't want Jesus talk, she can do that for herself. She is busy enjoying this world in the time she has left, lucky to have her granddaughter Annabelle living under her roof, Annabelle who was pulled out of school because it was holding her back, an ambitious reader who at the age of nine is done with children's books and making her way into Dickens. He believed in the contagion of good humor and kindness even in the midst of sickness and suffering, which I, the English major, felt was sentimentalism, the idea of laughter in the hovels of the poor, but Dickens knew it firsthand and so does Annabelle. Laughter is not a privilege, it's a basic element of humanity. And she loves his language. Like Dickens, she believes love is stronger than evil. And her grandma adores this child, curly black hair, brilliant smile, lying on the floor with her legs up on the sofa, book in hand. Arlene said to me, "I used to think that intelligence and happiness were somehow contrary, and I look at Annabelle and see that they go together hand in glove. She is my best gift to the world. My life seems worthwhile now that I know it leads to Annabelle."*

She was in a joyful mood that month. Not a word about illness and regret. She had watched the TED Talk by Alyssa and when you're dying, you needn't mince words. "The woman has shit for brains," she said. "*Stay in the moment.* She kept repeating it. Don't let your mind drift toward the past. *Stay in the moment.* But memory is one thing that distinguishes us from the moth and the butterfly. We have stories. Speaking of which, why do you write novels? Boredom? Prestige? You were hoping to get laid by an English major?"

I started writing novels when I gave up golf. It was the summer of 1982, I was 40. It was the ninth hole, I hit a perfect 5-iron shot out of the rough that rolled onto the green, and my partners clapped, it was my best shot of the day, the only really good shot—I was at 56 after eight holes—and it struck me, *I don't enjoy being with these guys and I'm no good at this game so why am I wasting my life?* I got the putt for a par 3 and said, "Sorry, I'm late for a meeting, thanks for putting up with me." I left my clubs in the clubhouse and took a cab home and made a list of other things to give up—all events at which someone stands behind a lectern and reads their own work, all choral concerts, any performance by a singer-songwriter who is not a close personal friend, all political fundraisers—and suddenly my life expanded. I started writing a novel and the first chapter was horrible but it got better by the third chapter so I threw away the first two chapters and started with the third, and it wasn't bad. It was actually worthwhile.

"I've written ten novels and I don't remember much of what's in them because they were all flawed and I knew it, whereas I remember some of the limericks I wrote because, with the limerick, perfection is possible. Like this one—

A liberal lady of D.C.
By day was tasteful and p.c.
And then after ten
She went out with men
Who were rednecks, vulgar and greasy.
"When it comes to the masculine specie,"
She said, "Believe me, I'm easy,
But liberal guys
Tend to theologize
And I am not St. Clare of Assisi."

Arlene said, "I liked your novel *Love Me* because it was about you at *The New Yorker* but the ones about our town bothered me because you left out so much great stuff, the adultery, the drunkenness, the pissed-off neighbors. You made us into *Rebecca of Sunnybrook Farm.*"

"I did not!"

"You absolutely did."

"What did I leave out?"

She sat up in bed. "You made it all happy and humorous. Why

179

deny your readers the real dirt? Why tippy-toe around, not look in the windows?"

"It was a performance. They call it comedy. Other people market despair and I'm not in that line of work."

She leaned toward me. "So if you write about me are you going to make pancreatic cancer into an acidy stomach and give me a bicarbonate of soda and we go off to the movies?"

"Of course not."

"I remember one thing you wrote that made sense. Maybe it was in *Love Me*. Maybe not."

"Only one thing?" I said.

"One that I remember right now. You said, 'Where you're from doesn't exist anymore and maybe never did and where you're heading for isn't there either and where you are is only good if you feel it's only temporary.'"

I told her that I never said that. She said I did. We went back and forth. She said it again.

"It's too big and mysterious for me to have said it," I said. "I don't think in triads. It's too Catholic."

"I'm so sorry. I really admired you for having written that."

So I quoted her some things I had written. I remembered four.

Some luck lies in not getting what you thought you wanted but getting what you have, which once you have got it you may be smart enough to realize is what you would have wanted had you only known.

Intelligence is like four-wheel drive. It allows a person to get into trouble in remote places where help is likely to arrive too late.

Good judgment comes from experience, and a lot of valuable experience comes from exercising bad judgment.

Too many people spend money they don't have—to buy things they don't want to impress people they don't like.

She smiled and shook her head. She said she liked the other one better, the one that wasn't mine.

And then her granddaughter Annabelle came in who wanted to read to me from Dickens, his account of his 1867 tour of America, when he visited

Minnesota and came to our town. A Dickens scholar from Newcastle College had come to Lake Wobegon on a Fulbright to research the author's travels as detailed in recently discovered diaries stored in an old laundry bag full of dirty shirts that the great man's disgruntled groom, miffed at poor pay, had stolen, meaning to sell them as souvenirs, but left them at the laundry where they wound up with a widow washerwoman who let her landlord have them, her rent being in arrears, but the diary was donated to Dickens's daughter Dorrit who put it in her chiffonier and simply forgot it, a diary in which Dickens wrote, on 4 April 1868:

Lake Wobegon was a cluster of humble wooden houses, huddled together beside a body of water, in a vast expanse of level ground with few trees, a great blank of earth that summoned the word "uninhabitable," a few birds wheeling here and there as if seeking a way out: and solitude and silence all around, oppressive in their heavy monotony, and I felt no pleasure to look upon it, no solace for the eye.

There was an hotel with a large dim dining-room with tin sconces stuck against the walls, and I seated myself at a table and asked for coffee and some eatables. Nearby sat four men with shaggy beards and enormous eyebrows, staring at me as if they had never seen a gentleman in a hat and waistcoat, and their boots reeked of manure. "A pleasant afternoon to you, good friends," I said and they made no reply.

The matron brought out a pitcher of coffee, which was tolerable, and corn-bread and chicken fixings, which was curious to me, by what poetical construction one might "fix" a chicken, but I made no inquiry. The four loafers nearby had cleaned their plates of a great heap of ham and sausage and various viands, and the one nearest me leaned idly to his left and from the seat of his trousers came a loud bark like that of a watchdog. "Yes, sir," he said. Whereupon his neighbor leaned forward and issued a loud report from his innards, like the chuffing of a horse, and they both said, "Yes, sir."

This tickled Annabelle who'd been in the Chatterbox and observed old men sitting in silence and then, apropos of nothing, come out with a "Yes, sir." She continued:

All around the dining-room, other fellows loitered in rocking-chairs, or lounged on the window-sill, or perched on a rail, who had not anything

to say to each other, other than the low rumbling of gassy eructations. An
odorous cloud hung in the room that reminded me of Liverpool and I stood
up from the table and approached a loafer nearby and inquired as to a water
closet where a gentleman might go to relieve himself.

"Do you need to pupe or tinkle?" he said loudly.

I had never heard the word "tinkle" except from small children. I cupped
my hand to my ear.

He said, "You can tinkle out in the street but to pupe, you will find a
little house out back." And then he emitted a blast of wind in which I clearly
detected the words "Canadian Rockies" and a moment later "Adirondacks,"
two mountain ranges spoken by a man's gas which caused me to laugh and
I commenced to laughing so hard I could not stop and then came the feeling
of warmth running down my left leg and the unmistakable dark stain on
my trousers and he saw it and pointed and whooped for glee and chortled,
and thus the English visitor was set straight, the satirist became the joke.
Laughter is a gift and I was the donor and I left the town better for my
having been there. I boarded the coach, a blanket over my lap, my trousers
tied to the baggage rack and flying in the wind and headed for St. Paul,
determined to write it all down, which now, dear reader, I have done.
Thank you for your attention.

The little girl read this in between bursts of laughter and Arlene was
pleased to hear her read beautifully, every word articulated with feeling.
The girl went off to enjoy her Dickens and Arlene said, "She is the joy
of my life and with Barbara Ann here, I get to see her all day every day,
which is about as much joy as a person can tolerate. I don't want to get
so overjoyed that I start writing an inspirational book or something—
God forbid. But I always wanted someone to call me Grandma and put
her arms around my leg. Duane's kids are so devoted to video. I don't
know that I've ever made eye contact with them. And most of my visitors
are here out of Christian charity, and charity gets tiresome. Not you!
Not talking about you. I appreciate your visits, but the world of a nine-
year-old girl is a magical fairy tale. She's homeschooled and hasn't sat in
a classroom full of critics and rivals so she's not afraid to show enthusiasm. There isn't an ounce of cynicism in her. No cruelty, except when

she mocks her mother, but that's just self-defense. You've never seen such pure love of reading. Nothing escapes her interest. A bird lands on the feeder and she's at the window. The Johnsons' dog comes over and lies in her arms. This girl lives every hour of the day at a high pitch. And I live through her—" Arlene dabbed at her eyes. "This is the happiest summer I can remember. Isn't that remarkable? My last summer and it's a high point of my life.

"But"—Arlene looked toward the dining room where the little girl was busy doing math—"I can't have her here when I die. I don't want to leave that mark on her. So B.A.B. is taking the kids back home in a few weeks." She was stunned at the thought. I got up to go. I put a hand on her shoulder. She gave me a little wave, part dismissal, part gratitude.

14

THE PASSING OF
THE CLASS

Moving Forward Together formed a task force that had a dozen ideas for civic improvements: a first-class fitness center, an up-to-date media center to replace our little domed Carnegie library, a tree-lined boulevard to replace our broad Main Street, and a modern airport to handle small corporate jets, instead of our grass landing strip with the old hangar and wind sock. It was there, in 2008, the TV evangelist Bradley Beemer made an emergency landing in ice fog and crashed into the eighty-foot pine trees that weren't shown on his map, which our local pilots had avoided for years, and he was killed, and his passenger, a young woman named Jasmine whom newspapers referred to as his "assistant" though she told the sheriff she knew him as Mr. Bowman and thought he was in real estate, she survived with slight bruises. The trees were cut down afterward lest some other adulterer attempt an emergency landing and MFT now wanted a 5,200-foot paved strip, with a beacon and PCL (Pilot-Controlled Lighting), and a small terminal with a manager's office and a conference room. A private luxury for the rich to be paid for with public funds: not a noble idea.

They presented their ideas to the town council in a fancy slideshow with handsome architects' renderings, which everyone but the designers knew would never become reality thanks to the expense and also the queer language—"connectivity," "visual resilience," "vernacular," "quality of life" are foreign words and what would you do if three men in furry hats stood up and addressed you in Russian? You'd listen and say, "Thank you," and place the proposal in a circular file, which was what was done. Let the millionaires pay for their own airport. Meeting adjourned.

I went for a walk and my feet carried me to the Chatterbox and I stood looking across the street where Bunsen Motors had been—no sign of it now at all, the showroom was an office of little cubicles where once two brand-new shiny Fords had sat. A plain reminder of the transitory nature of life. Someday the Lincoln Memorial may be a drive-up deli and the Capitol a car wash and Arlington Cemetery a gated neighborhood of mansions selling for $100 million a pop, the monuments all ground up for gravel. I thought of Clarence and how he'd suffered the bullying of his father and how that building had been his prison but he made the best of it, didn't complain, was a cheerful stalwart and one morning he woke up and his wife was in pain and that evening he was a retiree and a few months later there was no evidence of his work at all. I take this personally, having been in radio, which is invisible to begin with. Old carpenters can drive by homes they built, doctors see babies they delivered grow up, but a radio guy has nothing but a handful of air. All your ingenuity is blown away in a light breeze.

And then a car pulled up at the curb, a white Pontiac convertible, top down, a woman at the wheel, a guy beside her, fashionably dressed, city people by the looks of them.

The guy said, "So why are we stopping?"

She said, "I just thought it'd be nice to get out of the car and get some exercise."

"Oh," he said.

She said, "But you don't have to if you don't want to."

He said, "Fine. You want to go for a walk, let's go for a walk and get it over with."

She said, "I don't want you to go for a walk if you don't want to."

He said, "It's okay."

She said, "It just makes me nervous, feeling like I forced you to go for a walk and then you're going to be in a silent rage for the next two hours."

He said, "Well, if you'd rather I didn't come with, that's okay too. I'll sit and wait for you."

She said, "Just do what you want to do. I'll meet you back here in half an hour."

"Okay, whatever you want," he said, and he made his seat recline and then he said, "What's the name of this town again?" She told him.

He said, "This is the town that the guy talked about on the radio, that dumb show that you liked."

"Right," she said.

"Well, go have yourself a big time." He reclined way back. And then she spotted me standing under the Chatterbox awning. "Oh my God," she said. "It's him."

"Who?" he said and glanced at me. "What's your name?" I told him. He said, "My wife is a huge fan of yours. You live here? I thought you lived in New York."

I said that I'd come home for a funeral.

I started to turn away to go into the café but the woman walked over and wanted to take a selfie with me and then she wanted to buy me a cup of coffee. I said, "I've already had my allotment."

She asked me if Father Emil is still alive. I said no, he's in the cemetery. She asked if there are still Norwegian bachelor farmers around. "Three," I said, "but they don't come into town much anymore for fear they might run into each other. They hate each other and nobody knows why because we don't understand Norwegian."

She laughed. She thought it was a joke. Actually, it's not. Norwegian is a soft melodic language and I grew up loving the sound of its vowels and I miss it now. But it's hard to explain this to an outsider.

She asked if it's true that the high school teams are nicknamed the Leonards. I said yes, it's true. She laughed at that too. She asked me where she could find the garden where I threw the rotten tomato that hit my sister as she bent over weeding. I said, "It was next to our house but the land was sold and another house was built on it." I didn't want to stand there answering questions. I said, "If there's anything else you want to know, just ask Grace at the library. Have a nice day." And I walked into the café. Darlene said, "Who's your friend?" I said, "A tourist. What's the special today?" "Pork roast," she said. "Or squash soup." "Give me both," I said. Then I saw the woman heading for the entrance. I slipped into the kitchen and through the pantry, past the freezer. I told Darlene to pack up the lunch to go and I'd be back in fifteen minutes. I went out the back door and down the alley and scooted into Skoglund's lumberyard. I hid behind a pile of two-by-eights from which I could see into the Chatterbox where the woman was studying a menu and glancing down the hallway I'd disappeared into. She was a perfectly nice woman, I'm sure, and I appreciated her interest, but I didn't want to come between her and her husband and, what's more, I'm just not that interesting. I wish I were. I used to try to be, but you get to the age I'm at now, and you don't care to put in the effort. I crouched in the lumberyard until she got in their car and they drove away, and I went back in the café and sat down and ate my lunch.

"Who was your friend?" Darlene said. I said, "Her name is Francine DuBois and we were on a bus in Mexico that was hijacked by a gang and held for a half-million ransom in an abandoned castle and she and I became very close friends in the two months we were in captivity and a year later she found me and said she'd had a baby and claimed it was mine, a girl, which I was sure wasn't true—I'd been very careful, but she's still after me for child support though the girl is thirty-two years old. Supposedly she's writing a book and intends to name me as her father, and you know?—there's not a darned thing I can do about it."

Darlene gave me a long look and said, "You big fat liar. I don't believe a single word you're saying."

"Good," I said. "Then that means my secret is safe."

"Where did you ever learn to lie like that? I thought you grew up here."

"I was a big reader. I hid away in the basement reading novels. Piles of them."

She said she has a grandson who is like that and she means to keep a close eye on him.

15

SUNDAY MASS

It was a quiet week, sunny, in the 70s, big white pillowy clouds drifting overhead like in a child's picture book and green trees, light green from your Crayola box. All along the lakeshore, people were opening up their cabins for the summer, some rebuilding going on. Once there was a Memorial Day parade but all the World War II vets are gone and the Vietnam and Gulf War vets don't care to be paraded, so a few old stalwarts gather for a ceremony at the cemetery and that's it. A kid from the school band played Taps a couple years ago and hit a clinker so horrible he had a laughing fit and fell down on the ground and his mouthpiece came off and he swallowed it and might've choked to death but his girlfriend was there and clapped him hard on the back and he coughed it up.

I own a double plot in the cemetery but Giselle refuses to be buried there with me so I'm thinking I may put up a statue my friend Joe O'Connell the sculptor made for a Unitarian church in Minneapolis. He'd only gotten commissions from Catholic churches, this was his first Protestantt one, and they wanted Adam and Eve, another first for him after a long career of crucifixes and BVMs, and he worked four months on it, granite, life-size, and it was too detailed for them, with pubic hair, nipples, a foreskin, and so he sanded off the pubic hair and circumcised Adam and gave Eve a nipplectomy, but then the couple who'd modeled for the sculpture broke up and she threatened to sue for mental distress if the First Couple remained coupled so Joe sent Adam, apple in his hand, to an orchard in Stillwater and Eve is waiting in Joe's daughter's garage to take her place in the town cemetery, the mother of us all and still a great beauty, my lasting gift to my hometown. There will be a plaque on the base:

Gary Keillor is my name. And America is my nation.
Lake Wobegon is my home. And Christ is my salvation.
When I am lying dead and cold
And all the stories I have told are lost on moldy papers,
Remember me with gaiety by cheering up your neighbors.

One Sunday I went to the Spanish Mass at Our Lady because Arlene asked me to, she wanted me to pray for her granddaughter, and not a casual BTW prayer but an intensive one, that Annabelle would find God in her own way and time, and I went and got fully caught up in it. Our Lady was packed to the rafters, the Lutheran gringos mostly up in the balcony but many of them, Daryl and Marilyn, Clint, Darlene, mingling down below with the weeping Mexican mothers and I spotted Henry and his wife, Carlotta, kneeling at the rail, her arm around him, unloading their burdens on the Lord, and it struck me hard and I knelt beside him and put my hand on his shoulder. He was weeping. I had, of course, no idea why and then I felt my own tears trickling down my face. His brother Father Jorge stood at the altar, bread and chalice upraised, and I was moved by the mystery of it, there being no literal doctrine to guide me. We Brethren were descended from English intellectuals who spoke Greek and read Aramaic and dissented from the Anglican hierarchy of ignorant despots in robes and formed a radical minority based on their own studies, and here, weeping at the Catholic rail for reasons I didn't understand, I had turned back time and come to the antithesis of my Brethren upbringing. In the process of purifying Christ's church, the Brethren had squeezed out all the feeling as great intellects can do and here was the feeling all around me like warm rain.

I knelt, praying for Annabelle, so lucky in her choice of parents, growing up enjoying Dickens with hundreds more authors to be discovered. I prayed for her to experience, in due course, just such powerful mysteries as gripped me now. I prayed for her to avoid Thoreau and take her time getting to Shakespeare. I prayed for authors I care about, and old girlfriends, including the two who did me wrong. It was a meandering prayer. I prayed for readers of whatever novel I might publish next, that they find amid the wordplay and folderol some authenticity to inhale as I was breathing in the Catholic air, loving the Brethren's enemy as Christ commanded us to do.

I felt uplifted, joining myself to Catholics, none of whom, not even Henry, took notice of me. I am descended from hardworking people more like these *campesinos* than like the dissident dons of Oxford who invented Brethrenism. My people came in from a twelve-hour day in the fields when it was too dark to hoe corn and while the women made supper, the young men built a bonfire and played baseball, the pitcher throwing the ball through the flames, barehanded baseball, and after the meal they read from Ecclesiastes and prayed and if they prayed for hellfire to strike the rich and well-favored, the railroad bosses and mill owners, they kept it to themselves and fell into bed and awoke to cornmeal mush and coffee and another long day of labor. And some of them on Saturday night sneaked away to a town where they were not so well known and could go to the saloon with murals of naked ladies where a gin-crazed piano player walloped out the polkas and the Brethren boys could dance—Dance! One more innocent forbidden pleasure!—and hold a girl in your arms and if a fight broke out and two men started throwing big haymakers and rolling around in the sawdust, bartenders vaulting over the bar to break it up, you skedaddled lest you go home with bruises you'd have to explain. And on Sunday they sat in church and thought about death and damnation. And by the age of fifty-five or sixty, they were pretty well hobbled by hard work so that if they couldn't land an easy job as a watchman or janitor, they might suffer a horrible accident, lose a hand in a corn mill or be dragged by a team of horses and become an invalid and die of pneumonia. Those are my people and here I was, in their midst, weeping, putting my heart into a prayer for the granddaughter of a friend who was near death.

The Brethren were divided between the Closed, who believed in hygienic faith and so refused to drink from the same cup that had been touched by a brother in Error, and the Open Brethren who believed in wiping the rim of the cup and then not worrying about it. Both branches were in sharp decline, as tends to happen with perfectionists, and their children tended to migrate to the Church of Whatever and their grandchildren abandoned faith entirely for physical fitness or theater or veganism. I saw none of my Brethren cousins at Mass, only the Lutherans who felt it was a healing service though they weren't sure what exactly they were healed of. Something. Something they didn't want. English is the language of accusation, and Spanish forgave them. Father González fasts on Saturday and on Sunday clasps sinners to his vestments and weeps over them. Father Emil? Never. Father Wilmer, Father O'Connell? Not on your life.

Father Emil growled the Mass in the Minnesota accent of your grandfather asking why in the hell did you stay out half the night and why didn't you bother to put gas in the car. Father González sang the blessing and the people sang to him, *Y con tu espíritu.* It was beautiful and solemn. In English, it was just a shopping list but when I said *perdona nuestras ofensas,* I felt my sins lifted from me. All of my guilty regrets for forty years of weekly radio shows that never came up to the hopes and expectations of the audience that traveled great distances sometimes to see them, all of those offenses were pardoned. Gone. I ate the body, I drank the blood, I walked out of Our Lady head down, no small talk, and stepped into bright sunshine, fearing I might meet a Keillor and have to talk to him—"I hear that it's quite a show," he'd say and I'd say, "They're good people" and where does that conversation go? Nowhere.—but no, I drifted away and drove over to Arlene's.

She knew I'd been to church, she could smell the incense on me. She thanked me. She said she'd waked that morning with the feeling that I'd finally do what she asked me to do. She thanked me again. Barbara Ann had taken her family to an Episcopal church in St. Cloud and were going to have dinner with Barbara Ann's old boyfriend Brad who is the priest there. Mother and daughter had had a brief argument over whether Dickens could be brought to church. The mother surrendered, not wanting to sit next to a resentful child. Annabelle, Arlene said, feels pleasure intensely and displeasure almost as intensely.

Arlene was feeling displeasure this morning at the MFT faction that wanted to change the name of the town. "MeadowWood was dumb enough with the capital W in the middle of the word and trying to combine opposites: A meadow is a former forest; a forest is a previous pasture. It's like naming your town SunnyCloud or ValleyMount. But you question them and they're adamant: they want it exactly as specified, one word, capital W. And my own husband was in favor of it."

"Clarence?"

"My current husband, Clarence. He said the young will have their way eventually so why not now? He says that Alyssa and Sam and Mallory are the people who're going to save Lake Wobegon so let them erase it and start over. My husband goes to church regularly, for the same reason he goes to basketball games, to be sociable, not that he cares who wins or loses, and Pastor Liz has been preaching about resurrection and new beginnings and he figures MeadowWood is the way to go. And then they changed over to Manaadjitowaawin under the guise of paying respect to the Indians, but Minnesota's had hundreds of Indian names ever since white people arrived and where's the respect? I think that MFT wants Manaadjitowaawin because they can pronounce it and other people can't. A bunch of bullies and yikyakkers. My mother used to tell me, You've got two ears and only one mouth so plan accordingly. Barbara Ann tells me on good authority that Alyssa has screaming fits whenever her orders aren't carried out by her minions and she berates the waitress if the fork and knife aren't on the correct side of the plate. She can be very nasty if the subject of renaming the town comes up. The plain fact is, Manaadjitowaawin is the wrong name. Our Town would be a better name. You and I grew up and got used to outsiders making fun of Wobegon and either we concealed our colors or we wore them on our sleeve. I was proud of it. I dared people to laugh at Lake Wobegon. I was the only Arlene in school, named for a beloved great-aunt. They almost named me Gertrude and if they had, I would've worn it with pride. I'd have put the *rude* in Gertrude. It's good for a kid to grow up with that. Wobegon is perfect for a Minnesota town. You come from a town named Wobegon, it saves you from arrogance." She was rather emotional. She asked me to sing the town song for her and I did.

Wobegon, I remember O so well how peacefully among the woods and fields you lie.

My Wobegon, I close my eyes and I can see you just as clearly as in days gone by.

The song was written by Adolf Adolfson for the town centennial of 1948. "Imagine a man going through the Thirties and Forties with that name," I said. "Why didn't he change it to Yonny Yonson? Because he was named for his grandfather and you can't erase your ancestry. So he lived a quiet life and stuck close to home where nobody ever asked, 'What's your name?' And he wrote that sweet song."

The town referendum was scheduled and then Clint Bunsen pro-duced a letter from an Ojibwe savant on the Red Lake Reservation saying that "Manaadjitowaawin" is considered sacred by his people and that its use by non-native people for commercial purpose would be fought in the courts with all the resources at their disposal, and he cited a court case in New Jersey in which a sacred Ojibwe name taken by a clothing man-ufacturer had resulted in a $4 million judgment, and what's more, Clint brought out an old Ojibwe dictionary compiled by missionaries that clearly listed "Wobegon" as an Ojibwe word, meaning "the place where we waited for you two days in the rain," and he discovered, in the Minnesota criminal statutes, a law stating, *No person shall aid, abet, allow, assist, accommodate, or authorize alteration of the Indian name of any geographic feature or location, any governmental unit, or any building open to public access or commerce, without the prior approval by unanimous resolution of the state Indian Affairs Council formed under Minn. Stat. § 3.922. Whoever violates this provision may be sentenced to imprisonment for not more than five years or a fine of not more than $10,000, or both.*

And so Manaadjitowaawin vanished under threat of punitive court judgments and the issue simply evaporated. MFT proposed that a non-sacred Ojibwe name be found such as *Asibikaashi*, but when people said it aloud, it sounded to them like someone trying to cough up a hairball, so it was dropped.

Clearly, there was a boom in Lake Wobegon, regular people driving Chryslers and Cadillacs and our high school graduates now had good job opportunities right at home, and real estate was selling for two and three times what it would've gotten a few years before. There was no doubt that the millennial entrepreneurs were responsible and the town owed them a great deal of gratitude but nonetheless there were limits. The airport bond issue, for one. Mayor Alice saw that the take-off path on the extended runway would have jets screeching a couple hundred feet over a big chunk of town, including the high school and Our Lady of Perpetual Responsibility. Lots of people take afternoon naps; school classrooms should be protected; Our Lady doesn't need a jet screaming over during 10 a.m. Mass. So Alice at a meeting of the council in executive session inserted a clause deep in a dense paragraph of multifarious clauses linked with a host of ifs, ands, and buts, a clause forbidding airport use between sunrise and 3 p.m. Central Time, and this little phrase was the bird the lady swallowed that ate the spider that wriggled inside her and wouldn't let those jets fly.

The MFT folks argued but the runway extension quietly disappeared into a pile of paperwork, along with the plan to add right-field bleachers to the ballpark and the plan to build a $15 million glass conservatory, along with the idea of widening the sidewalks along Main Street to make a mall. Leave well enough alone, Alice said. What's the rush? Act in haste and repent at leisure.

I stuck around for another week and visited Arlene who was in a mournful mood. Her dose of morphine was up and she said it made her feel indifferent and she didn't like indifference. Passivity and lassitude were not her style. She said, "You and I are the last historians around. The others don't care—Clarence claims not to remember the time he took me to Venice. It was the most money he ever spent in one week. He flung thousand-lira notes around like they were fives or tens, his credit card was in his hand, he knew no limits. How could a person forget it? He doesn't remember the tornado of 1965 that flung pickups and John Deere tractors a quarter-mile away and impaled cornstalks in plate glass windows. He doesn't remember going out to the Flanagan brothers' farm to pick apples. How could you ever forget that?

"How could you forget Peter and Paul Flanagan?" she said. "It's like forgetting what happened on November 22nd or Nine/Eleven or December 7th, the day of infamy. It's like forgetting my mother's and my father's birthdays, May seven and October twelve. But Clarence insists he can't remember. So it leaves it up to us, you and me, to keep track of the past. They can change the name Lake Wobegon to MeadowWood or NightView or BeachLake but they cannot be allowed to eliminate the Sons of Knute or the Thanatopsis Society and the Proust Roost, or *Syttende Mai* or Jack's Auto Repair or the Flanagan twins. Or the Lake Wobegon song. There are people residing here who've never heard it because it's hardly ever sung because only old people know it and old people hesitate to sing in public. And that is going to be your responsibility, not mine." And she closed her eyes and sang, very sweetly.

It's never far from wherever you are,
And when you're old it never leaves you.
You sit alone and thoughts of home
Come and stand around your chair.
What's their name I knew back when,
Never liked them that much then,
But memory is kind and they weren't bad,
I'd love to see those folks again.
Wobegon, my home.

Peter Flanagan of the Flanagan twins died in a cabin in northern Wisconsin, a member of a right-wing militia The Enforcers, hiding from the law after he was indicted for defacing a portrait of Thomas Jefferson in the attack of January 6, 2021, on the U.S. Capitol. His head was shaved and a four-letter word was written in big letters on his forehead.

He wore a cape of fox skins and leather pants and boots with sharp spikes protruding from the toes. The face of Donald Trump was painted on his bare chest. He was anti-vaccination, anti-gun laws, anti-speed limits, anti-public schools, and he believed that Aaron Burr had been cheated of the presidency in 1800 by Jefferson and that had set the country on a course of liberalism. He wrote a song that the Enforcers sang at rallies:

You liberals and this nation you are leadin'
You're trying to make us like Sweden.
Or Italy or France
Where women wear the pants.
Why don't you go be Dutch
If you hate America so much.
You are not long for this world
I've got a gun and my finger is curled.
Better leave the USA
Before I blow you away.

The Enforcers kept a list of left-wing optometrists who use secret eyedrops to induce mind control and render their patients submissive to the CIA, the U.N., and the AFL-CIO. Peter believed in maintaining purity of bodily fluids by drinking water from lakes and rivers where he bathed. He sent secret messages to his fellow Enforcers in Gaelic. His cabin had mirrors on the roof to deflect the rays of government satellites so FBI agents couldn't get a bead on him, he allied himself with Proud Boys and QAnon and Swamp Dogs and other groups and was waiting for the signal from Mr. Trump that the new revolution had begun, and when he got the signal, he headed for Washington and the Capitol. He was treating his colon cancer with Clorox, which didn't help, and he died of COVID, alone, after posting his farewell on Facebook in Gaelic and texting his sister Doris that the deep state had marked him for extinction and she drove to Wisconsin and brought his body back home.

Peter and Paul, the Flanagan twins, were famous at one time and appeared in *Parade* and *Look* and *Life* and other national magazines. Back then, there was a sign south of town: *Lake Wobegon, Home of the Flanagan Twins.* They insisted it come down and it was taken down but nonetheless they were our celebrities. They were twins joined at the hip, what we called Siamese twins back in less sensitive times, and they were almost separated when they were nine but their parents got an offer from the Sorenson Circus of Oddities that was too good to turn down so the boys joined the show and spent fifteen years traveling to fairs and carnivals, displayed with the Fat Lady, the Penguin Boy, the Alligator Woman, the Human Pincushion, a sword-swallower and fire-eater named Vince the Invincible, and Mister Posthumous, a corpse in a coffin who spoke from the Other Side, thanks to a ventriloquist, and answered theological questions that over the years changed from Wesleyan to Charismatic Catholic to atheistic depending on location. For a time, a midget joined the show, billed as the World's Most Silent Man, and the barker offered ten bucks to anyone who could make him talk and the man sat solemn-faced and endured ten minutes of vile and vulgar abuse, people paying an extra quarter for the privilege.

Peter and Paul enjoyed the road life. The other freaks treated them as normal people and eventually each married and got his own trailer and spent a night in one and the next in the other and fathered five children between them. They came home and bought two hundred acres north of town and built two houses and planted an orchard, raised beautiful sweet corn and award-winning Irish setters. They wore special shirts and shared a pair of four-legged pants and some of their little kids liked to button their overalls together and go around in tandem like their dads. The brothers got along well enough though Paul was a Democrat and married Lutheran and attended church regularly and Peter was an atheist and conservative Republican, but he attended church with his brother and slept through the service.

Thanks to the Flanagans, Lake Wobegon never had a leash law. Other towns did, for the benefit of children who were afraid of dogs, but the brothers campaigned against it, arguing that leashed dogs cannot protect property from marauding raccoons and deer who will walk into town in broad daylight and eat your garden and you'll no longer have fresh berries. They insisted that a child should learn to deal with an aggressive dog by looking it in the eye, speaking calmly, and pointing a finger at it. You never turn and run from a dog, they said; you point a finger and speak. Every year, spring and fall, the Flanagans led a wildlife chase, the town's dogs running deer and raccoons and foxes out of the woods and miles away to protect our gardens and fruit trees.

The brothers ran into trouble in their late thirties when Peter heard that average life expectancy for conjoined twins is only forty-seven. He heard it on the radio as the brothers were bathing and reached for the radio and it fell into the bath and Paul said he heard no such thing but Peter fell into a deep depression and tried to cut his wrists and Paul had to wrestle the knife away from him and watch him carefully from then on. And soon Peter's wife divorced him on grounds of incompatibility. She said he was crazy, paranoid, was devoted to Ayn Rand's novels, hung pictures of Ayn Rand on the walls, quoted her, had the words *No one can stop me* tattooed on his right arm.

The divorce was a grievous thing and Peter refused to talk about it and was furious if Paul mentioned Ann and one night when she and her new boyfriend Ray came to pick up her kids, Peter, who had joint custody, reached into his pocket and pulled out a pistol and shot the boyfriend dead on the spot.

Paul had no idea his brother had a gun in his pocket though they shared the same pair of pants. The county attorney brought the case to a grand jury, which declined to indict Peter for murder because his conviction would mean sending Paul, an innocent man, to prison. The jury figured nature had punished the two enough already. So life went on though Paul was moved by the tragedy to teach Adult Bible Study at 8 a.m. on Sundays, which irked Peter the atheist, being roused from sleep to go to town and sit and listen to his brother natter on and on about Deuteronomy and Leviticus. Peter kept interrupting, saying, "You have no proof of that. It's superstition and mythology is all it is." He insisted that no merciful deity would create two human beings joined together at the hip. And he announced, not once but several times, that he was in love with Paul's wife, Virginia. "How could I not be" he said, "having listened to them make love for the past twenty years?"

This information caused Paul severe erectile dysfunction and he considered getting a surgical separation but the verse in Scripture, "Those whom God hath joined together, let no man put asunder," stopped him. And in the meantime, the Flanagans were carrying on a bustling business of hosting weddings at their orchard. They had bought a circus organ, which the two of them played on a flatbed trailer in the Fourth of July parade, playing "Tea For Two" and "Side By Side" and "Under The Double Eagle" and advertising their Chapel of the Apples where young people who didn't want to be married in church and go through a charade of faith could have a festive secular wedding with whatever music suits your fancy, played on a circus organ by two men joined together and if they could live as one, then surely you and your Chosen Beloved could too.

But one Sunday morning in Bible Study, Peter heard Paul read from 2nd Corinthians, "Wherefore come out from among them and be ye separate, saith the Lord, and touch not the unclean thing." He decided to separate himself and he got Paul drunk that night and drove him to a veterinarian in Cold Spring who used a local anesthetic and cut the connective tissue and that was that.

Paul felt lost and empty as a solo and Peter felt happy as a bird released from a cage. He took up bicycling and tennis and started dating women. Paul felt his life lacked a purpose. "I am living with a ghost," he said. "I'm living on a narrow precipice looking a thousand feet straight down." He desperately missed his twinhood.

Meanwhile the DA came after Peter on the old homicide charge and he went underground, joining the Enforcers. He roamed the country, camping in tents or sleeping in his 1978 Impala or crashing with fellow Enforcers, but wherever he went, he stayed in touch with his brother. Paul told me so. "He was a crazy fascist and I'm a standard liberal but when you're a twin, none of that matters, you're still brothers."

Doris wanted Peter buried in the cemetery next to his parents, and asked me to say a few words at the grave. She said, "My brother Paul is utterly distraught. He is speechless with grief, sitting in his house, phone off, unable to deal with this. He is wearing a knapsack full of sand on his left hip where Peter was attached to him, in memory of his brother. This is a terrible time for our family, for Peter's kids, all of us, because a mob of militia and who knows what weirdos are on their way here to honor our brother. I don't know how we're going to endure this. But if you could stand up and speak for him, it would mean everything to us. If you don't want to, I can understand, but if you could find it in your heart, we'd be everlastingly grateful."

How could I say no to a weeping woman who had endured her brothers' bizarre celebrity and now the death of her insane brother, so I said yes. Two hours later, Arlene called and said she admired me as never before. "You are my hero," she said. "Please don't get yourself shot." Pastor Liz called and said she'd be there to say a prayer, but one that omits divinity out of respect for Mr. Flanagan's unbelief. She said, "Maybe you and I should hire out as a team. There is a growing market here: families of unbelievers who want solemn funeral rites but godless ones. There was a song we learned in seminary—" and she sang it to me over the phone.

Dig a hole in the ground,
Three feet across and six feet down,
Borrow the dough, pass the basket,
Give the bastard a high-class casket,
Get your ass to the funeral Mass.
Kneel and close your eyes in prayer,
Thank God it's him, not you, up there.
Line up for a last reviewal
Once the man was cold and cruel,
Now he's sweet, quiet, calm,
That's what happens when you embalm,
Close the lid and say goodbye,
You really ought to try to cry,
Fold up the flag, give a salute,
Too bad the waste of a pretty good suit,
It was the best suit that he had,
In another two months it's gonna smell bad.

201

Doing the Funeral, doing the Funeral, doing the Funeral Rag.
Sickness sucks and death is a drag,
But when God calls you can't turn back.
Everybody's doing the Funeral Rag.
When you leave and you're out the door,
They love you more than ever before.
When you lived they wouldn't look at you,
When you're dead they put up a statue.
It's the Funeral, it's the Funeral Rag.

I told Arlene and she said, "You know that Liz has a crush on you, don't you? I used to think she was gay and couldn't face up to it, but now I think she's in love with you. So be careful, pal. You do adultery with clergy and you're digging a deep hole for yourself. She'd make you feel guilty ten ways from Sunday."

I assured Arlene that Liz and I were only friendly acquaintances and that I would not cross the line into anything romantic, not even a wink or a pat on the shoulder.

She said, "I have no right to be jealous but if I ever hear that you've gone skinny-dipping with her in the lake, I will find a gun and go shoot you and I believe no charges will be filed against a dying woman, they'll just sentence me to a hospice."

I met my guys for lunch the day before the Flanagan funeral and Daryl said he'd seen an armored personnel carrier with swastikas on it parked by the railroad tracks, and four men in armored vests cooking over an open fire.

"I can't speak for you, but I plan to attend," said Billy. "A classmate is a classmate forever."

Clint pointed out that the Flanagan twins never attended public school, they were taught by their mother at home.

"Okay, but a neighbor is always a neighbor. And he wasn't a bad person until he cut himself off of his brother."

Dave: "I just don't understand how somebody from our town can turn into a Nazi stormtrooper."

Clint: "He comes from a crazy family. His grandfather spent his life trying to prove that the Chinese bombed Pearl Harbor and FDR covered it up on account of his communistic sympathies and Wendell Willkie knew it but the FBI put tranquilizers in Willkie's coffee that made him listless when he ran against FDR in 1944 and he lost the election and FDR went to Yalta and gave Europe to the Soviets."

Billy: "Old man Flanagan believed that? How come we never heard about it?"

Clint: "They kept him hid in the barn. It was a big barn. He called it the Wendell Willkie Presidential Memorial and filled it with flags and campaign posters and pictures of Willkie and he stood at a lectern and read Willkie's speeches and he put on a torchlight celebration for Willkie's birthday and the barn burned down and they put him in an asylum in Iowa and he died down there. He had an exciting life, fighting for what he believed in, which happened to be nuts, just like Peter."

And then Clint looked out the window. A crowd of fifty men passed by, many of them in camo, carrying assault rifles, one with a flag ("Don't Tread On Me"), some with "Trump 2024" signs, some with Enforcer armbands and insignia, and some wearing helmets, some horns, one carrying a tape deck playing a military march, and Clint turned to me and said, "There's your audience, friend. Hope the eulogy is up to their standards."

Dave said the funeral was going to be at Lundberg's but then he put up a sign, *No Firearms Allowed Beyond This Point*. So they switched it to the cemetery.

Clint said, "And they're scattering the ashes to the four winds."

"You're kidding," said Dave. "How do you know that?"

"You work on cars, you roll under the car, people forget about you, they say things. I know everything that's going on in this town. I know things that'd astonish you."

"Such as what? Tell."

"All in good time. Don't worry, if I give the eulogy at your funeral, I'll leave out the stuff about the fishing trip to Manitoba and that woman at the campground."

"Bullshit."

"Memory loss is a common thing at your age."

And the next day, we gathered at the cemetery. Doris and Paul and Liz and I walked in and the Enforcers were already there, about forty of them in formation, two caped figures on horseback behind, holding long lances with black pennants. They had built a stack of wood for a ceremonial fire and dragged in a cannon and they were bristling with rifles and some of them wore swords but they didn't look dangerous to me, more like children at Halloween impersonating evil. Paul held the urn with Peter's ashes. About a hundred townspeople were on hand, standing facing the Enforcers, Liz and I standing in the middle.

"It's a shame Peter had to miss this. And miss it by just a few days," said Liz.

"It makes you wonder if the man's life had any meaning at all."

"Well, he proved that Clorox doesn't cure colon cancer," she said.

"Are you going to speak?" I said. She said, "The sermon that really matters is what we do with our lives, and you and I are going to face these creeps and not flinch. These aren't people, this is pathology."

The man wearing antlers was chanting something—Liz said it was Gaelic—and it went on, a sort of keening, rising and falling, and he'd pump his fist and his men shouted "Ho!" and Liz leaned over and said, "If you want to get out of doing the eulogy, how about I get up and sing a song?" and she sang quietly in my ear:

Kneel down, pay your respects.
Pray as everyone genuflects.
Everybody put the fun in funeral.
Good grief, it isn't often
We get a fresh one in the coffin,
One more bastard off to glory,
Maybe gonna stop in purgatory.
You do the eulogy, I'll give the sermon,
He was a jerk so we'll do it in German.

His misdeeds do not concern us,
Stick him in a bag and throw it in the furnace,
Throw the trash in the cemetery,
Let's get shit-faced and be merry,
Everybody, let's put the fun in funeral.

"Dare me to do it?" she said. "Give me twenty bucks and we'll be out of here."

The Gaelic had ended. The antler man walked over and said, "Which of you is doing the eulogy?" Liz pointed to me and said, "And I'm doing a prayer."

"I just did the prayer," he said. He glared at me. "I hope this isn't going to be a long speech or anything." I shook my head. He said, "And I hope you're not on the other side."

"Other side of what?" I said.

"Oh, we'll know. We're not stupid."

I stepped forward and the crowd shushed and I spoke up in a loud clear voice and said, "I knew a different Peter Flanagan perhaps from the one you knew. You knew him as a patriot who followed a lonely path and remained true to his own vision of what is good for America and we as Americans have always honored solo visionaries, but I knew him as a poet, another lonely calling in life. And as we lay him to rest, I think it appropriate that we harken to his own words."

There was profound silence when the paramilitary bunch and the townspeople heard the word "poet." It was a very fertile silence. Pastor Liz turned and looked at me. Arlene looked up from her wheelchair and Paul Flanagan, who had his arms around his wife, stood up straight and paid attention. Nobody had ever used that word in connection with Peter. When you're telling a story, it's very rewarding to hear that sort of silence. I continued:

Breathes there the man, with soul so dead,
Who never to himself hath said,
This is my own, my native land!

Whose heart hath ne'er within him burn'd,
As home his footsteps he hath turn'd,
From wandering on a foreign strand!
But success is counted sweetest
By those who ne'er succeed.
To comprehend a nectar
Requires sorest need.

Not one of all the purple Host
Who took the Flag today
Can tell the definition
So clear of victory

As he defeated—dying—
On whose forbidden ear
The distant strains of triumph
Burst agonized and clear!

This thou perceiv'st, which makes thy love more strong
To love that well which thou must leave ere long.

When you tell a bald-faced lie, you put yourself on the line, but when I said the last line about "love that well," an armored man in front yelled, "By God, that is a hell of a poem" and other Enforcers joined in the shouting, there were high fives and several rifles fired into the air and then a whole volley, they loved it and whooped and yelled and one yelled, "Do it again!" so I did and they liked it even more, meanwhile the people who knew that Walter Scott wrote the first part and Emily Dickinson the middle and Shakespeare the last two lines kept their mouths shut. A man in a raccoon coat asked for a copy and I gave him mine, the only one. Doris looked dubious but withheld comment. Mr. Antlers took the urn from Paul as a torch was put to the pile of wood and flames flew up and he let out a war cry and flung the ashes into the air, but misjudged the wind and the remains of Peter Flanagan, a solid cloud of them, were blown back into the Enforcers, men ducking, coughing, spitting, wiping ashes from their eyes, brushing off their faces and hair, and Mr. Antlers who had swallowed a mouthful of the decedent was bent down and spitting vigorously as Liz and I and our fellow Wobegonians slipped out the gate and hightailed it downtown.

Doris decided against a funeral lunch lest some Enforcers show up and the table talk turn to politics after the interment, but Liz and I headed for the Chatterbox and there were Clint and Dave and Daryl and Billy and we ordered tuna hotdish in honor of our school lunch program and Billy had a bottle of Bordeaux from the municipal liquor store, a price tag of $18 on it, and Darlene brought us glasses, strictly against the rules, and everyone but me took a glass and I stuck with coffee.

Four funerals in less than a month—Norm and Ronnie (aka Mr. Nookie) and Larry Becker the Nowhere Man, and the town Nazi—a wave of death of my contemporaries, kids I'd stood in line with at the cafeteria to be served macaroni and cheese, and meanwhile the town we knew and loved is vanishing under the weight of millennial idealism and Arlene was dying; she said so herself. She said, "And when I die, please say that I died and I am dead. Do not say I 'passed.' I passed high school English. I passed Anoka many times while driving north. I've passed gas. This is not passing. This is dying." Clarence rarely ventured out of the house, he couldn't bear to receive sympathy, people reached out to hug him and he recoiled as if it were a virus. Weeks had passed and people still dropped off flowers, food, loaves of bread. "Get the damn banana bread out of here," Arlene said. "The smell is disgusting." Barbara Ann sent her kids back to Minneapolis with her mother-in-law. Dorothy moved in with her bag full of morphine. Clarence sat nearby, a helpless observer, hands in his lap, the ringer turned off on the phone, listening to the silence.

Arlene lay propped up on pillows, an oxygen tube nearby, books stacked on a side table—her three old favorites, *Buddenbrooks, The Great Gatsby, Alice's Adventures in Wonderland,* that she'd read often and wanted one more round—"People keep bringing me books of poetry—what in the hell do I want with poetry? Poor Clarence keeps putting Bach on the CD player. I hate Bach. The man has been married to me for fifty-six years and he doesn't know this? That's why I quit choir. I hear Bach and I feel like it's January in Germany and there's sauerkraut for breakfast. The man was angry at the church for paying him so poorly and he wrote music to make them suffer." She missed her granddaughter. "We Zoomed a few times but I look terrible and she asked me, 'Grandma, what's wrong?' and I don't want to explain death to her. I don't want her to know about death. It's a drag," she said. "I am not myself. I have about one good hour in the morning and half an hour in the afternoon. After six p.m. I am a zombie."

She turned off the TV. "I don't miss much from the old days but I do miss the Fourth of July after the bikers and Trumpers messed it up. And I miss the Polar Plunge on January the First. It was so weird and wonderful. Our dad and our uncles and all the men of town except your snobby Brethren men would head downtown in their bathrobes, sit in their cars with the motors running, and a horn honked and they walked out on the dock and when Mr. Nelson blew a big blat on the bugle, they dropped their robes and you saw an amazing sight, hundreds of big butts jumping into the freezing water and they thrashed around for a minute and climbed out and went home."

"You saw this?" I said.

"One year I watched from the bandstand in the park. I brought binoculars. It was craziness, grown men who'd no sooner go naked in public than they'd sing grand opera, but it was a tradition and so they did it without question because it always had been done. It was probably the only insane thing they did all year and it helped make them sensible. It was as close as they came to debauchery, jumping naked into freezing water, a very private experience—they didn't look at each other and anyway when it's that cold there isn't much to be seen, but still it was brave of them. And when they climbed out of the water, they felt all happy and proud of themselves. All those dignified men who ran the town and stood for common sense and sobriety, and on that one day they did that big crazy thing and they were proud of it.

"It was an old Viking custom. You jump in to overcome your fear of death and thereby get more pleasure out of life. And then one year some women threatened to join the Plunge and that threw a wrench into it. So that year they all wore swimsuits and that killed it. That was the last Polar Plunge. People talked about reviving it but once it was gone they couldn't figure out what the purpose was so they forgot about it. It was wonderful. Men whooping and yelling, naked in icy water. It looked crazy but it was very meaningful, which you didn't recognize until after it was gone and then it was too late. Just like so much in life.

"And now that I'm down to a few months, I wish I could go back and redo some of it. Not my marriage—I'm fine with Clarence—but I wish I'd taught my husband and children how to clean the house so I could sit and read a book all day Saturday. That's the way to read a good book, two hundred pages at a sitting. And I wish I hadn't tried so hard to be nice to everybody. Some people aren't worth the effort. I went to so many awful dinners and luncheons. At a certain age, I think your social obligations cease and you stick with people you enjoy. Oh well. Regret, regret."

She was in a mournful mood when I arrived but she talked a blue streak and got livelier and livelier. "With the kids, I was one out of two and that's par, as far as I'm concerned. Barbara Ann was a horrible teenager and she married a delinquent and shaped him up and made herself into a terrific mom, I don't know how. She has weird politics but who cares about that? She's been a blessing. Duane is a robot. He judges a hundred video games a day, is considered an expert in his field, but he never went to Europe, only went to Japan once for a video convention and he never left the hotel. He's never been to a play except at his kids' grade school, has no interest in music or fiction, and if left to himself would live on glazed doughnuts, frozen waffles, peanut butter. The times he's come to visit us, he could only stay for an hour or two; the guy is lost without super-high-speed internet and he has to go back to the hotel. Once he got off the toilet and was pulling up his trousers and accidentally dropped his cellphone in the pot and tried to fish it out with his shoe and lost his balance and hit the handle and flushed it and when his phone disappeared, he was utterly lost and bewildered. He was like a four-year-old child. Sometimes I'm not a hundred percent sure he knows who I am—I'm kidding but not by much. I hold out my arms to give him a hug and he takes a step back, it confuses him.

"But enough about that." She said, "Why did Brethren men not take part in the Polar Plunge? Because of nudity?"

"There was drinking involved and a lot of whooping and hollering. And they believed in maintaining distance from unbelievers."

"When did Lutherans become unbelievers?"

"Brethren read the Scofield Bible, which printed the dispensationalist interpretation along with the divine text so that you could understand it correctly. Lutherans just read the text."

"So God left out the directions and Scofield had to provide them? Oh, never mind. I'll be seeing God soon enough, I'll ask him directly."

She said, "And I'm going to thank him for planting me in Minnesota in the middle of the twentieth century. I got to go ice fishing, which Barbara Ann never did, nor did she ever eat lutefisk or dance the Shim Sham or the Lindy Hop. We had sweet songs about holding hands and about the teenagers who fell asleep at the movies on a date—'What're we gonna tell your mama? What're we gonna tell your pa? What're we gonna tell our friends when they say, "Ooh la la?"'—We got to own a Mustang convertible. I got to drink gin cocktails and got to see Obama elected and I also got to live through the most disgusting incompetent presidency in American history and the country survived. Too bad they didn't find a cure for cancer, but hey, I had my share of fun. So how are you doing? If you're writing another book, I wish you'd finish it so I can read it before I die. But don't rush on my account."

I came to visit Arlene a few days later, hearing she was near the end, and she got up out of her chair and put her arms around me. "I love you," she said. She said she remembered a day the sky turned black and Mr. Bradley was leading us on a nature walk and we ran toward school as the rain came down in buckets and she turned as she went in the door and saw me, face turned up to the sky, laughing, drenched, hair plastered to my head, clothes soaked, enjoying the downpour. I remember this but differently. She saw me as a joyful adventurer, but I was happy because, having gotten drenched, I could go home and skip Miss Story's fifth-hour English class and the discussion of *King Lear*, which I had not read, but it's an honor to be admired by someone for sixty years, even for the wrong reason.

One night Arlene asked Dorothy to play a song that was popular at dances long ago, it was the last dance of the evening, and Dorothy found it on YouTube:

> *I miss your warm embrace,*
> *My cheek against your face.*
> *Your voice was my delight,*
> *I heard your breathing every night.*
> *Soon I'll lie in bed alone, mi amor, mi corazón*
> *You gave all you could have given*
> *Lay at my feet the cloths of heaven*
> *You kissed me and my heart stood still*
> *Yes, I said, O yes I will*
> *Now I go to worlds unknown, mi amor, mi corazón.*

Arlene went to the powder room and Dorothy said, "I can appreciate a good love song so long as I don't have to live it. I never married because I got a good look at my parents' marriage and it told me to stay out of that swamp. Mother was faithful to a loveless marriage and went to church every Sunday like an old firehorse but she didn't discover her true self until Daddy keeled over, her ball and chain, and she took a lover who took her dancing and traveling and Lord knows what and she got to live ten years before she died at eighty-seven. I found a blue ribbon in her dresser drawer for a tango contest at the Miranda Casablanca Hotel in Las Vegas. Remarkable. So I skipped the incarceration and went straight to the happy ending. I've had a few beaus and I thank God I dumped them before they became a bad habit. Romance leads in one direction: down. Put that in your pipe and smoke it."

I was about to say a word in behalf of marriage and Arlene called for me and she said, "Make me laugh" and I said I had told her all the jokes I can remember except the one about the two penguins on the ice floe. "I've heard you tell that and I still don't get it. What about the one about the dying Republican?" I said, "What's that one?"

She said, "A man was dying who'd been a Republican all his life and just before he died he switched to the Democratic Party because, he said, 'I'd rather it happen to one of them than one of us.'"

And she laughed. She said, "Remember the song we sang in Miss Person's class? It was a speech class but we always started it with a song that she knew from her college choir at Gustavus."

The winter wind may blow
And sorrows overflow
But let us gather near in friendly company,
And let us not discuss
The ills befallen us
But let us only see how fortunate we be.
Let no one stand alone
But make each one our own
And climb aboard the boat and all head out to sea.

She was clinging to life so she could see what would happen to Lake Wobegon and then she collapsed, didn't know where she was or why. She asked Dorothy, "Is he okay?" She couldn't remember Clarence's name but she worried about him. Dorothy said, "He's just fine, darling. It's okay for you to go now." Arlene said, "Then I think I shall," and the next day she died.

Barbara Ann went upstairs and flung herself on a daybed and sobbed so hard, people down the street heard it. She was a capable corporate woman but she allowed herself to fall apart and then came downstairs and made coffee. Clarence wandered in and said, "I have no idea what to do" and wandered back out. Dorothy fixed Arlene's hair and washed her face and Mr. Lundberg took the body away and it was burned and two days later he brought them a cloth bag with the ashes. Pastor Liz conducted the funeral and spoke on stoicism, the verse *For God hath not given us the spirit of fear; but of power, and of love, and of a sound mind.* She also said that we are jars made of clay and shine with God's light. Clarence collapsed and did not go with the others to the cemetery where her ashes were scattered on the graves of her Gunderson ancestors, the Whippets having turned down the request to scatter them along the third baseline at the Wally (Old Hard Hands) Bunsen Memorial Ballpark. ("If we allowed one, we'd be inundated by dozens of others," said Otto, the groundskeeper. "People'd want to be deposited in the batter's box. On the mound. There'd be no end to it.")

"Let the rains come and join her to all who've gone before and let her memory live in our hearts as she joins the great throng of faithful in perpetual light around God's throne of mercy," said Liz. Barbara Ann had brought Annabelle who stood proudly at attention, holding her grandma's American flag.

I went back to the cemetery that night and walked through the tall grass where she was scattered and sat on her parents' tombstone, Marjorie and Harold. It felt like it was about to rain. I felt a little adrift without her. My old friend, my fellow Democrat, my reader in her St. Olaf sweatshirt who was thrilled to pieces when the college fielded a women's hockey team with forwards named Tiffany and Annika and a goalie named Grace. They were living a life she had wanted for herself. I had known her since childhood, since before I learned to impersonate adulthood. She knew Mrs. Shaver, Mrs. Carroll, Mrs. Moehlenbrock, Miss Hallenberg, and when I'm gone, who will be left to tell about those days?

In my mind, she is seventeen, riding an old green bicycle and I'm on a red one, tooling along the old county road to Millet, past the pig farm and over the wooden bridge and along the creek, talking about the *Herald Star* and how carefully it avoids all the news that's of interest, in favor of good feeling. It was 1959. One night that March, I stood at the free-throw line, Lake Wobegon down 59-58, two seconds on the clock, the St. Margaret fans whooping and screaming, trying to distract me, their team of flat-footed farm boys jumping up and down, and I held the ball up and a still small voice said, "Sorry, mister" and the ball landed on the rim and rolled around and fell off the rim, and the St. Margaret fans were rapturous, and my teammates and I walked in stunned silence to the cold locker room and sat staring at the floor and nobody said a word, there was no consolation. Their janitor had turned off our hot water so we took cold showers and we dressed and walked to our bus through a mob of jeering St. Margaret fans and rode home in cold silence. We had been considered a cinch to go to State, and losing to St. Margaret was unthinkable and there I was at the line, the savior of my people, knowing I'd screw up and I did. It wasn't a game any longer, it was the valley of the shadow of death. But the next day Arlene invited me on a bike ride and said, "I'm sorry for those St. Margaret kids because last night was the high point of their entire lives, but you're going to have a great life and do wonderful things and I'm happy for you."

That was Arlene. She became my lover that night long ago at the lake and maybe I would've married her and maybe I would've gone on the radio and written a book and another one and maybe we'd be good together but when I first brought Giselle back home to meet everybody, Arlene told me I'd done the right thing, so there it was. When I said goodbye after the Flanagan funeral, she looked rather fragile and looked up and said, "I love you. I hope you know that."

"I love you." I wanted to embrace her but she looked breakable.

She said, "I'm proud of you. I liked your writing, especially the things that made me cry. You thought you were writing comedy but there was a lot more to it."

I took her hand, didn't know what to say.

She said, "Bye, Good Lookin'. See you in the next act." And I grinned and walked out the door and wept all the way to the car.

16

PLAIN FACTS FACED

It was the best of times, it was a dreadful time, you could FaceTime a friend in London from a porch overlooking a Minnesota lake, and Google had all the facts at hand, we were on the verge of breakthroughs in enlightenment but common sense was in short supply and COVID was picking off the innocent and naive.

A brutal storm came through one Tuesday night, Old Testament clouds rolled in and the sky turned dark green and purple, the world got very still and even agnostics could imagine God opening his Book and then came the thunder and lightning and a power surge and computer screens went dark before you could hit SAVE and Carla Krebsbach, driving home from the hospital where she works in Pediatric Intensive Care, looking after desperately ill children in a crisp upbeat style, pulled over under an overpass, bawling and couldn't stop, thinking of the anguished parents and the terrified children, the COVID cases, the sky was blowing up overhead, bombs of thunder bursting, rivers of rain, justice proclaimed: *you, the privileged and comfortable, think again, you own a house but you do not own the sky.*

I went to bed when the storm passed and the next morning saw in the *Times* that in the Bronx poor children playing with used hypodermics found in a park had thereby contracted HIV, a heartbreaking story, and under the flight path leading into LaGuardia a brutal concentration camp was maintained by the city on Rikers Island that nobody knew what to do with, and in Lake Wobegon after the storm went through, there were ominous rumblings of hostile wagons rolling into position, marauding entrepreneurs, gunslingers, CPAs, government lawyers, a day of reckoning at hand.

The Federal Trade Commission sent two horse-faced lawyers from Washington to discuss with Universal Fire's legal reps certain claims about the health benefits of inhaling smoke from logs treated with sea salt. *Does it truly energize the creative powers, realign one's awareness of the harmonious Present, and provide relief from anxiety by harnessing the calming powers of the Pacific?* The FTC doubted it. *How does one measure "harmoniousness" as a byproduct of a woodfire?* Rob McCarter's lawyers argued that he was a poetic visionary, not a scientist, and the claims were metaphorical. The FTC didn't put faith in metaphor. His lawyers mentioned the First Amendment in a hopeful way and the FTC lawyers laughed aloud: "arguing freedom of speech when it comes to public health would make any judge reach for his sledgehammer," they said. They said, "Where did you get your law degree? Bard College?"

Same with RedMedic's claims about lycopene's effects on male virility and sperm motility. A study of male RedMedic users showed the same rate of erectile limpidity as found among the elderly and infirm. The FDA and the FTC plus the FMT and the FGH sent a team of six lawyers from the firm of Patterson, Peterson, Corcoran, Cassidy, Kilpatrick, Keppler, and Cohn, six seasoned courtroom coondogs who'd brought down some giants like Continental Capacitor & Converter Corporation and American Attachment, the nation's top two distributors of selectors, scanners, repeaters, rectifiers, magnetic detectors, tracking transmitters, and pressure switches, lawyers in black leather vests with rows of battle ribbons made from snippets of the underwear of enemy attorneys, and they informed RedMedic that they were not amused by fraudulent claims in respect to the consumption of tomatoes. Mr. Cassidy said, "We'll see you in court in a week and a half. Show us your balls or we'll cut off your tits."

RedMedic and Universal Fire had never anticipated getting involved in street fights. In their hearts they belonged to the nonprofit quality-of-life world of nature preserves, preschools, and public radio. Ugliness came as a shock to them. They had hired gentlemen lawyers who enjoyed rare book collecting and wilderness hiking and French cookery in their spare time. The federal lawyers were roughnecks who used the F-word the way other people use commas. They were nobody you'd discuss croissant baking with; their game was figuring out how to bake you.

The case against RedMedic would be tried in the courtroom of Judge Hadassah Heins, the last living Truman appointee on the federal bench, an old union stalwart who sees the letters *C-O-R-P* and adds an *S* and *E*. The complaint was 1,600 pages long and weighed two pounds with extensive footnotes in 4-pt. type and apparently written in Aramaic. Cassidy delivered his line about balls and tits, and the locals were about to propose arbitration and the meeting was over.

The tomato and firewood lawyers felt that the claims were protected by whatever common law principles protect other imaginative writing. When Allen Ginsberg wrote that he had seen the best minds of his generation destroyed by madness, did he need to present the results of IQ tests and psychiatric diagnoses? Surely not. But word of the complaint got out and LifeCycle stock dropped like a turd in a tornado and Universal's dropped similarly. They had never considered the possibility of an FTC crackdown just as they'd never imagined poisonous snakes coming up out of the toilet. Shudders went through the millennial community. They believed they had introduced a new era of harmonious diversity and now were under attack by trolls living under the bridge.

People started quietly divesting and word got out and the shudders became serious shakes and shimmies. Millennials met at Sunny Gardens, trying to steady themselves with a plate of cauliflower calamari and an excellent Peruvian Barolo, and then they saw the price of the wine, $21 a glass, and decided to go with the California instead. Sam was speechless. He'd assumed growth in perpetuity, that a leaking ship won't sink so long as it maintains full forward throttle, and now shareholders of Indigenous Interactive Investment discovered that they held bonds issued by LifeCycle and RedMedic that, due to disadvantageous jiggery-pokery, were now worth slightly less than a basket of autumn leaves.

They finished their lunch and asked for the bill and put down their credit cards and a very nice waiter came back and asked if they had another Visa card, this one seemed to have a problem.

Alyssa and Prairie thought they were sitting pretty, with an offer from Federated Foods for $55 million for the Aunt Mildred brand, but Mildred herself had become unmanageable, accusing them of cheating her, and had to be sent to a wonderful care center in Minneapolis, Sister Carrie Home, and Alyssa headed to Maui to look at a property there, eager to find a place in paradise once the Federated deal was done, and Prairie felt suspicious, felt she was being ditched. She remembered a line from Alyssa's Instagram page—"I am the one who makes my life complete, nobody else." Prairie's mother was right when she said, "People are people. You can trust them about as far as you can throw them. Don't get screwed by the one you love."

So Prairie visited Aunt Mildred and they called a lawyer, Betty Buttrick, and Prairie told Betty, "My partner is pulling a fast one on me—she told me there was no need to draw up partnership papers, that everything was halfsies, and I believed her because I loved her."

"Were you two married?"

"She said that marriage is a relic of Eurocentric colonial paternalism, totally unnecessary."

"Oh boy." So Ms. Buttrick drew up papers on the spot, and Mildred signed over half of AuntMildred's.com to Prairie and Ms. Buttrick filed a claim against Alyssa for half of all assets. Meanwhile, Alyssa was busy on Maui, having made the deal with Federated, $55 million to the good, and looked at a palm plantation named *Puʻuanahulu* on a hill above the sea, a white chateau with a wrap-around veranda, the windows open year-round, a path through the orchard, fresh fruit within reach overhead, parrots perched who spoke Hawaiian, the lap of waves on the shore below, and there she met Yvonne, a tall crew-cut blond with orchid tattoos on her shoulders, the caretaker of the place, which had been an Evangelical Pentecostal Independent Church retreat center for troubled preachers. Yvonne had been a massage therapist there, working with godly men who were under stress to conceal their depression and maintain a joyous demeanor even while plagued by sexual urges and suicidal impulses, which, in EPIC, amounted to the same thing.

Over time, the EPIC found that relaxation led to heresy and preachers abandoned the faith to become Pre-Resurrectionists or Apocasolipsists, so they sold the place, and now Alyssa felt free and easy there and she and Yvonne became lovers. Why not? Love was in the air, but the next day she learned from her lawyer that the sale of AuntMildred's.com was off and Federated Food was suing her for misrepresentation and the check for the down payment on *Pu'uanahulu* had bounced and so had the check to the lawyer who wished to be released from the case because she was becoming a wellness instructor.

So Alyssa had to come home. Yvonne accompanied her. They flew tourist class, back in row 46, a long fall from paradise, and she encountered Prairie two days later in court, Prairie and Betty Buttrick and Aunt Mildred, a fierce threesome, a hearing that took less than an hour. Prairie and Mildred walked away with five million and Alyssa got five thousand. "Nice knowing you," said Prairie. "Give your girlfriend some money so she can do something about her hair."

It was a stressful time for a number of people. Sam's picture was on the front page of the *Star Tribune*—it was a slow news day, the top story was *House Committee On Committees Resumes Hearing On Norman Nomination*—and below it was *LifeCycle and RedMedic Cited On Fifteen Counts Consumer Fraud.* The sales of composting worms and maggots went flat as a memorial tablet. Lycopene was a joke on the late-night shows, pronounced *LIKE-o-peeny.* The millennials were distraught: *what had they done wrong?*

It reminded me of the time I skidded off the road in a snowstorm and wound up in the ditch and the highway patrolman stopped and called a tow truck. I told the cop, "I can't believe this. I wasn't speeding at all." The cop said, "The speed limit sign doesn't know that it's snowing. You do. You were speeding. You went off the road. Other cars didn't. It's the same highway for everybody."

Sam didn't get it. He said he didn't want to spend the next two years getting torn limb from limb in a Maryland courtroom, he wanted to go hiking with Molly in Alaska, so RedMedic was sold off to Benvenuto Canned Cannelloni for a fraction of its assessed value, and what had been a lucrative trade in masculinity enhancement became a simple matter of tomato sauce. Some of the Mexican families stayed to harvest the tomato crop but fewer and fewer, and the Spanish Mass came to an end.

Sam sold his breeding stock of composting worms to a breeder in Barbados and when the crate was opened, it was empty. The worms had devoured each other completely. Years of worm eugenics, down the tubes. And he sold off his Floating Home branch to Continental Cardboard, for $5 million, which was almost enough to pay off Sam's loans.

The company was in the tank, accounts payable towered over the receivable, assets depreciating and deficits accelerating and liquidity evaporating while liens had factored up and cash flow fluctuated down and long-term balloon loans were staring him in the face and about to pop, poor guy.

Disaster led to disaster. LifeCycle owned half of *Let's All Go Rithm* and Conscious Lunches but both had been taken over temporarily while Sam's sister Lainie was in Tibet with the boyfriend she then dumped while at the Buddhist monastery and the boyfriend's sister Trish wasn't aware of Sam's half-ownership nor was the boyfriend who believed he was entitled to half, as did his sister, so you had four people splitting 200 percent of a sinking ship, which is not easily resolved, especially since the assets included a portion of Lambikins Tissue and Whatever Ginger Ale. Vanguard Trucking was in debt, having sold 324 custom vans and built only 180 of them, and Prairie had bought one and paid $97,000 for it and it didn't get delivered and Stan the Vanguard man convinced her to invest a hundred grand and gave her a promissory note but it wasn't the note itself but a carbon copy, which her brother the lawyer said was no good in court and she called Stan and his number was disconnected. His brother said he was on a spiritual pilgrimage in Mexico.

The boom went down like a row of dominoes. Rob McCarter shut down Universal Fire, got in his pickup and drove away and his employees took ownership, divvied up the dough, and split, socialism in action. Willow was about to sell Wholly Shit when a lady customer complained of contracting a rare hoof-and-mouth disease and had to be sent to a veterinary podiatrist and in two days W.S. stock hit the ground like a box of rocks. The failure of LifeCycle, the biggest game in town, sent ripples of dread through the Moving Forward Together ranks. Totality Totes had a big year and then faded fast: there is a limit to the demand for tote bags. Alyssa and Prairie's publishing house, Becoming Press, was in the red—the market for memoirs by trans women of color is limited and their latest, *A Trucker's Tale: Freightways to Negligees,* was named Worst Memoir of the Year by *Fatigue* magazine. NutriSoft nontoxic face cream was sued for two million by a customer whose face had turned orange and scaly and her lower incisors had grown into sharp fangs. The LazyMan robotic lawn mower plant shut down—one of their lawn mowers got its wires crossed and crashed into a rabbit pen and slaughtered a dozen baby bunnies, the sort of bad publicity you never recover from. Front-page photos of weeping boys and girls holding bleeding furry bodies and every parent had the same thought: what if a LazyMan ran amok in a playground and chopped up your children? The mowers were derobotized and sold for scrap.

First Ingqvist State Bank had stayed clear of the boom because Eric Ingqvist considered the newcomers fly-by-nights. He didn't trust them. He'd been paranoid since his cashier Maude departed for Buenos Aires and the bank's detective discovered a whole neighborhood of small-town Midwestern lady bank tellers in Buenos Aires, seven Maudes, eight Gladyses, three Florences, and two Myrtles, living in stone mansions behind high brick walls, with swimming pools, tennis courts, manicured lawns under the palm trees, and many of them with young gigolos bringing them gin fizzes. He refused to lend money to strangers—so the young entrepreneurs had banked among themselves, interest-free loans that turned into investments, all very informal and chummy, no paper, let your yea be yea—until deficits struck and the entanglements were pulled taut and friends avoided each other on the street and text messages went unanswered and gradually the whole ball of yarn started coming loose.

But through all the turmoil of tall trees toppling, Dorothy stayed true blue. She found ways to feed the poor of which there were many who'd never expected to be. She found cheap rooms to rent, temporary jobs, guys who'd fix your car for a few bucks or clean your furnace. She told me, "Alyssa has been through some very hard knocks but she is still a very positive person, maybe even more than before. You should get to know her and give her another chance. I hired her friend Yvonne to try to develop that Cream of Happiness soup of my mother's into a commercial product. She and Alyssa bought a cabin a few doors from yours. Take a hike down there and say hello. Let bygones be bygones. Okay, maybe she tried to pull a fast one on Prairie but she paid a big price for it and it's time to move on. Mildred is very happy at the Home and Prairie has run away with someone to La Stephenie and changed her name to Mary Lee so let's put away the grudges, forgive and forget, today is a new day."

So I walked down the shore to Alyssa's cabin and she offered me a cup of honeysuckle licorice tea and said not a word about Federated, Prairie, or Mildred—she was very excited about Dorothy's nephew Douglas's son Jimmy whom Alyssa said she is now managing and who is a hot item in the streaming emo-gospel hip-hop field and has a half-million followers on TikTok and hit No. 3 on Billboard's gospel rap chart. "Hybridity is the thing in pop music now," she said. "There's no such thing as straight gospel or straight pop or anything else, everything is an amalgam and all over the map. It's wild. I have another client who is queer, neut, demi-trans, irreg, and country, and s/he is doing very well at it. Look her/him up. Mailer Twist is the name. Big new song, 'Like You Care,' it's setting the charts on fire." Alyssa sang me the chorus:

Saw you today,
Just standing there.
"How're you?" you say,
Like you care.

I asked her what emo-gospel is and she said, "It's like when you're tired of praising God and you're pissed and want to hurt his feelings even if its heresy. In the Bible, it's called lamentations, but we call it emo." She played me a Jimmy hit:

Jesus, you don't know me
You're so into divinity
You said you love me
And I keep tryin'
To find green pastures to lie in
But all my homies are dyin'
And now I'm cryin'
I say there ain't no Zion.

"Homies? I met this Jimmy. He's white."

"As I say, it's a wild world out there. He records under the name J Guy and posts to Sound Ground and I'm talking to Effen Music about signing him to a stable that includes DaBabe, Post Modern, Sir Hoodie, and Lil Whitey, because they're very into his groove. A man from Effen is flying out in a week or two. The kid is seventeen and all he lacks is confidence and I have enough of that for both of us." The breakup with Prairie, the loss of the meatloaf fortune, the failure of Becoming Press, the NutriSoft lawsuits, the loss of *Pu'uanahulu*, it was water under the bridge. Troubled water but over and done, yesterday's news. Yvonne was not at home; she was at the Chatterbox, cooking, working up a new menu. Since Sunny Gardens closed, Dorothy is adding a vegetarian menu and Yvonne is handling that. "She grounds me," Alyssa said. "Prairie was so needy. Always looking for a hand to talk to. It was draining to be with her. She was the CEO of need. I felt like I was only a lap for her to rest her head. When I met Yvonne, I could feel the validation. We were beautifully aligned. Her behavioral patterns fit what I wanted for myself so when we came together, I joined up with the person I want to be."

I've heard affection expressed in more lyrical terms: to me, validation is about licenses and alignment is for tires. "Sounds like you're a happy camper," I said. "Glad you're doing well." She had lost a fortune and got booted out of paradise but she hoped to win it all back on the strength of Jimmy's teenage self-pity or maybe a queer cowboy/girl. A remarkable woman, assuming that is her current status.

I'd heard rumors of Liz moving to Maui and opening a Buddhist Lutheran nudist camp, but no. She said, "Prairie and I talked about it, the idea of giving up material things starting with the clothes on your back, but Maui's out of the question. I'm allergic to sea salt. I tried burning Universal firewood and the next morning I was covered with blisters. I'm staying right here in Minnesota."

Meanwhile, Mallory walked over from her cabin to bring me a bouquet of something—I'm not a scholar of flowers—and seemed very contented as well. She had found a spiritual partner named Scott who had put her in touch with herself in a way she'd never experienced previously. "He is teaching my spirit to step back and not be so busy trying to make people fit my specifications but enjoy them in their entirety, including their imperfections."

"Is he what we used to call a 'boyfriend'?" I said. She said, "We've discussed taking our relationship to that level and decided we'll stick with noninvasive proximity. We do harmonic breathing together and he puts his hands on my back and he talks backward very fast, he'll do the Pledge of Allegiance or 'Jabberwocky' or even sing 'The Star-Spangled Banner.' Backward at top speed. It makes me laugh harder than I ever laughed before. He comes to bed after I'm asleep and we sleep together, his hand on my arm, but I'm asleep so I don't feel trapped, you know?" She pulled a card out of her pocket and said, "I read this twice a day to keep me on track."

Live your life from the inside out. Keep the exterior outside, don't give it access to your inner being. Be in the moment. Feelings are not beliefs, and beliefs are not the soul. Everyone's got their thing and many people's thing is anger disguised as rightness. The thing you desire is love and it begins with paying close attention, lying in tall grass observing winged insects and feeling my fate intertwined with theirs. Lie with my mouth open and if a fly enters, take it into myself, and if a grasshopper lands in it, laugh and she will fly out.

I wanted to ask her a few questions but it's no business of mine anyway—if a woman wants to co-breathe and sleep proximitously, good luck to her. But lying in tall grass and watching insects is not an option for me. She quoted a poem by my old English professor James Wright, a great poet, who wrote a poem about lying in a hammock on a Minnesota farm and looking at a butterfly and listening to cowbells and noticing horse manure, a poem that influenced several college friends of mine to head for the pasture and hang up a hammock and wait for the light to dawn and they awoke a decade later, middle-aged, no light had dawned, there was nothing to put on their résumé, and hammocks are not good for your back. Nothing had happened. I didn't mention this to Mallory. We talked real estate instead. She'd decided to tear down her cabin and Scott would build a new and simpler one with a glass dome to give them a view of night sky. She said, "Are you planning to live in your cabin? Are you and your wife separated? Somebody in town said they thought you were."

"No, she is on her way here as we speak. Wednesday she arrives. She's been hiking the Adirondacks under the big sky. I'm an indoorsman, I need a flat surface and a power outlet."

The collapse of the millennial boom occurred in a flash and a couple of bangs and was taken calmly in town, as one might expect. Panic was never our style in Lake Wobegon. We admire Florence the farmwife who ran from her house in the tornado of 1939 with the infant Delores in her hands and was blown into the limbs of a tree and climbed down and said, "Where is my purse?" It was in a town fourteen miles away, blown onto the steeple of a Congregational church and a roofer found it a year later and he happened to have known her husband, Harold, and she invited him and his wife to dinner, by way of thanks. Those are my people; we take things in stride.

One day Clint said to Daryl, "So I hear that Sam and Molly left for Alaska. Is the farm still for sale?"

"Far as I know. Looks like the real estate market is a little soft. Probably not a good time to sell."

"I was planning to stay anyway."

"Sounds good. So you okay then?"

"Far as I know. And if not, so be it."

"Ever been to Alaska?"

"Nope. I've seen pictures but why would I go all that way when there are beautiful parts of Minnesota I've never seen?"

"Good point."

What saddened Clint was the fact that Daryl's brother Dave had moved to Rochester and his son Charlie had left for Iowa State and so the family EZFreeze had closed after 77 years in business. Never a big moneymaker, it had given four generations of teenagers their first job in retail, meeting the public with a smile, learning to make the frozen milk in the cone with the twirl on the tip, handling money, flirting with fellow employees. And it also meant people stopped saying, "It's the biggest thing to hit here since the bug zapper came to the EZFreeze." Dave shut off the lights and locked up, and suddenly we were a town without a punchline.

The firewood and RedMedic and organic manure empires came crashing down like children's blocks and now it was easy to find an empty table at the Chatterbox and the airport bond issue disappeared and the money MFT raised to promote it was instead spent (thank you, Alice) on a beautiful plexiglass rendering of four Norwegian bachelor farmers sitting on a bench by the bank, one with his finger alongside his nose who is about to exhale forcefully. (One NBF, Mr. Mundal, had died, leaving three, but the sculptor refused to lower his fee so they stuck with four, figuring maybe some kid might come along and catch the bachelor bug and pick up the antisocial skills.)

Roger and Cindy returned from La Jolla where (they said) they felt out of place like two chickens in a barn full of owls. "People kept asking us where we're from and when we told them, they couldn't think of anything to say, they said, 'Minnesota. Oh. It gets cold there, doesn't it.'" So they returned and a semblance of normality resumed, the cassoulet at the café became hotdish again. Orlando left to play ball in the Texas League and the Whippets resumed their losing ways. Mr. Bauser at the post office was cranky about the same things as had irritated him for years, other people's dogs, other people's kids, and, with few exceptions, other people themselves.

Outside the *Herald Star*, I ran into Myrtle Krebsbach, who seemed unaffected by the collapse. She said, "I'm supposed to go to the hospital to see about my aorta. It's a congenital thing and it could explode at any time and blood would come gushing out of my ears and nose and I'd be gone out of this world and off to the next, leaving Florian to fend for himself. God help us. Jesus Mary Joseph—the thought of him on his own, how long before the house blows up—your guess is as good as mine. Thank God, I won't be here to see it. Anyway. They're not sure they can repair the aorta because my heart is so fragile due to emotional stress, they're not sure I can tolerate going under the knife though compared to a good many other things I've endured, the knife would be a minor irritation, but anyway they may just run a little tube up a vein and squirt some adhesive in and see if that does the trick. I don't know. I may not have long and if so, so be it. If it gets to be too much, I may just ask Florian to load the shotgun and put me out of my misery. I just need some poor soul to write my obituary. You're a writer—how about you give it a shot? You have a few minutes to give an old friend a good send-off?"

The truth is that I don't know Myrtle that well—though she has talked a good deal about Florian, their son Sheldon, the oddities of the Krebsbach clan, their painful silences and chilliness to their children, their inability to throw anything away such as bank statements from the Seventies, for God's sake, but she says very little about herself. I don't even know if she is a Democrat or Republican, prefers creamy peanut butter or crunchy. She said, "I don't want one of those standard 'Beloved wife and mother, dearly missed by all who knew her' obituaries, your basic dollar-ninety-five memorial—I want something more specific. Like 'She cared for her family more than they ever knew and even when they turned their backs and didn't listen to a word she said, she never stopped loving them. It simply wasn't in her nature to lose faith in people, even those near and dear who avoided her when she needed them most.'

Florian hates it when I talk about death but we are dying the moment we arrive. We are born astride the grave. The light gleams for an instant, then it's dark once more. I read that somewhere. You might want to quote it in the obituary. And what about 'All the world's a stage and we are only players'—I love that one." I asked her if she needed a ride to the hospital and she said, "No, I don't want to bother anybody. Florian has the car keys, I'll get them from him and drive myself, and if I die on the way, I just hope and pray I don't kill someone else. Have a good day. Thanks for listening."

I saw her the next day and she had canceled the trip to the hospital and was feeling somewhat livelier. She was eating a lamb shank and enjoying a glass of red wine and reading my weekly column in the newspaper. "I hate it when you get onto politics," she said, "but this is about spring and I like where you say, *A person has to have suffered to fully enjoy a spring day and that is the beauty of May in Minnesota—we're not fully thawed out until the middle of July but we can see it from here.* You sure do have a way with words." A compliment from a strong-minded critic.

17

A FINE JOB

Except for a pair of window blinds that came crashing down when you tried to adjust them and a row of electrical outlets up under the kitchen cupboards that required you do a headstand to plug in a toaster, Carl and Henry had done a fine job on the cabin. New toilet with shower (green tile, the color of the linoleum), a proper bedroom with walls, an electric range, white oak flooring, a great improvement over the cabin of 1960, maybe too improved. It pretty much obliterated the memory of that summer and the kid in shorts reading Thoreau with his hand on the girl's bare leg. This was a fully respectable cabin now, not merely aspirational. The Gundersons, who built it to celebrate their hard-earned leisure, were dead. It belonged to a sentimental old guy married to a New York lady who possessed very good taste in décor. The wicker chairs no longer belonged, nor the yellow kitchen table, but were kept for authenticity. My old paperbacks sat on a shelf above the sofa bed, *Walden*, *The Myth of Sisyphus*, *The Poorhouse Fair*, *The Enormous Radio*, *Selected Poems of W.H. Auden*, but otherwise the historic site I'd set out to preserve had been mostly modernized. The historic site interpretive center with the curator Meredith explaining the Fifties to the Online Generation was not a workable idea. As for the window shades, if you want sunshine, you can sit on the porch. No need to fix the awkward outlets: accept them as a challenge.

There was a new book on the shelf, *The Permeable Family* by Mallory's roommate Scott, a gift from Alyssa who, now a neighbor, seemed to want to be a friend. She loved the book, the idea of a freely chosen family instead of the inherited nuclear one, and she underlined passages she thought I should take note of—"our friends and partners and sisters are our family and blood relations are merely gene donors and critical onlookers," she underlined—and "each family develops its own customs and protocols, its rituals of bonding, and you will be better served if you find your own rather than adopt your parents' mode of living" and in keeping with that, she was busy organizing a Bonfire of Soul Sisters, which, it occurred to me, was rather similar to the Sons of Bernie Polar Plunge except it took place in June rather than December and ice was not involved except afterward in drinks. It was scheduled for the next week on Tuesday, the day before Giselle arrived, and Alyssa and Yvonne were handing out invitations. Dorothy showed me one: *The patriarchal paradigm is a male with a sword standing at the castle gate to defend his seed, his bounden wife, and his brood against seducers and false prophets and marauding adventurers. It is a myth that is no longer useful. Past the age of twelve, everyone has free access to information and ideas and begins to choose her or his own family based on cooperative reinforcement of common ideals. We choose our relations so as not to be defined by heredity. The permeable family values inclusivity over hierarchy and diversity over exclusivity: and therein lies the answer to gun violence, opiate addiction, rejection of racial and gender minorities, the violation of nature, and contempt for women, which are variations on the very same theme: the wound of male narcissism. I call on my sisters regardless of creed or belief to gather at Arcadia and let us drop the costumes that distinguish us and seek a common identity around the illuminating fire of sisterhood. We declare our love for each other and from this love springs miraculous good beyond understanding.*

It was quite a manifesto to find in your mailbox, and a good many Wobegon women immediately made other plans for that day. Even those who admired Alyssa's brass found urgent distant errands or elderly relatives who deserved to be paid a visit.

I was tempted to go out north of town toward Arcadia, the old

Moonlight Bay Supper Club where post-prom parties took place long ago, and observe the festivities, same as Arlene and Irene had snooped on the Sons of Bernie. It wasn't about nudity—you can find all the nudity you wish on the internet—it was about social psychology: could the women I know, Midwestern Christian women, interact happily with each other without clothing as a topic of conversation? I can't imagine two women scoping each other out and one saying, "I wish my boobs looked more like yours." The Sons of Bernie did the Plunge because Bernies before them had done it, it wasn't idealism, just an obligatory custom, but the June skinny-dip would be in the interest of Openness and Transparency, and many women weren't in the mood for transparency and were making other plans.

I saw a pair of binoculars in the cabin; I wasn't looking for them but there they were, under a pillow. I was sort of tempted. Sisterhood dancing naked around a fire is a lovely concept for a ballet but women's gaze is merciless and it would be only too clear who the young and comely are and who would be clinging to the shadows and reaching for a towel. The Sons of Bernie didn't look at each other but women are more curious and I guessed it would be a rather select group dancing.

So I was looking at the clock, thinking I might go for a ride, maybe accidentally drive by Arcadia, and then suddenly Giselle was there, a whole day early, in jeans and a denim jacket and one of my black T-shirts, grinning, arms out, her head against mine, her lips, her hands all over me. A young driver had picked her up at the airport and she handed him a roll of bills and sent him on his way and kissed me and said, "I came early because I suddenly couldn't bear to be without you." I didn't ask why, she just put it out there. "I can't wait to undress you," she said, but then she was distracted by the cabin and walked around examining the workmanship for a few minutes. "Those blinds are all wrong, it makes no sense to hang cheap blinds," she said, "and we'll have to change those outlets so we can actually use them." She put a cucumber salad and a bottle of champagne in the fridge. She said, "You can have some as soon as you kiss me with feeling. Or whatever else you had in mind." So I hoisted the T-shirt off her and unsnapped her jeans. She kissed my neck, my shoulder, and I could hear the Shondells singing, "I Think We're Alone Now"—*the beating of our hearts is the only sound.*

"What're the binocs for?" she said. I said, "I've taken up bird-watching." She snorted: "You couldn't tell a mourning dove from a nighthawk. You've been looking at young women sunbathing. Fine. And in a minute, if you like, you can look at a mature woman. Up close. But only if you wish."

"Do you love me?" she said. I told her that I adore her, which is a variation of love with artistic intent in addition to friendship, admiration, lust, the other stuff. Growing up Sanctified Brethren I'm wary of sensuality, which can slide into licentiousness and before you know it, you're lying in bed all day, drinking wine, never getting dressed, and the yard has gone to underbrush and the bank is filing foreclosure papers and the water and power have been shut off. For me, a naked embrace is thrilling, like leaping from the roof in the dark. Whereas for Giselle of the Village, sex was a part of normal adult life and if you were good friends with someone, it was not a leap in the dark to lie next to him and engage in intimacy if you were in the mood and he was respectful.

"First, a shower," she said. "I got all sweaty looking forward to the anticipation." She winked at me and disappeared into the new bathroom and I went out on the porch and my ghosts,

Norm gone and Arlene, the first girl I loved. Marj had endured poverty and the grief of hearing her father weepy and drunk in the barn and the wind blowing the topsoil away and the taste of dirt in the morning oatmeal and for her the memory of misery made a summer night all the sweeter. "We were so poor," Harold said, "that Dad ate his cornflakes with a fork so he could pass the milk around for the rest of us to use." Watching the sun set, Marj and Harold sitting in their customary places, I could almost see the red coals of lit cigarettes and smell the lemony cocktails and hear the murmur of voices. They didn't tell stories, they just mentioned places and names, like flipping through index cards in a file drawer, laughing at each one. Arlene and I had no knowledge of misery. My hand on her leg was an innocent hand, with no agenda in mind, she wanted to be loved, so I loved her, then I went my way and she went back to St. Olaf and waited for me to write to her and I didn't so she married Clarence. Why had we lost touch? Sheer happenstance. You turn left instead of right and you happen onto a path that leads you here rather than there, and that's the story of my life. It was 1960, I didn't have a cellphone with a lady in it telling me where to go. I was content being lost, waiting for Miss Fortune to guide me.

Giselle was in the shower, steam leaking around the door. I opened it. Water flowed off the bather, a waterfall down her pale breasts. "Soap my back," she said, so I did, scrubbing her elegant shoulders, her shoulder blades, and the small of her back and her buttocks, down and up and down, lingering, and then I soaped the front of her. She accepted this without objection but I didn't linger. "My legs ache from hiking. We did thirty-two miles a day, sometimes more. I'm too old for that. I'm an old lady but when you touch me—" she hummed a low note and I took the nozzle off the shower head and washed her legs—"you make me feel like I'm in a porn movie, *Linda Love Goes To Grover's Corners*," she said. I wrapped her in a towel. She stepped out of the shower and gave herself a critical glance in the mirror and I kissed the nape of her neck and my fingers traced the fine architecture of her shoulders and collarbone and breastbone and stopped short. She grabbed a pinch of flesh at her waist. Not fat, just flesh. "I'm old and I'm fat," she said and she sighed. She was neither old nor fat and any old fat person would be honored to be compared to her. So it was up to me to arouse her and I said, "Then why am I so excited by the sight of you?" "So what are you waiting for?" she said.

I kissed her in several delicate places, thinking of pictures of Eve and Venus and Aphrodite I had seen in my innocent youth, and a slender beauty by Goya, and she placed her hands on my chest lest I get carried away. "I'm helpless to resist you," she said. "Then why bother?" I whispered. I knelt at her feet, my arms around her thighs, and thought of Gauguin and how delighted he would be to see her. I led her to the bed and helped her lie down, as Modigliani would wish, slightly on her right side, her right leg at an elegant angle, and she pulled me down on the bed and kissed me in an intense interrogatory way and gave me a penetrating look that I interpreted as permissive and our bodies intersected

and interacted and she looked startled as if this had never happened
to us before, which in a sense it had not, not in showing this glory of
the apotheosis of female form in the Renoir posterior with the delicate Degas spine like Bathsheba or Cleopatra and I thought of Roman
marble goddesses, *Amo, amas, amat, amamus, amatis, amant,* as light
mists curled around us, which I saw was smoke from the cigarettes
of slender men, mustachioed, with wire-rimmed spectacles, standing
in vests and shirtsleeves before canvases on easels, painting furiously,
thwapping, swopping, swooshing, muttering in French, trying to
capture the rapture and action of the moment and especially the arch
of her spinal column and her pale arms thrown back, her head slightly
raised, all of her elevated, crying, sighing, and though I was busy I
happened to notice that I the naked male lover was not in any of the
canvases except as a faint shadow, only she, her exquisite neck, her
elegant tendrils, her regal ears, the classic serenity of her breasts, and
I smelled the cigar of a surrealist portraying her as a naked woman
holding a waffle iron with a cormorant sitting on her head—"No, no,
no!" I cried, trying to interrupt the *swish swash* of brushes, the *squort
shvitz* of paint, and saw Matisse making her a stained-glass window and
Monet a reflection on water and Cezanne an assortment of fruit and
Magritte a bird perched on a marble bust and Renoir made her Parisian
and Gauguin Tahitian, Munch an apparition, Goya a mystic vision,
Miró a constellation, Vermeer a location, Warhol a libation, Van Gogh
an outpatient, O'Keeffe a carnation, Titian made her ancient, Hopper
a filling station, Botticelli a virgin adoration, and amid this crowd of
chaos one man said, "*Encore, s'il vous plaît. Lentement. L'homme au
sommet*" but then there was an *Oh God,* and a string of *Oh Gods* and
shuddering as our old friend Ecstasy grabbed the lady by the shoulders
and we rolled over, she breathing hard, murmuring things in her own
language. Giselle does delight more dramatically than anyone I ever
was naked with, and a man, I believe it was Modigliani, said, "*Ancora.
Ancora uno*" and I reached under the pillow and pulled out a pistol
and fired three shots at the crimson moon someone had painted they
grabbed their palettes and canvases and wine bottles and ran, even

Picasso and Magritte, the entire platoon of painters fled out the door and down to the shore, and I pulled a sheet up over us.

"Are you okay?" I said.

"I haven't been this okay since the last time I laid eyes on you."

And then she said, "What is that clicking sound?"

"It's my heart valve pounding."

"I'm serious. It's like an alarm or something."

So she had to roam around the cabin and track down the clicks. I took her a bathrobe and she pushed it away: "What's modesty to a fallen woman?" she said. She said, "I thought I told you not to get those blinds, they get awful reviews online. Linen shades would be much nicer." She looked under the bed. She went in the kitchen. It was the refrigerator clicking, the door was slightly ajar. She got out the champagne.

"How was the Adirondacks?" I said. I wanted her to come back to bed.

She said, "I love grandeur but then you sit around the campfire at night and people pass around their iPhones so you can see the pictures of grandeur they took. You should be talking about global warming or the life of John Muir but instead you're admiring little pictures of woods and hills you walked through today. Why do people keep trying to put everything into small rectangles?"

"Well, you married a writer and I put things on a page."

"If you write another Lake Wobegon book, leave the lovemaking out of it," she said. "I don't want my nieces to be embarrassed. Anyway, I'm tired of travel. I'm in the mood for marriage." And I heard the pop of champagne and the fizz of pouring and she returned, naked, with two half-glasses and a volume of Emily Dickinson. "Just published last week, I picked it up at the airport. *The Secret Verses.* They were glued to the bottom of a dresser drawer in her bedroom in Amherst. The secret Dickinson."

Marriage—is counted Sweetest
By Those who never—Wed:
And the next One whom—I meetest
I Plan to take—to Bed.
Not one of all—the Purple Team

Who played—the Game today
Are Men of whose—Amour I Dream
As You—who walk my Way,
Intelligent—Dramatic,
On whose Astonished—Ear
Falls my Voice Emphatic:
"Remove your Pants. Come here."

She jumped back in the shower and rinsed off and I sat on the porch and awaited my next move. I had been thinking it over for several days. I was determined not to go through the discussion of "How long are we going to stay here?" and "What do you want to do with this cabin?" and all of that. I had packed my bag already. The car keys were on the counter. I had heard Thoreau's bugle call here and made love with Arlene and accepted the hospitality of Republicanism while standing my ground against its stubborn closed-mindedness: I had honored the faithful friendship of the Gundersons and paid tribute to my coming of age and now I was free to go back to New York.

I had worked it out with Mallory two days before. She came over for a drink and we talked about the entrepreneurs and what a remarkable band of oddballs they were and she admitted that, though she missed Vermont where she'd gone to college and New Mexico where she'd taught yoga, she felt that Minnesota was her home. She had hired Henry to tear down the shack she'd bought down the shore after she put out rat poison and a family of rats ate it and in their death throes they chewed through the ceiling plaster and their dead bodies dropped on the bed where she and Scott were reading poetry to each other. So they were looking for a rental and I offered her my cabin. One of those instant right decisions that the world needs more of. "Pay what you like and if you decide you want to buy it, we can negotiate a price. It'll be dirt cheap. I just want to get back what I put into it, a few thousand bucks." I told her. "You could move in tomorrow."

She said, "I thought your wife was coming back this week."

I said that when Giselle comes to Minnesota, she isn't coming *back.*

I'm the back-comer in the family and she comes to pull me away and get me back to where I belong, which is walking around the Upper West Side of Manhattan and buying cheese at Zabar's and walking around the Central Park reservoir and going to the opera and confessing my sins at St. Michael's. Nostalgic backsliding is my specialty and hers is the resumption of forward momentum.

So when Giselle walked out on the porch, warm and damp, champagne in hand, I looked up and jingled the car keys and said, "If we leave now, we can catch the late flight to New York." I was serious. She was astounded. Her astonishment was wondrous to behold.

She said, "What's the rush? I just got here." I told her that I only lured her here to have sex with her and now I was done with the place.

She said, "But you went to all this trouble."

"And it paid off."

I love when I can mystify her. Usually she reads me like a book for third-graders. "I'm done here," I said. "My people are gone. The family who owned this cabin were good friends and they're gone now and I fixed the place up in their honor and I'm done. I know a couple who are all ready and eager to move in. Let's hit the road. We'll sleep in New York tonight and in the morning we'll go to City Diner for bagels and visit the Met and look at the impressionists."

It was a beautiful authoritarian moment, which a man only achieves once a year or so. She shook her head but she didn't argue. She put on her socks and shoes. She picked up her bag. She stepped off the porch and took a few steps down the walk. "It's a lovely lake," she said. I said, "It's a fabulous lake if you grew up here and otherwise it's just another lake. We have thousands of them in Minnesota and each one is sacred to some people and to everyone else it's just a watershed. I can't look at that lake without thinking about my lost friends, and when I remember them, I go around and around in circles remembering—but I'll never know any more than what I know now. So let's say goodbye and go to New York where every day of your life you see something you never saw before."

She started to say something but nothing came out. I tossed the bags in the car and got behind the wheel and she sat close beside me. It was exciting to bewilder her, the woman who is ever and always fully in charge of situations. She'd been anticipating two weeks, three, a month, hanging around old neighbors, being polite to Dorothy and Carl and Liz and Clint and my strange Brethren cousins, trying to remember who is who, the names of their children and which children they're eager to talk about and which not so much, who is in med school and who is in treatment for substance abuse, sitting patiently through reminiscences about people she never heard of, old farmers and teachers, old ballplayers, thundering preachers entirely alien to a girl raised among dedicated iconoclasts, sketchy recollections of bygone times in desperate need of footnotes, and now here we were backing out of the driveway, past the foundation of the old outhouse and the pile of firewood under the lean-to, past the mailbox with "Gunderson" in big black letters. "I hope you're not doing this on my account," she said.

I drove slowly through town, I wanted to savor this. "Don't you want to stop and say goodbye?" she said. "If I stop to say goodbye, they'll think I have lung cancer," I said. I was happy for having liberated my wife from my past, doing of my own volition what she hadn't dared ask me to do—leave town—and, best of all, mystifying a woman who knows me much too well. She sees me glued to baseball on TV, she smiles at my simple puns, she accepts that I wear a black T-shirt and jeans wherever I go, and when she is driving and sees a White Castle ahead, she pulls up to the drive-up window so I can get a couple sliders and large fries, and she gives me her talk about aging and cholesterol. I am not a complex guy. So this was my opportunity to acquire some mystery. I said it had been a beautiful two months and I had experienced a revelation that we are jars of clay that carry God's light. "Pottery, plain pots, crackpots maybe, some more artistic than others, but even so, containers, and we hold light in darkness. The love of God shines in each of us. *We are hard-pressed on every side, but not crushed; perplexed, but not in despair; persecuted, but not abandoned; struck down, but not destroyed.*"

"Did you write that?" she said. "No, the apostle Paul did," I said.

"'Persecuted' is rather dramatic in my case and I can't say I've been 'struck down' but still here we are, on the loose and we do not lose heart, we need to live and live abundantly."

I was about to pull onto Interstate 94 to head south to the airport when my phone rang and I made the mistake of answering. It was Carl. "I'm at your back door with some new window blinds."

"It's not my back door anymore. It's Mallory's. Ask her to let you in. I'm on the interstate, heading for the airport."

Actually, I'd pulled over on the shoulder. It makes Giselle nervous if I drive and talk on the phone.

"Who was that?" she said.

And then the phone rang again. It was Dorothy. She was crying. "You can't run away now. I didn't get to say hello to Giselle. I just made a beautiful Caesar salad and tuna sandwiches and I am on my way to your cabin. You *can't* leave without saying goodbye. I would never forgive you."

The phone was on speaker. "I want to see Dorothy, turn around and let's go back," said Giselle. So I made a big U-turn and headed back home. I know a direct order when I hear one.

It turned into the classic Minnesota goodbye, like when you load up the car in the driveway and the family stands around leaning on it, talking through the open windows for a couple of hours. Taciturn people can sit silent for hours but when the guests go to leave, everyone has a great deal more to say.

We pulled into the driveway to the cabin and there were a dozen cars parked in the yard and people sitting on the porch, waiting for us. Clint and Irene had come and brought gallons of iced tea and Dorothy had jiggered the front door latch with a credit card and gotten in and laid out her salad and sandwiches and Alyssa and Yvonne had arrived with chilled seafood soup and a jug of Portuguese wine and Daryl and Marilyn and Mallory and Scott and Henry González and his wife, Carlotta, and Grace the librarian and Ralph and Marion and Judy and Dick Wilcox, and word got around and more people arrived, everyone bringing potluck.

Scott had his guitar so Henry went home and got his, and they both knew some tunes so we sang "I can't help it if I'm still in love with you" and "Remember me when the candlelights are gleaming" and Giselle was touched, sitting by me on the swinging couch on the porch. She was so touched, she accepted a cigarette from Yvonne and smoked it. "My first since I was in college," she said.

She went out on the dock and stood in the water and she came back, weeping, and put her arms around me. "It's so beautiful. The cabin is beautiful. I want to stay."

I told her that this is a Minnesota goodbye. You get ready to leave and everyone feels bad for having ignored you and so they gather around and embrace you, but it doesn't necessarily mean you should postpone your departure. "It's complicated," I said.

Bill showed up whom I beat in the sixth-grade spelling bee on the word "eleemosynary" and then I beat Marilyn on "perspicacious," but she was perspicacious enough to marry him instead and there she was, tall and elegant as ever. Alyssa and Yvonne brought their parrot Gwendolyn who could say, "B.S." and "Now you're talkin'." Lyle brought his dog Roxie who took a shine to Giselle and she asked him what kind of dog it was and he said, "She used to be a hunter but she changed her mind. Hunters are a rough crowd and she prefers the comforts of home. Speaking of which, where in New York do you live?"

Giselle said, "I grew up in the Village, but we live on the Upper West Side now." And Lyle said, "We had a fellow from the West Side of New York who came out here to write a book about the economic decline of the Midwest, which, according to an article by him that I read in the New York *Times* was tied to a cultural decline, which he hadn't mentioned to us but with the internet you can gather intelligence quickly that back in the day would've taken longer than you'd care to spend. Anyway, I didn't care for his point of view. I think the word for it is 'snotty.' Whitby was his name. Little guy in a fancy suede jacket and black horn-rims and a broad-brimmed hat that when he took it off, you saw he had a goldarn hairpiece, black and silky with a white stripe down the middle. Maybe it was high fashion back in New York but out here it made you think of a skunk. The guy struck me as a phony and he was out to write us up as a bunch of illiterate rubes and hang us out to dry so I decided to sic the dogs on him. We made a campfire in the woods and served clams on the half shell and fixed beef stew, which I told him was squirrel, and he got sort of pale but he enjoyed the clams and he had a glass of brandy and asked Daryl if his dog Seamus was a hunting dog or a show dog and Seamus picked up the sarcasm in his voice and he moved in and sniffed Whitby's hairpiece and could tell it was made of cat hair and he growled and Whitby shoved him away and you don't do that to an Irish setter. The dog glared at him. We were tossing bits of beef to the dogs and Whitby, Lord knows why, grabbed a clam and tossed it to Seamus who thought it was beef but it hit him in the mouth and he tried to spit it out but reflexively swallowed it and he lay on the ground gagging and choking and finally stuck his paw down his throat and made himself vomit. Well, Irish setters have a long memory. They hold onto a grudge. So we started the deer chase and loosed the dogs to rustle up the deer and we thought of the hatchet job this writer could do on Lake Wobegon if he got bit by a dog, so we put him in a deer stand up high in a tree, which usually goes to the elderly and infirm hunter, which was last used by Old Man Olson, his last hunt, but we stuck Whitby up there, and suddenly the dogs started baying and barking because here came three deer, a buck and two does, into the clearing, three drunken deer who'd been feasting on windfall apples that'd fermented lying on the ground and the deer could hardly stand upright, so we had to herd the three of them to safety, meanwhile the dogs were going crazy."

Lyle looked at Daryl: "I forget what happened next," he said.

Daryl said, "So we had the drunken deer to herd down the path and away from the dogs who were crying for blood, the deer staggering, had to be helped up, and petted and encouraged with bunches of fresh grass, and then we heard people singing, *Standing On The Promises of God* and it was the Olson family, Old Man Olson's survivors who'd gathered to scatter his ashes where he last hunted deer. The three deer melted away into the underbrush and we joined the Olsons and paid our respects, though he was no great hunter. He made the mistake of pissing from the tree and the deer could tell from the smell that he was an old man and not to be feared so they paid him no mind, but anyway he liked to be part of the action, so all was well."

"Anyway," Lyle said, "Whitby was sitting up in the tree stand while we were with the Olsons and we had given him two squirt guns in case Seamus came after him, one full of vinegar, one full of urine. You spray the urine to draw a boundary, and if he crosses the boundary you spray him with vinegar. So we were with the Olsons and the hymn singing was very moving, we sang *Amazing Grace* and *Nearer My God To Thee* and *It Is Well With My Soul* and then the pack of dogs came baying and barking and driving a young buck and they drove him so fast he ran right up the big pine. We heard the rattle of hooves up the trunk and Whitby calling for help and ten feet above him, was the young buck spread-eagled on two limbs, panting hard, terrified. He'd never been up in a tree before. Whitby squirted piss at him and suddenly there were acorns falling down on him except they weren't acorns, they were soft and moist."

"The deer ran how far up the tree?" said Daryl.

"I don't know. It all happened so suddenly. I wasn't carrying a tape measure."

"You said he ran up the tree up above Whitby? Who is in a deer stand ten feet up? And the deer is up above him?"

Lyle said, "You want to go out to the woods and find the tree with the hoofmarks on it? Fine. Anyway, the deer came crashing down on top of Whitby and then he was flat on his back on the ground with the terrified deer on him and Seamus was closing in and Whitby fired a stream of vinegar but Seamus had loved pickles since he was a pup and he opened his mouth and swallowed all he could get and then sat down in the grass, full of wonderful memories. We came and chased the deer off Whitby and his hairpiece had fallen off and we saw that his head was bald and he had a tattoo up there, a red rose and a pair of crossbones, and we stared at it in amazement, and he said, 'My mother's name was Rose and when she died all my hair fell out.' Anyway, he went back to New York and we kept waiting for the book about the Midwest to come out and three years later he published a children's book about penguins and polar bears having a birthday party.

"Anyway," he said, "when you mentioned the Upper West Side, I couldn't help but remember him. He never did write the book, by the way. I think probably when a deer shits on you and you fall out of a tree with him on top of you, it sort of knocks the piss and vinegar out of you. In any case, no harm done."

Giselle kissed Lyle on the cheek and made him a gin and tonic. "That is the longest story I've heard in years," she said. "You could never tell a story that long in New York, people would've interrupted you to talk about their dogs or tell you something they read in the *Times* about deer. We don't give up the floor in New York unless the person talking is holding a gun." I was about to tell Lyle he'd left out some crucial facts, such as a stranger who came by and turned out to be a game warden who gave Daryl a ticket for allowing his dog to run the deer up the tree, but I decided not to. Giselle was having a wonderful time, the center of the party, standing on the lawn surrounded by my old hometown friends. A number of them said how beautiful she looked and indeed there was a bright gleam about her for which I, her lover, take some credit. Nobody commented on my appearance, it is what it is.

"So you still like it in New York?" said Daryl.

She said, "You just have to shut some things out. Sirens, helicopters, and crazy people yelling at you. You tune them out and the rest is quite pleasant."

Myrtle was there and caught the end of the story. "I just wanted to get a look at you," she told Giselle. "Your husband came from rather eccentric people but I suppose you've figured that out. Not much point in trying to change him at this point so he's damn lucky to have you, and don't let him push you around. That's my advice. Would you mind if I give you a big hug?" And she wrapped her arms around Giselle and squeezed.

"We need to go," I said.

Henry and Scott had been joined by Scott's brother Joe on harmonica and an old Finnish guy named Peltoniemi had dropped in with a button accordion and Henry was singing "La Bamba" and someone had built a fire on the beach and some people were dancing. Peltoniemi had been fishing, heard the music and dropped by, and he knew tangos, and two women canoed up to the dock, Jearlyn and Jevetta, and they sang "O Happy Day" to a tango beat, and the song traveled across the water, so soon a couple fiddlers arrived and a drummer and a bassist named Speed, more beer arrived, and Carl's daughter Amy and her St. Olaf friends.

"I love this, I love these people," Giselle said. "This never happened when I visited here before."

Ralph's butcher Bud brought a sack of brats and buns and Yvonne set up a grill and the sun went down and I pulled Giselle into the shadows and said, "We have a plane to catch. We can come back next summer." I towed her away toward the car. "We can't say goodbye, it'd only bring the party to an end," I said. I could hear them singing "Come and sit by my side if you love me" as we got into the car and coasted silently down the hill to the county road and drove away, headlights off, and headed for Minneapolis.

It was a starry night. Giselle found out the flight had been delayed so we had plenty of time. Stars shone in the southern sky, some that had died long before but their light still shone, just like on the classic country station Chet Atkins sang "I Still Can't Say Goodbye" and Peter Ostroushko played "Heart of the Heartland" and Bill & Judy sang "Late last night in the pale moonlight, all the vegetables had a spree" and Don & Phil sang "Bye-bye, Love." My phone vibrated in my pocket but I didn't pull it out.

Giselle sat, looking straight ahead, listening. I couldn't recall another time when she'd been so silent. She is never at a loss for words, she has always been quick with a smart retort, and now she was speechless.

And then she said, "Are you sure this is south? It feels like north to me." She has a sure sense of direction but this time she was wrong. She said she thought it was rude of us to leave the party, but she was wrong about that too.

I said, "I went to five funerals this spring, two of my best friends, and two jerks and one miscellaneous, and I saw my past disappearing into the misty hills, and I could be dismayed and perplexed and I decide not to be. This is what we do in Minnesota. The blizzard comes, the wind rages, blinding snow, the Highway Patrol says 'Stay home, no driving today' and we start up our car, scrape the windshield, and head for town. Life goes on. Anyway it was a great party and people will talk about it for weeks to come, the party so great that nobody noticed the hosts had left. And what you did for Lyle was a miracle—usually the man is silent, nobody ever heard him talk that long, that dumb story about the writer and the dog and the deer—he did that for you, you liberated Lyle from himself just like you liberate me. You're a powerful woman and I'm not from here anymore, I belong to you."

And I looked over and Giselle was fast asleep. So I talked some more about Arlene and me on the dock and how that repaired the injury I suffered from missing the free throw against St. Margaret's and it changed my life forever. And then we got to the airport and she woke up in a good mood and asked when could we go back to Lake Wobegon. "January," I said. "We'll go ice-fishing. Spend the night in a shack with a propane heater and walk across the ice under the stars and cook meatballs and spaghetti over an open fire."

We missed the flight to New York, the plane pulling away as we ran through the terminal, so we crashed in a hotel and Giselle asked if I didn't want to go to Murray's or visit the U or look at the Fitzgerald Theater or houses where I had lived with previous lovers, and I said no. I was too beat. We slept until ten and caught a noon flight to LaGuardia where the taxi took us over the East River and onto the FDR and west on 96th Street and at every red light where we stopped, I watched the people crossing the street, people I'd never know, navigating the canyons in Manhattan's shimmering show of lights, children of God, hard-pressed, perplexed perhaps, but not forsaken, still giving off reflections of divinity. We came home, said hello to Gus the doorman, declined the offer of help with the bags, rode up to the 12th floor, walked out on the terrace, watered the pine tree and the plants, and looked out over the roofs of brownstones, a couple on a balcony below listening to opera on the radio, a fire truck racing up Amsterdam with its horn roaring, a helicopter hovering over Central Park, a train rumbling under the street, a troop of nursery-schoolers roped together headed for the playground where we could hear the shouts of a serious basketball game. I went in the kitchen and made coffee. The male couple in the apartment across the courtyard walked around in their underwear, shades up. I got down the "Minnesota" coffee cup with the loon on it that my mother gave me when I moved to New York and poured the coffee and went back out on the terrace where Giselle was listening to a man down on the street yelling about something, and she said she had met him years ago, that he used to be a famous writer, and she said, "Hold me," so I did, my chin on the top of her head, her cheek against my beating heart, and she said, "I love you so much. You're my favorite. I need you." And now that I knew why I was here, it felt like home.

American Pride